A Ghost in Shining Armor

Kensington Books by Therese Beharrie

And They Lived Happily Ever After

A Ghost in Shining Armor

A Ghost in Shining Armor

Therese Beharrie

ZEBRA BOOKS
Kensington Publishing Corp.
www.kensingtonbooks.com

ZEBRA BOOKS are published by
Kensington Publishing Corp.
119 West 40th Street
New York, NY 10018

All Kensington titles, imprints, and distributed lines are available at special quantity discounts for bulk purchases for sales promotion, premi-
ums, fund-raising, educational, or institutional use.

Special book excerpts or customized printings can also be created to fit
specific needs. For details, write or phone the office of the Kensington
Sales Manager: Attn.: Sales Department. Kensington Publishing Corp.,
119 West 40th Street, New York, NY 10018. Phone: 1-800-221-2647.

Zebra and the Z logo Reg. U.S. Pat. & TM Off.

First Zebra Trade Printing: October 2022

ISBN: 978-1-4201-5340-8
ISBN: 978-1-4201-5341-5 (ebook)

10 9 8 7 6 5 4 3 2 1

Printed in the United States of America

For Grant, my human in shining armor, which doesn't sound *quite* as right as the title of this book, but has somehow been exactly right for more than a decade.

For my sons. May you grow up knowing you are worthy exactly as you are, and deserving of every single good thing. You are everything to me.

I love you all.

AUTHOR'S NOTE

This book is a lighthearted, sparkly romance, but it does deal with themes of adoption, death, and parental abandonment. If any of that is difficult for you, it's okay to set this book aside and come back to it if and when you're ready.

—Therese

PROLOGUE

The day Gemma Daniels turned eighteen was memorable for many reasons, the main one being that a man appeared in her room, claiming to be a ghost.

Initially, she did what any sane person would do: She threw her hair dryer at him. With impeccable aim. It hit him right in the forehead.

That's what you get for breaking and entering, she told him mentally. In reality, she merely watched him, her body tense, ready to defend itself.

As it turned out, her impeccable aim didn't matter. He hadn't moved, completely unbothered by the fact that she had thrown a heavy piece of machinery at him.

In fact, he stood unnervingly still. He watched her from behind glasses that sat on a pointed nose, framing kind eyes that shouldn't have been on a burglar. Nothing about him reminded her of a burglar. Not the cardigan that looked like it should have been thrown away a hundred or so washes ago, nor the faded brown pants and scuffed brown shoes. He stood with his arms folded behind him and resting on his lower back, as though he were a kindly old grandfather. Or a bewildered older teacher.

Wait—he didn't look like a burglar at all. He looked like . . . he looked like her biology teacher.

But that was ridiculous.

"I have a hairbrush," Gemma warned. "And I'm not afraid to use it."

"I don't doubt that, my dear," the man said calmly. "In my days as your teacher, I've never seen a hair out of place."

No. No way.

"Mr. . . . Mr. Harris?"

"Yes."

She took a second. "Not to be rude," she said slowly, "but why are you here? In my bedroom," she clarified. "At seven in the morning."

"It's your birthday, I believe?"

"Yes. What does that have to do with anything?"

"Well, Gemma," he started, placing his hands in his pockets, "I've been asked to talk to you about how your life is going to be from now. I was honored." His voice had taken on a measure of pride. "To be asked to be your first."

It sounded like a compliment, and Gemma's chest filled with pride and happiness until the words filtered through the sunlight.

And then there was considerably less sunlight and a lot more cloud.

And rain. Lots and lots of rain.

"Oh. Um . . ." She swallowed. "This is very . . . um . . . kind of you." It wasn't, but she didn't want to offend him. On the other hand, if there *were* a time to offend someone, it would be now, when her elderly teacher was offering to be her *first*. "But I don't think that's a good idea."

He frowned. "I'm sorry?"

"Well, you're married, for one. For another, there's a significant age difference. Not that it matters, mind you." She tilted her head. "Well, in this case, it probably would matter. Plus!"

she added triumphantly. "The power dynamics between a teacher and student!"

"Gemma, what are you talking about?"

She blinked. "You offering to be my first lover. Which technically, I suppose you would be. But if we're not talking 'technically'"—she lifted her fingers in air quotes—"you're a little too l—"

"Gemma," Mr. Harris said again, in that long-suffering way too many adults used when they were speaking to her, "I'm not offering to be your lover." He looked a bit green. "I'm your first *ghost*."

She stared. He waited, then went to her bed and patted the space beside him. She looked at him, at that space, and somehow her legs took her there, though she had no recollection of asking them to do so.

"You see, my dear, you have the ability to see ghosts."

With a shake of her head, she said, "No."

"Yes."

"Mr. Harris, I saw you yesterday. You told me to have a good day. You aren't dead." She shifted to face him. "Is this an illness? Are you having a breakdown? Maybe I should call my mom."

She moved to get up, but Mr. Harris took her hand. His skin was soft against hers, the wrinkles giving away his age. Comforting her.

"I died last night. Brain aneurysm. Barely felt a thing. My Sandy found me this morning. Terrible," he said, his mouth downturned, "but she'll be okay. She's always been the strong one." Now his lips curved into a smile, albeit a sad one. "When I got to the Waiting Room, They offered me the opportunity to guide you—"

"Hold on," Gemma said, lifting her hand. "The Waiting Room? Like at a doctor's office?"

"No, more like the place you wait before They decide the next phase of your existence."

"Who are *They*?"

"Well, now." He frowned. "I don't know that."

"You . . . don't know?"

"There isn't much time for asking questions. You are either given an assignment or not, and when you are given an assignment, you have to decide whether you'll accept it quite quickly."

"That sounds overwhelming."

"It's not that bad," Mr. Harris said conversationally. "They do tend to speak to you as if you're a child, but I suppose to Them, human beings are the equivalent of—" He broke off. "Gemma, you're distracting me."

"I'm only asking questions."

"Exactly."

"Okay, fine." Gemma waved her hand for him to continue. "Tell me more about how you're supposed to help me with my ability to see ghosts."

The door to her bedroom opened. She heard a faint *pop*.

"Gemma?" Gemma's mother came into the room before Gemma could investigate what the sound had been. "Who are you talking to?"

"Mr. Harris."

She gestured to him with her thumb, but Jasmine blinked at her. "Mr. Harris? Your biology teacher?"

"Yes. He's right over here."

She turned. Saw that he wasn't right over there. Stared.

"Oh, honey," Jasmine said, sitting down where Mr. Harris had just been sitting. She put her arm over Gemma's shoulders. "I didn't realize you already knew."

"Knew what?"

"Mr. Harris died last night. We got an email from the principal." She paused. "You *did* already know that? Why else would you be speaking with him? Wasn't it to say goodbye?"

Gemma took a second to figure out how she was going to approach this.

"Yes, I knew that. I was saying goodbye. To his ghost," she said, watching her mother's reaction carefully. "His ghost that came to visit me."

"Oh."

Her mother frowned. It was a delicate frown that suited her delicate features. One of Gemma's school friends had once said that Jasmine looked like a doll, and Gemma secretly agreed. Jasmine wore her black hair in a tight bun at the nape of her neck every day. Her makeup was flawlessly applied, another daily occurrence. The only times Gemma saw her mother look any different was when Jasmine was ill. But every other time, Jasmine made sure she woke up before Gemma and Gemma's father did, and went to bed after they did.

Jasmine never acknowledged that she did this; Gemma's father never said a word about it, either, and Gemma never had the courage to ask. So the entire family accepted Jasmine's habits, though personally, Gemma found the standard it set impossible to achieve herself.

Jasmine didn't act like a doll. She wasn't laid-back or fun. She was strict and uncompromising, funny with the driest sense of humor, and she loved her family. It was especially that love that made Gemma feel all warm and fuzzy.

Now that she thought about it, she wasn't sure dolls were laid-back. Maybe they were exactly like her mother. Maybe her next visit would be from a doll telling her to stop being so ignorant. If ghosts existed, it was plausible dolls could be alive, too.

"I didn't realize you and Mr. Harris were that close," Jasmine said.

Close enough that his ghost came to visit me? Neither did I.

But Gemma didn't say it. Because her mother's reaction didn't exactly scream *Yes, ghosts exist. Welcome to adulthood.*

Gemma shrugged in answer.

"You're in shock." Jasmine squeezed Gemma's shoulder before moving aside. "You said he was sitting here, correct?" She didn't wait for Gemma to reply. "Why don't we say goodbye together?"

Jasmine cleared her throat, directing her words to the space where Mr. Harris had been sitting before she came in.

"Mr. Harris, you were a great biology teacher. You never complained about Gemma, and I know that must have been difficult." Gemma opened her mouth to protest, but her mother continued. "I was also particularly pleased that you taught my daughter about the anatomy of the human body and explained the technicalities of sexual intercourse." Jasmine sniffed. "I will forever be grateful."

"Mom, you're being pretty irreverent right now."

Her mother gave her a look. "Seems I should be thanking your English teacher instead."

Gemma sighed. It was the kind of sigh she saved for special moments, like when words were simply not enough to get the message across. Or when she had to get a significant amount of tension out her body. This sigh was a combination of both, which was likely why Jasmine sobered.

"Gem, are you okay?"

"No," Gemma answered honestly. "Can you give me a few moments?"

Her mother hesitated, though she got up. She gave Gemma a once-over, and left with the words, "It's your birthday, honey. I'm sure Mr. Harris would have wanted you to celebrate it."

Gemma wasn't sure about that, but she waited until her mother left. As she expected—heaven only knew why—Mr. Harris reappeared.

"You better tell me more about this ghost business, Mr. Harris," she said gravely, softly, so her mother didn't hear her.

Mr. Harris nodded and said kindly, "Call me Arnold, dear. We should dispel with the formalities if we're going to discuss magic."

CHAPTER 1

Twelve years later

"What about him?" Gemma pointed to the man standing at the bar. He looked lost, which was exactly why she had chosen him.

No. That was a lie. She had chosen him because he was tall. Really tall. The kind of tall where people—not her, per se, but people—looked up and thought about climbing things. And by things, she meant *him*.

Luckily, those people were not her. She preferred climbing more traditional things. Trees. Ladders.

That man.

"Who?" Lacey Maritz, Gemma's closest friend since university, asked.

Lacey's bride-to-be sash had fallen off her shoulder and was now a hula hoop at her waist. She was swirling the champagne in her glass; a controlled movement, despite how much she had already drunk. Not that that mattered. Lacey was never sloppy, even drunk. Gemma's eyes rested on the liquid as it circled the glass, not a single drop spilling over the top.

"Never mind."

"Gemma," Lacey said, eyes narrowing. "Tell me who you were talking about."

"That guy over there." Gemma pointed to a completely different man.

"The one with the nipple ring?"

"How do you know he has a—" Gemma broke off when she saw the man she'd pointed to had taken off his shirt to reveal . . . yes, that *was* a nipple ring. Gemma studied it, but no length of time made it seem like something she wanted to know more about. "I'm sure he's a perfectly lovely man—"

"Gemma, we don't want you to marry him," Izzy, Lacey's soon to be sister-in-law, said. "We just want you to kiss a stranger. Come on." Her voice turned sharper. "It's a bachelorette game, not a life decision you have to ponder."

There was an awkward beat of silence, the kind that had settled over their group a couple of times that night. Izzy wasn't the most pleasant person, and she and Lacey bumped heads often. At least they did when they weren't playing nice for the sake of the wedding.

Lacey had told her fiancé, Chet, that she'd make him choose between her and his sister if Izzy didn't behave. She didn't mean it, Gemma thought, but the threat was good enough. So they had both been on their best behavior. For the most part. Izzy tended to take out her frustrations on the group; Lacey responded by ignoring it completely.

Until now, it seemed.

"Izzy—"

"At the bar!" Gemma cut in. There wouldn't be an incident because of *her.* "Tall. With the beard. The one whose skin looks like gold and brown had a baby."

"Who?" their friend, Pearl, asked.

"At the bar," Gemma said again. Why was it so hard for them to see him? He stood out like a . . . like a tall tree. "Wearing the green shirt with the buttons down the front? The blue jeans?" When they still didn't seem to get it, Gemma continued. "Standing next to the man in the leather pants?"

"Oh!" Lacey said.

"*Oh* is right," Izzy agreed.

They all went quiet in mutual admiration.

"How did you manage to find the hottest guy here?" Pearl complained. "I don't think I've ever seen you date someone mediocre."

"It's the energy you put out in the world, Pearly," Gemma said with a grin.

"Oh, you mean your 'my face is an artist's dream' energy?" Onu, Pearl's girlfriend, teased. "Because some of us don't have that kind of energy to harness."

"And some of us do," Pearl replied, stealing a kiss from Onu.

"Break it up, you two," Lacey said, waving a finger at them. "Gemma has a task to focus on, and she can't do that if you're Frenching."

"I'm pretty sure I can do it fine with them Frenching," Gemma offered. She smiled when Lacey quirked a brow. "Do I have your approval, madam?"

"Indeed you do."

Gemma reapplied her lipstick, made sure her hair was still doing what she'd told it to do, adjusted her boobs, and ignored her friends' teasing. A feat, truly. With one last look in her mirror, she slid out the booth and made her way to Mr. Tall and Beautiful, rubbing her thumb over the back of her ring for luck.

The bar was full. Unsurprising for a Saturday night at the end of the month. There was an unspoken agreement among the people of Cape Town that when they had energy and money to spare, they partied. Gemma usually preferred to do so at one of the rooftop bars in Cape Town. She loved air and space and the feeling that she wasn't about to risk her life simply by breathing in the same oxygen as the people around her. And this . . . wasn't it.

No, this was one of the dodgy Cape Town clubs where air, space, and avoiding disease—of many kinds—were not the priority.

They'd descended a long flight of stairs to get inside, been ogled by the bouncers, then ogled by everyone else, since the entrance led directly onto the dance floor. There were no windows, the floor and the walls were different shades of the kind of brown that didn't bring to mind anything good, and it smelled like sweat and alcohol. When they walked past the bathrooms, the vague scent of throw-up threw its hat in the ring of smells.

Gemma shuddered.

Fortunately, the booth they'd reserved was relatively clean, but that didn't stop Gemma from giving Pearl the stink eye.

"What?" she'd asked.

"*This* is what you chose?" Gemma demanded.

Pearl shrugged. "Lacey wanted dirty."

"I don't think she meant that literally."

"No, I did," Lacey interrupted, a faintly alarming expression on her face. "It's perfect."

"This wedding is damaging your brain," Gemma informed her.

She'd gotten a deranged smile in return.

Shaking it off—while also shaking off the feeling that she was walking with a blanket of fleas over her dress—she dodged bodies, swearing at them under her breath since doing it out loud wasn't polite, until she reached the man at the bar.

"Hi," she said when she got to his side.

He didn't respond, his eyes scanning the room in front of him. Was he looking for someone? A partner? Spouse? Friend with benefits? She had no interest in interfering with that.

But surely, he could handle the situation better than ignoring her.

"Hey," she said louder.

Nothing.

Maybe she was too short. "Hey," she shouted, adding a little jump. It made her feel stupid, but it worked: He looked down at her.

Suddenly, she felt a strong urge to make climbing her new hobby.

Up close, he was even more attractive than she'd thought. The kind of attractive that made her wonder if she'd ever really seen attractive before. All of it framed by such angry *hair.*

It wouldn't make sense if she didn't see it herself. She wouldn't have thought it attractive if she didn't see it, him, herself.

But there it was—his angry, beautiful hair.

Thick, full black eyebrows that curved so slightly, they looked like squares. A thick, full black beard that highlighted the sharp curve of—surprise, surprise—angry-looking cheekbones. And thick, full black hair that wasn't wavy, but wasn't straight either, on top of his head.

Gloriously aggressive, all of it.

Her stomach did a swoop, and she told herself it was alarm. Alarm, because who described a man as *gloriously aggressive* shortly after thinking of him as attractive? Those two things were not aligned. Not for her; no sirree. She was not drawn to beautiful men with angry hair and intense brown eyes. She did not care for full lips that looked to be in a permanent pout, contradicting nearly everything else about his face. Not to mention that *earring.*

An earring!

Gemma, focus.

Right. Yes. She needed to focus on her task.

"Are you looking for your partner?" she half-shouted, because it was still loud, even though he was now looking at her with those piercing eyes.

Those unnervingly *serious* eyes.

She got so distracted by them she almost missed the shake of his head.

"So you're single?"

He angled his head. Nodded.

"Do you speak? Or do you only do the head thing? No," she said, hearing it and immediately banishing the dirty thoughts it brought to mind, "you know what? It doesn't matter."

She paused. Considered. Glanced at her table and saw her friends being obnoxiously supportive.

"I'm going to level with you, okay? It's my best friend's bachelorette party. One of the games is 'kiss a stranger.'"

"That's a game?"

"Oh, so you *do* talk."

He gave her a look. She realized she'd said it out loud.

Okay, Filter, remember we had this talk? You need to do your job. Otherwise, I'll give your position to Conscience. You know he's been wanting it for years.

"Anyway," she said brightly, "they picked you." *They.* "If I don't do this, I'll be the only one to lose the game. So I guess I'm asking—can I kiss you?"

There was a long silence.

A long, long silence.

She prepared to walk away.

But then . . .

He nodded.

Levi Walker had always been competitive. Once upon a time, he'd worked through it by playing sports. That changed when his parents got divorced. He'd channeled all his competitive energy into helping raise his sister after that, but perhaps that wasn't the best idea. Not if the mere mention of a game had him agreeing to kiss the last woman he should be kissing.

It was most certainly that making him agree, and not the large brown eyes staring up at him from the most striking face. It was a unique face: dark lashes and brows, high cheekbones, a wide mouth that was painted a fierce red. Her hair was long, making her seem shorter than she probably was, though that was true of most people for him. He tried not to notice the red outfit she wore, the skirt of which ended in the middle of truly impressive thighs. Tried not to lower his gaze to a rather spectacular chest, either.

She hadn't looked like this in the video They had shown him.

There, she had looked innocent. All smiles and politeness, bouncing around the world as if she truly believed in its goodness.

Or maybe that was what They wanted him to see.

Not this version of her. This . . . this *seductive* woman standing in front of him with her body and her dress, asking him to kiss her. He was supposed to help her get her life together, but here he was, kissing her.

Somehow, he was *kissing* her.

He wanted to say it was terrible. He *wanted* it to be terrible. That way, he wouldn't think about it as he continued his mission. That way, he could tell himself it was a mistake and pretend like it didn't happen.

Except it wasn't terrible. It *sparked*. As if he were being kissed by some impossible mix of light and happiness. It made him feel like he was suspended in the air; a cosmic entity that wasn't part of the earth, but still belonged to its orbit.

He could—and probably would, at some point—put it down to a technicality. *Technically*, she made him feel like he wasn't part of the earth, because *technically*, he was dead.

Technically, it was all bullshit.

Technically, she was the most enticing person he'd ever kissed.

Her lips moved gently, innocently, against his. At first. If he didn't know better, he would have said she knew how he'd perceived her, why he'd agreed to help her, and was mocking him for it. Because when her tongue slipped into his mouth—when fire took the place of his blood, and for a second, he thought he'd failed at his mission and ended up in hell—innocence flew out of the window.

He tossed his restraint out with it, too, slipping an arm

around her waist and pulling her flush against him. Since he'd only been a ghost for an hour, he wasn't sure what his body was capable of. Turns out, it was quite a lot.

She moaned into his mouth, the vibration traveling through him, turning into goose bumps on his skin. Her hands slid up his arms, rested on his shoulders. Her fingers dug into the muscle there, and he thought it might be involuntary. A reaction to whatever was happening between them.

She shifted, her breasts pressing against his chest. He imagined them bare against him, and his body once again proved that it was indeed alive and well, even if his soul—or whatever—was dead.

"Hmm," she said as she pulled back, her lipstick smudged, her lips glistening with a faint sheen of moisture, parted slightly in surprise.

He might have read her reaction wrong, but she said, "Well, that was surprising," and confirmed that he hadn't.

He loosened his grip, only then realizing he'd been holding onto her too tightly, and nodded. "Yeah."

"I'm sorry."

"Don't," he said, his voice a little gruff in its command.

"Don't what?" she asked, frowning.

He frowned right back. In truth, he didn't see the point of her question. His *don't* had been clear.

Don't apologize for kissing me. You asked, and I said yes.

Don't apologize for kissing me. It was incredible.

His frown deepened. Perhaps the second one wasn't as clear as the first.

But it would remain unclear. He would never admit it out loud. Certainly not to the woman he was meant to be guiding through a particularly messy situation in her life. Certainly not when he was sure he had simply added to the mess by agreeing to kiss her.

Why had he agreed again? Right, because of the game. Because he wanted her to win.

If he wasn't so annoyed, he might have ignored the mocking laughter some self-sabotaging part of himself had echoing in his head.

"You're not going to answer that, are you?"

He blinked down at her, saw that she was staring at him thoughtfully. No, she was *studying* him. Studying with those bright brown eyes.

Had he noticed the intelligence in them earlier? Or not intelligence; wisdom. The kind that made being studied by her awfully uncomfortable.

He shifted.

"No," she spoke again. It took him a second to realize she was answering her own question. "You won't answer me because you're trying to figure out why the hell you let me kiss you. Don't take it personally." She grinned. "I'm the kind of person who whittles their way through defenses until one day, you find yourself asking me to be the godmother of your first-born. Not to mention the fact that I'm really cute."

She fluttered her lashes at him, laughed, as if she couldn't believe she'd done it.

"Anyway, it was a great kiss, and if you ever want to do it again . . ." She trailed off with another laugh. "What am I saying? As soon as I leave, you're going to pretend this never happened."

With a pat on his chest, she thanked him and disappeared into the crowd.

He stared after her.

"That might not have been the best way to approach this task," a voice said from beside him.

Levi turned. It came from a lanky guy hunched over his beer at the bar. He was wearing a loose T-shirt with leather pants. Levi stared at those before resting his eyes on the man.

"Who are you?"

"No pleasantries?" The man looked at him. There was something different about his eyes. A light, or perhaps a darkness, that Levi hadn't seen before. "No, 'you offered me an opportunity to return to my life, and I should take your advice'?"

"Oh, you're one of Them."

"No need to sound so dismissive."

Levi grunted.

The man smiled.

There was a long silence. Levi usually didn't mind those. He wasn't one of those people who felt the need to fill silence whenever they encountered it. Hell, some might even say he preferred it. Yes, he did prefer it.

So why was he suddenly feeling the intense desire to say something?

His mouth was opening before he could stop it, and he hoped he'd say something that wasn't stupid.

"It wasn't my fault."

Nope. Stupid all the way.

"We probably shouldn't talk about it here."

The man took Levi's hand, leading him to a dark corner of the club. Once they got there, Levi felt as though he'd been swept into a hurricane. He braced, but the sensation was already over.

Except for the nausea. The dizziness. That stayed.

"What did you do to me?" Levi asked, looking around to find a seat.

And found that he was now in a hotel room.

It was swanky, with its plush blue carpets on sleek wooden floors and views of the ocean. Much larger than he was used to, too. It didn't only have a bedroom and bathroom, but a dining area, a kitchen, a lounge.

"We *poofed*," the man said, waving a hand and distracting Levi from his perusal. "It's the way ghosts move around when we have to. Well, some ghosts." He paused. "Sometimes, anyway."

There was a lot in that, but Levi was stuck on one thing. *"Poofed?"*

But the man continued, as if he hadn't heard the question. "Being dead is complicated, Levi. As you've already discovered." He leaned back, holding out his hand. "I'm Jude, by the way. Your Guardian Ghost."

Levi took the hand while his brain tried to figure out what a Guardian Ghost was. "I thought *I* was a Guardian Ghost?"

"I suppose you are. To Gemma. But we don't call you that."

"What do you call us?"

Jude smiled. "Shall we talk about what happened tonight?"

Whatever They called people like him—ghosts—wasn't flattering.

He might have cared more if he weren't still processing that he was dead, that the key to his reincarnation was a woman he had kissed, and that the kiss had made his body believe it had already been reincarnated.

"You said it wasn't your fault," Jude prompted when Levi didn't speak. "I suppose I misheard when you gave your consent."

"She asked me," he replied, as if it were an adequate defense.

"When people ask you things, Levi, do you always acquiesce?"

When someone like her asks for a kiss, yeah.

He blinked. That was *not* how he felt. Certainly not.

"It will complicate things if you have feelings for her."

"I don't have feelings for her," Levi replied. "It was one kiss. It didn't mean anything."

Jude studied him. It felt a lot like before his parents' divorce, when he was still a carefree kid who did stupid things because he could. When he got caught doing them, his mom would look at him like this.

Maybe not exactly like this. Jude made him feel as if . . . as if he were transparent. And because he was a ghost, that might have actually been happening.

"If you say so," Jude eventually said, tone all mild and innocent even though Levi knew—he *knew*—Jude thought he was full of it. "Regardless, you've made an introduction now, so she should be willing to let you stay with her from now on."

"What?"

"Where do you think you're going to live?"

"Here?" Levi asked.

"Unfortunately, this room is only available for a week."

"You only booked it for a *week*? I'm supposed to be here an entire season." He paused. "Unless time here works differently than in my universe?"

"As I explained previously," Jude said patiently, "everything here would be the same as in your universe. Alternate realities only differ when it comes to people, although often that does lead to some significant changes in the structure of the world." He paused. "It's a bit complicated to explain, but not important. *This* reality is exactly the same as yours, except the people you share your world with don't exist. There are also insignificant details that differ, such as who won what during award season." He scrunched his nose. "We get those things wrong sometimes, so we like to course correct in different realities."

Levi exhaled. He might have got in too deep by agreeing to this.

"Besides, I didn't book this room. I just happen to know the next guests will only arrive in a week."

"So, what?" Levi asked in a measured voice. His best option seemed to be keeping calm. "I stay here and hope no one comes to investigate?"

"Essentially, yes."

"What if I don't find another place to go?"

"You will. She'll help."

"'She' doesn't even know who I am. 'She' doesn't even know *what* I am, and you expect her to house me for three months?"

"It will be okay, Levi. Trust me."

Jude didn't wait to see if Levi had any reply before he disappeared.

CHAPTER 2

Gemma stared at the book on her kitchen table. The box it had come in had arrived right before she went to work that morning, so she'd set the package down on the floor and hustled out of the house. She'd made it exactly on time. A thing that happened regularly and never failed to give her a sense of satisfaction. Which was probably why she never woke up earlier than she absolutely had to, so she wouldn't *have* to rush.

But who cared when there was the box and what the box held: the book that was currently on her kitchen table. One of many books, in fact, each of which was a possible key to a part of her life she hadn't known about for twenty-eight years.

The key to her *sister*.

She shuddered, as if the term were a curse. But it was merely a word. Or a relation, technically. A sibling. The sibling she had nagged and nagged her parents for from the time she could understand that she wanted friends and that siblings often meant built-in friends.

Back then, her parents had given her all sorts of reasons why that wouldn't be happening. It had become a game, and her parents had come up with playful answers.

If you have a sibling, we would have to share your birthday cake between four and not three people, and we're not willing to do that. After which they'd give her another slice of birthday cake.

A sibling would mean less time tickling you. After which they would keep tickling her.

We simply cannot afford to send another child to obedience school. After which they would wink and give her a command in some made-up language that almost always sounded like German.

She struggled to see it as innocent now, when the private investigator she'd hired had told her she had a sister. He'd given her a nice little package of information about the home she'd been adopted from, about the family who hadn't wanted her, and about the sister who had never been adopted.

Why? Why didn't you adopt her?

"A really good question," Gemma said out loud. "If only you had the courage to ask them about that."

Unwillingly, her eyes moved to her phone. There were dozens of unread messages from her parents on that phone. Dozens of missed calls.

She'd told them she was busy with the final arrangements for Lacey's wedding, and she hoped that excuse would buy her at least another three weeks before she had to face them. Unlikely, considering their messages and calls had come after she'd told them that. In fact, she was fully expecting them to pitch up at her house any day now. So she was treating every knock on the door with suspicion, something she had never done before in her life.

She had never stared at a book before, either. Hadn't walked back and forth between the kitchen table and her counter so she could look at an author's picture. Or read their bio.

Her phone rang. The screen showed Lacey's name. It was probably wedding-related—as every Lacey call had been for the last few weeks—and in truth, she was happy for the distraction, so she answered.

"Come out with us," Lacey said.

"What?"

"I said, come out with us."

"Lace, I *just* went out with you. Last week."

"Yes, that was for my bachelorette, which you were legally obligated to attend because you're my maid of honor. This is you and me. And Chet," she said, like it was an afterthought.

"I'm not going to be the third wheel on your date. On a Friday night," she added.

"You are not the third wheel. You've never been the third wheel."

"I've always been the third wheel."

"Well, it's never bothered you before." Lacey paused. "You've been acting weird for a while now. I bet you think I haven't noticed because I've been distracted, and you're partially right. I *have* been distracted, but that's why I haven't asked you about it. But I definitely noticed."

This was the problem with having best friends: They knew when things were off. And the problem with having Lacey as a best friend was that she wasn't always polite enough to leave things like this alone. She would pester Gemma until Gemma finally gave in, tired of being tortured.

But that was only if Lacey got Gemma alone for long enough. They hadn't been alone in almost a month. Lacey's official countdown had begun then, and every moment had been spent on discussing the wedding with family or friends or with Chet. And that would likely continue for another three weeks at least.

"Nope," Gemma lied cheerfully. "Nothing's going on. I'm fine. Everything's fine. But I can't come out with you tonight, because I'm . . . going to the bookstore."

"To the *bookstore?* Who are you?"

"I read," Gemma said defensively.

"Babe, reading your social media feeds doesn't count."

"Are they not words? Do those words not make sentences? Do those sentences not form stories?" Gemma demanded.

"You're proving my point."

"Fine." She gave herself a second. "I have . . . developed . . . an interest in romance novels."

There. That wasn't a lie. She *had* developed an interest in romance novels, because her sister wrote them.

Gemma couldn't help the irrational thrill that thought brought. Irrational, because she barely knew the woman, but she was already proud of her achievements.

"Which part of romance novels?" Lacey's voice was deceptively innocent. "The parts that involve climbing?"

"I will never forgive myself for telling you about that."

"Yes, you will, because it was an incredible kiss, and it was all because of me."

She wasn't lying. But Gemma had pushed that kiss—in all of its amazingness—to the back of her head. She had other priorities, other things to think about. Things that weren't the tingling in her body from a kiss with a man who hadn't seemed remotely interested in her after.

"You're keeping me from my bookstore activities, Lace," Gemma said, leaning against her kitchen counter, staring at the box that held two copies of every book her sister had written. "I'm going to go now."

"Gemma, if you put down this phone, I will drive right to your house and force you to tell me what's going on with you."

"Good thing I won't be home."

"Gemma—"

"Love you, Lace."

Gemma put down the phone, feeling only half bad, and focused on that box.

"What is that you say?" she asked the books brightly. "We should drop a set of you at the secondhand bookstore so I can avoid reading one of you and possibly getting some insight into the sister my parents didn't adopt or tell me about?" She nodded. "Sounds like an excellent plan. Let's do it."

* * *

Levi watched as Gemma tried to navigate this meeting with her sister.

It was obviously unexpected. She'd brought some books to the bookstore, but had dropped them on her way in. A man had come to help her—her sister's man, apparently. Gemma hadn't known that until Gaia had come to stand with this man, and now Gemma was . . . *floundering.*

"This is painful to watch," a voice said from beside him.

He startled, straightening since he'd been leaning against a tree. He'd been ready to defend himself, but the voice came from a small woman with long dark hair tied into two braids. She wore a cute little dress that flared at her hips and had black and white polka dots. She was young, possibly in her early twenties, but something about the way she looked at him made him think she was older. Nothing about her was threatening, though; he almost felt embarrassed at his initial reaction. But he was also standing in the trees beyond the parking lot of the bookstore, clearly watching the people in that lot having a conversation. Stalking, essentially.

But, based on what the woman had said to him, she had been stalking, too.

"You don't have to worry," she said mildly, "I won't report you to the police."

He opened his mouth, but she turned to him, grinning. It was that grin—and those eyes that were shadow and light again—that made him see it.

"Jude?"

"As I live and breathe." The smile widened. "Well, maybe that isn't the best phrase to use, all things considered."

"You're different today," Levi commented, as if that were the most important thing here.

"Yes."

There was a moment of silence while Levi waited for more,

but he got nothing. Accepting that this was merely how it was—that Jude would appear however she wanted to; that there was no point in questioning it—he turned back to look at Gemma and her sister.

"It is painful," he muttered.

The entire thing had been. Initially, because Gemma had been talking and talking to her sister's man, smiling and laughing and generally being comfortable with him, as if she hadn't only met him today. That was a strange pain, hot and prickly, sinking into his gut and making his skin feel too tight. He ignored it, because it felt a lot like it had something to do with the kiss they'd shared, and that was impossible.

Now, the pain was . . . sympathy. She seemed dumbfounded by her sister's appearance. She stared, shifted her feet, clutched the books as though they were a lifeline. She talked and talked, again, but this time it was colored by nerves and not a ridiculous sense of comfort with strangers.

When she all but ran inside the bookstore, he started to follow her. He wasn't sure what he would say once he reached her, but there was a deep desire inside him to *do* something. He probably would have, too, if Jude hadn't stopped him.

"Where are you going?" Jude asked.

"To talk to her."

"Why?"

"She needs . . . support," he said, his frustration seeping into his voice. "Isn't that why I'm here?"

"Yes, but you can't sort through this mess for her." For the first time, Jude's demeanor turned entirely serious. "She has to experience her current emotions so she can move forward with her sister."

Levi gritted his teeth. It helped anchor him. Helped remind him that he *wasn't* there to solve Gemma's problems for her. That was the first thing he'd been told when this assignment had been presented to him.

You won't be able to solve the problem for her.

It was a particular skill of his, not solving people's problems, only helping them. That's why he'd so easily agreed. He had spent his life supporting his father through the divorce, then with raising Haley, his younger sister. He had years of experience.

But why did that feel so disingenuous now? As if there were something wrong with the way he had framed it?

He shook it off. It was probably the transition from the life he had known to this life. To this different time, this alternate universe. It was probably nothing to worry about.

So why did it feel like something he should worry about?

"Do you know everything?" Levi asked, trying to get out of his head. Another thing he never did. What was it about Jude that made him want to *speak*? "About everyone's lives?"

"No," Jude said. "But we're given a file on our charges and their charges." She waited a beat. "I know what I need to know, and I guide you when I need to guide you."

Levi gave her a level stare. "Lots of wishy-washy stuff, that."

Jude shrugged. "You're a ghost, Levi. You're as wishy-washy as they come."

Damn. She was right.

"So when can I—"

He stopped speaking when he realized Jude had disappeared.

"Great," he said. "That probably means you think I don't need guidance anymore." When he got nothing, he continued louder. "I'll go speak with her now." He pretended to walk forward, even took a couple of steps. Still, nothing.

"I have to speak with her now," he said to himself. It took him a few seconds, but he managed to move his body. Before he could make much progress, a car passed him, Gemma in the front seat, her eyes glued to the road in front of her. He stared after her.

What was he supposed to do now? He had come here with

a taxi that had been paid for by whomever had left that note in his room telling him to take the taxi. He assumed it was Jude, and it probably had been. But now he was stranded with no transport and no money. Not only that, he didn't know the first place to start looking for Gemma.

In his time, his world, whatever universe he had come from, he lived in the Northern Suburbs of Cape Town. Kuils River was relatively large, the areas within it ranging vastly in terms of social and economic status. His family fell somewhere between the rich and the poor, but that only meant Levi had been exposed to both lifestyles, neither of which appealed to him. Having spent his entire life there—school, work—he was familiar enough with it that he'd be able to wander around and find things if he had to. But even there, he wouldn't have been able to find a complete stranger.

He wasn't in the Northern Suburbs now, nor was he in the world or time that he came from, anyway. According to Jude, nothing major had changed.

But Jude had also left him stranded outside a bookstore.

It should have concerned him. That he had no transport to get back to the hotel, that he only had one more night there, that he was a ghost whose entire existence depended on a woman he had shared an okay—fine, spectacular—kiss with. It should have worried him, and yet he could only think about Gemma.

How was she handling this first meeting with her sister? What had she said? Did she regret it? What would be her next steps? They were illogical thoughts, illogical questions. Why did these things matter? They didn't, he told himself. And he couldn't stop them for the life of him.

It must have been because he was a ghost whose purpose was Gemma.

That *must* have been it.

Now he had to find his way to her.

As he thought it, he felt that feeling of being swept into a hurricane again. Only this time, it felt as if the hurricane was *inside* him. No—as if it *were* him. As if his cells had come apart, spun around at a high speed, and come together again.

It left him nauseous and dizzy, as it had the first time.

It also brought him to a different place.

It took all of a minute to figure out what that place was.

Gemma took the ice cream and her phone and sank down to the floor.

"I can't believe you did that," she said out loud. "I can't believe that when you met your sister *for the first time,* you decided to *lie* to her. Now she's not only going to think that you're a weirdo, she's going to think that you're a *liar,* and I don't even know which is worse."

Gemma took a generous scoop of mint and chocolate and shoveled it into her mouth. "You've had a bunch of stupid ideas in your lifetime," she said, speaking through the frozen deliciousness, "but this? This was the stupidest thing by far."

Gemma stared at the pile of books she'd packed on the counter before taking the spares to the bookstore. They were bright, her sister's name on their spines in different colors, but the same font. It was impressive. To see how many books there were, all with GAIA ANDERS on them. Again, she felt that unreasonable pride. She had no doubt she would feel even prouder if she picked up a book and read it.

But she still couldn't bring herself to. Her actions that evening certainly wouldn't help that. When she was reading now, she would spend the entire time thinking about how she had made up a plot of a book when Gaia had asked her which one of Gaia's books was her favorite. And Gaia had gone along with her nonsense, too. Either because her sister was too polite to correct her, or because Gaia was testing her.

Gaia's first impression of Gemma would always be the lie.

"Stupid, stupid, stupid," she muttered, closing her eyes and knocking her head lightly against the cupboard behind her with each word.

"You're not stupid," a deep voice came from the shadowy area of her front room. "You panicked."

Her initial reaction was to throw her spoon in the direction of the voice. She got as far as lifting it, but then she realized that if she threw it, she would have to get up to get a new one.

She stayed on the floor with her spoon.

"I really want to help you," she said, "but I've had a rough day. Can you come back in the morning? I'll be in a much better space then. Might even be okay with you coming into my home."

No ghost had done that since the first year of her gift. Back then, they'd appear anywhere. Didn't matter where she was or whom she was talking to. Mr. Harris told her that if she didn't speak with the ghosts, no one else would see them. If she acknowledged them in any way, though, they'd materialize, and she'd have some awkward explaining to do. Like when her father had seen Benny the Ghost half-naked in her bedroom.

After that, she'd explained to the ghosts that she wouldn't engage with them if she wasn't alone. The ghosts soon acquiesced; she could only thank the Powers that Be or whomever had decided to cut her a break.

Least they could do, since you're the only person in the freaking world with this ability.

To be fair, she didn't know if that were true. She was only sure that the people in her life didn't share the ability. She'd had a hell of a time finding that out—it had taken some very creative inquiring—and their answers might as well have meant she was the sole person in the world to see and help ghosts.

She didn't mind helping. It was tricky to manage, but she'd quickly realized that her gift was bigger than herself. And if she was honest, she felt honored that she'd been chosen, out of everyone, to do this thing. So she would handle tricky, even if at times it meant ghosts invited themselves to her pity parties.

"I didn't mean to," the voice answered.

It was low, deep.

Familiar.

No.

She chose to agree with her inner voice.

"You didn't mean to what?" she asked.

"Come into your home."

"But you're here."

"Yes."

The word floated in the air. No other words joined it, so she was left without an explanation. She didn't ask for one, though she desperately wanted to. She liked the ghost's voice. Liked how soothing it was, how the low pitch made her skin feel all prickly.

Ha! Now she knew she was in a state. Fantasizing about a ghost's *voice.*

Maybe it was because it told her she wasn't stupid. It was always nice to hear that. Besides, she *had* panicked, so maybe that assessment was right.

Wait a minute.

"How did you know I panicked?" she demanded. "No—how did you know what I was talking about?"

"I watched you."

"You . . ." Maybe she did need to get this spoon involved. She stood, setting the ice cream on the table, tightening the grip on her weapon. "You should leave."

"You're kicking me out?"

"You appeared in my house uninvited, and you told me you watched me. What else am I supposed to do?"

"I thought you'd be used to this kind of thing, since you see ghosts."

"None of them stalk me."

"Funny you should use that word. As I understand it, that's exactly what you've been doing with your sister."

She opened her mouth to ask what he knew about that, when he stepped into the light.

It was *him.*

The man she wanted to climb.

The man who kissed as if he'd been born to kiss.

The man who kissed as if he'd been born to kiss *her*.

"You're a *ghost*?"

He spread his arms, as if to say, *there you go.* As if she were some kid who'd gotten a math equation right on the first try. Which was ridiculous—she had never gotten a math equation right on the first try in her life.

"I kissed you," she accused. "We kissed. In front of people."

"We did."

"Why? Why would you let me kiss you?"

There was the slightest beat before he said, "It was a good way to introduce myself to you."

"Was it?" she said sharply—and did not like it. She was not a sharply spoken person. She was a kindly spoken person, damn it.

"I admit, it was a lapse in judgment."

His expression was stoic. All emotion, any emotion, safely tucked behind that angry hair. Behind that *deceptive* hair. She should have known it hid a dishonest person. Aggressively sexy was not a thing, and here he was, proving it.

"You know what this means, don't you?" she asked, her voice all light and fluffy, like a cloud.

Like a storm cloud, yeah.

No one asked you, she snapped at that stupid voice in her head.

He was staring at her when her eyes met his. Waiting on something. It took her a while to figure out he was waiting for her to answer her own question.

"It means that you exist now. In this world."

He frowned. "I don't understand."

"Of course you do," she said, more gently than she felt. "I've never met a ghost who didn't know the rules of their existence."

"You've never met a ghost like me."

Some secret part of her trembled at the way he said it. With a confidence that rarely came off as undickish, but did now. She wouldn't even blame him if it were dickish, because dickish did seem like the right adjective when it came to him, for more literal reasons than she cared to admit.

He was right, though. Not once in the twelve years since she'd lived with her abilities had she seen a ghost like him. Sure, there were attractive ghosts. Sure, sometimes she wondered what it would be like to know those ghosts when they'd been alive. But she had never crossed a line with a ghost as she had with him. She had never wanted to kiss a ghost, let alone actually kiss them.

Except this one.

What was so special about him? Her eyes scanned him without her permission. Her cheeks blushed without her permission, too, when she realized her heart was beating faster because of her perusal.

So, okay, yes, fine, he was exceptional-looking. Besides his height and his aggressively sexy facial hair, his shoulders were broad. And yes, there were many men who had broad shoulders, but none that looked like *that*. It was somehow a combination of *come, let me help you with your burdens* and *come, let me throw you over my shoulder because you've been misbehaving.* The earring made her think the punishment for misbehaving would be very good indeed . . .

She blinked. Her thoughts were never this depraved. She could recognize an attractive person, of course, but usually, she didn't think about them in this way. She certainly wouldn't have imagined scenarios where she wanted to misbehave so that she could test her hypothesis about a set of shoulders and an earring.

Maybe there was something special about him.

Even so, that something special was confined to his appearance. To his eyes that were piercing and somber and appeared to be the same color as that special blend of brandy she liked. To his mouth that was grim and thin but could kiss her as if she were a fairy-tale princess who needed true love's kiss to return to life.

This was already the most complicated ghost relationship she'd had, and she didn't even know his name.

"I can't imagine your superiors are happy with you," she told him lightly, putting her ice cream back in the freezer and taking out mugs for tea.

When in doubt—or confused about the effect a ghost had on her body parts—make tea.

"What makes you say that?" he asked.

"You kissed a human."

"I'm human, too."

"Yeah, but you died." There was silence after that, and she stopped her tea-making when she realized how it sounded. "Oh, that was thoughtless. I'm sorry. For that, and about your death." She waited for a reply. Didn't get one. Continued. "Would you like to talk about it?"

He only stared.

"I only ask because sometimes they do. Other ghosts," she clarified. "They tell me how they died, and I say something re-assuring like, of course it wasn't silly of you to run toward the knife and not away from it!"

"You've said that?"

"Of course," she said, going back to the tea. "The first step in dealing with your death is acknowledging one, that it hap-pened, and two, that it's pointless to think about how you could have prevented it. So"—she turned, offering him the mug—"would you like to tell me how you died?"

He looked at the mug, took it as if she were offering him poison, and didn't answer her question. She would have been bothered if it weren't for that look on his face. Discomfort . . . no—embarrassment.

She'd met her fair share of ghosts, so she'd heard enough em-barrassing death stories. A number of people had died because they'd taken selfies in unsafe places. There was that man who'd died trying to shake a coconut out of a tree. He'd gotten the coconut . . . because it had fallen on his head, and sadly, he'd become one of the one hundred and twenty-three people killed by a coconut that year.

And then there were the ghosts who died from experimenting sexually! Those were the *worst* ghosts to talk to. They refused to accept they'd died. Because having sex on a glacier was *so* safe.

"Is it a sex thing?" She sipped her tea. The peppermint flavor coated her tongue, and she gave a happy shake of her shoulders. "No need to be ashamed."

When she looked at him, he was gaping.

"Not a sex thing," she said with a nod. "Got it."

"How many people die of sex things?"

"Too many to mention. But if yours is not a sex thing," she went on, "what is it?"

"That's not important for you to know."

"The whole point of this"—she gestured between them—"is for me to know. How else am I supposed to help you?"

"Help me?" he repeated. "I think there's been a mistake."

He put his undrunk tea on the table and folded his arms, leaning against her counter. Her stomach did a twirly thing, which was strange, because she was certainly not one of those people who was impressed by leaning. Especially not when it came from someone with his *attitude.* Like he was taunting her.

"You're not supposed to be helping me," he told her. "I'm here to help *you.*"

She snorted. "You're here to help *me*? How? No—why? I don't need help."

He studied her. It was the best word to describe it, because it did feel like he was studying. Like she was a subject he would later be tested on.

She pursed her lips. She did not like that at all.

"Correct me if I'm wrong," he said, "but are you not currently trying to build a relationship with the twin sister your parents didn't tell you about?"

"How . . . how do you know that?"

"It was part of the presentation They gave me when They offered me the opportunity to help you."

"They *offered* you this *opportunity*?" she asked, her voice dripping with sarcasm. "Helping someone who doesn't need help—helping someone who hasn't asked for help—isn't an *opportunity*."

He didn't reply, only went back to studying her. Annoyance skittered down her spine. Another thing she did not like. She already had all those feelings about meeting her sister swirling inside her, and now she had to deal with this?

She was about to ask him to leave—as politely as she could manage—when the doorbell rang. It was obviously Lacey, which would have been fine under normal circumstances. But these weren't normal circumstances; she had a ghost in her house.

A ghost she had kissed. In front of her friends.

"Oh, shit," she said. "You have to go."

"Excuse me?"

"Right now. Do your ghostly *poofing* thing."

"You call it *poofing*, too?" he asked, clearly not understanding the urgency of the situation. "It's terrible."

"Yeah, yeah, awful," she agreed. She would have agreed with anything at that point. "But can you do it now, please?"

"No."

"No?"

"I don't know how to."

"You don't know how to," she repeated slowly, though she wasn't sure why. "How did you get here?"

"I can hear you in there," Lacey called from the door. "And I can hear you're with someone, you liar!"

Gemma swore. Then, because that didn't seem like enough,

she turned around and knocked her head against the wall. Lightly, of course. But it achieved its desired effect.

"That is not necessary."

She whirled around. "Of course it's necessary. My best friend *heard* you. Now I'm going to have to answer some pretty awkward questions."

"Tell her you were on the phone."

"That won't work. She heard you."

"I'm a ghost," he said simply.

"Yeah, you're a ghost, but I kissed you in front of my friends."

"Why do you keep saying that like it's significant?"

She stared. "You really don't know, do you?" At the shake of his head, she sighed. "I've acknowledged your existence. You're pretty much human now."

"I still don't understand."

She could hear the frustration in his voice, but she couldn't help him with that. "Neither do I, but that's the way it works."

"Do you . . . acknowledge"—the word sounded strangled—"many ghosts?"

"I did, in the beginning. I was young and didn't know any better. There was this time I did it with a ghost in my bedroom, and my dad—" She cut off when she saw his face. Suddenly, it clicked. "Acknowledge in *any* way. Not just kissing." She leaned in conspiratorially. "You're my first. No need to be jealous."

"I was not jealous."

She winked. "Sure."

"Gemma Daniels! If you don't open this door right now, I'm getting Chet to kick it open."

"I'm not kicking the door open," came Chet's voice.

"Of course you will, my love," Lacey said. Gemma could almost see her patting his chest. "But you won't have to, because Gemma is going to open the door for us."

She said the last part louder, as if Gemma and the ghost hadn't been privy to their entire conversation anyway.

Gemma turned to the ghost. "Look, if I hadn't acknowledged you—talked to, looked at, gestured to, whatever—you'd be able to stay here while I deal with this. But because we kissed, everyone can see you, so you need to leave."

"I can't—"

"Hide, then," she hissed, walking to the door. She was half afraid Lacey would kick it in herself if she didn't. She glanced over her shoulder to check that he was gone—he was—and opened the door.

"Lacey, I told you not to come," Gemma said brightly.

"And I told you I would, because . . ." Lacey trailed off, frowning. "Because you're acting weird, and I'm worried about you." The concern in her tone warmed Gemma's heart, but Lacey quickly pushed past her, scanning the room. "Where is he?" she demanded.

"Who?"

"You know I'm talking about the man you had in here."

"A man?" Gemma scoffed. "You must be mistaken."

"No, I heard him, too," Chet said from behind her.

She turned to him. "Did you now?" she asked, and gave him a look that clearly said she expected him to be on her side, especially after everything she'd done for him over the last few weeks. Helping Lacey with the wedding, coming over when she was having a meltdown, talking her down when she made threats. Just the day before, he'd called her because Lacey hadn't liked her hair trial and had the scissors in her hand, ready to cut her hair off.

Chet seemed to remember that, too, because he winced and mouthed, "Sorry."

"Apology not accepted," she replied out loud, before turning to Lacey. "Your energy is a bit chaotic right now, and I need you to take it down."

"To what level?"

Gemma considered it. "You're probably at about an eight, and I need you to be a three."

They did this. Spoke about emotions in a more practical way to manage them. It didn't happen often, but in situations where emotions ran high, it was helpful. She knew if she told Lacey about the thing with her parents, her sister, Lacey would tell her she was being a level ten unreasonable, and Gemma would have to take it down, too.

Actually, Gemma wasn't sure that was true. Lacey always took her side. That's how they'd become friends in the first place. On the first day of orientation at university, a girl had refused to let Gemma sit down next to her, because she was keeping three seats open for her friends. Normally, Gemma would have respected that, but the classroom was packed, and it was either one of those seats or none at all.

Lacey, who'd been sitting in the next open seat, had kindly but sharply stepped in, and since her best friend was a little scary, Gemma had been given permission to sit down. She and Lacey instantly clicked, and Lacey had been a steadfast and loyal presence in Gemma's life since.

She hadn't told Lacey this huge news because . . . well, she was waiting until after the wedding. It would be selfish to distract her friend with her feelings before such a pivotal event.

Level ten unreasonable.

Gemma ignored the voice in her head.

Lacey took a deep breath, exhaled, and spoke in a much calmer voice, respecting the agreement she and Gemma had made. "I did hear someone, Gemma. Chet heard someone, too. So you can stop lying now and tell me where he is. No—tell me *who* he is. I have a pretty good idea of where he is."

She grinned, and Gemma realized Lacey was talking about the bedroom.

"It was the television," Gemma lied, resisting the wince. She hated lying.

"Your TV isn't on." Lacey folded her arms. "Try again."

"I switched it off before I opened the door for you. That's why it took so long."

She folded her arms, too. They stared at each other, and Lacey said, "Fine. I'll go and find him in your bedroom."

Gemma considered tackling Lacey to the ground, but she might break something, and Lacey would never forgive her for that right before the wedding. So she accepted her fate, and hoped with all her might the ghost had gone to the spare bedroom instead.

CHAPTER 3

He had to admit it, this was not the way he wanted their first meeting to go.

"Technically, this isn't your first meeting."

Levi spun around. A man stood in the corner, tall and dark, his dreadlocks falling to his shoulders. He had a soothing voice, wore loose clothing, and regarded Levi with a steady—and familiar—gaze.

"Jude?" Levi asked. The man nodded. "How many times are you going to change bodies?"

"I never know who I'm going to appear to you as, so I don't know how to answer that question."

"What does that—" Levi broke off. Sighed. "How did you know what I was thinking? Can you read my mind?"

"I have the ability to . . ." Jude gave him a serene smile. "You know what? I'm not sure you want to know the answer to that." Changing directions, he continued. "How do you feel about how things have gone so far? I assume you're not entirely happy?"

"Why didn't you warn me about the rules?" he asked. "I *poofed* here because I thought about her. Is that how that works? Is it possible for me to return to the hotel room if I think about it?" And because he was compelled to keep talking around Jude, his tongue apparently a hamster on a wheel, he said, "While we're on the topic of you not telling me things, why didn't you warn me that if she acknowledged me, I'd stop being a ghost?"

"You're still a ghost, Levi," Jude said mildly. "And I thought you knew you existed now. Why else would you ask me about booking the room or staying with Gemma if you didn't realize it?"

Jude was right. Some part of him must have thought he was human.

No, that wasn't it. He'd asked about it because he was still thinking in human terms. He'd been human for thirty years, damn it. Of course he was still thinking in human terms.

"Nice try," Levi told him. "But it won't work."

"I'm sure I don't know what you're talking about, Levi."

Levi snorted, though he could begrudgingly admit Jude's commitment to his aloof guardian role was impressive. The actual approach, however . . .

"You're not the kind of guardian who likes to give their charges helpful information, are you?"

"I am," Jude said, sounding offended. "I told you things that first evening."

"Nothing helpful."

"Hmm. Almost makes me not want to tell you what I came here for."

Levi lifted his brows.

"Fine, you've convinced me." Bright smile. A little creepy, to be honest. "Your best option here is to take Gemma's lead. If you do, you'll find answers to the other problems you have, as well."

Levi was about to ask what he was talking about when the door pushed open, and a woman walked in.

She was tall with loose copper-colored hair falling in waves over her shoulders. She had big eyes lined with dark pencil, her lips were painted a dark brown, almost brick color, and her cheeks were dusted with a shade marginally lighter than her lips. Her eyebrows were perfectly shaped, with one quirking as she stared at him. Her mouth dropped, and she whirled around.

"You *sly* dog!"

Gemma walked into the room, too, heard her friend, saw him, and sighed. It was cute. His brain told him to cut it out, and he realized the emotion behind that sigh was resignation. As if she'd known this would come, and she was already tired of dealing with it.

Defensiveness rose like a wave inside him. It also crashed like a wave pretty soon after—he probably could have made more of an effort to hide. He hadn't thought about what would happen if her friend investigated. He'd been so distracted by her room at first—bright orange and green décor against whites and creams, and a *ton* of plants—and then Jude had appeared.

So he took Jude's advice and waited for her to take the lead.

"Lacey, how old are we?" she asked her friend.

"Clearly not old enough to tell the truth when we have a man in our bedroom." Lacey turned to Levi. "Hi, how are you?"

Levi glanced at Gemma. She made a *go on* motion with her hand.

"Fine." When Gemma did the motion again, he barely resisted the urge to roll his eyes. "How are you?"

"Delighted to have found you in my friend's room." There was a beat. "What are you doing on the twenty-third?"

"Lacey, no."

"Gemma, *yes.*"

"He and I have known each other for one week. I am not taking him with me to your wedding."

Levi wanted to interject and say that he had very little interest in going with her to the wedding, but he didn't. She was clearly uncomfortable. Besides, if he put himself in her shoes, he'd be uncomfortable, too.

She'd kissed a ghost without knowing he was a ghost—

although how was that possible when she'd seen ghosts for twelve years of her life?

It didn't matter.

She *had* kissed him, her friends had seen it, and now, he was in her house. It was an awkward situation, as she'd predicted. Made even more awkward by a friend who didn't seem to understand boundaries.

"Of course you're bringing him! Unless by then your new relationship has fizzled, which is a possibility, considering you've gone from kissing him before knowing his name to having him in your bedroom a week later." Lacey turned to him now. "What *is* your name, by the way?"

Man, she was pushy.

"Levi."

"Hi, Levi. I'm Lacey." She offered her hand. He took it, but only because it seemed like something Gemma would want him to do. "This is my fiancé, Chet."

If long-suffering had a face, it would be this man's. He was only slightly taller than Lacey, cleanly shaven, with smooth brown skin and tired eyes. Those eyes held a devotion Levi had only seen in dogs before, which was probably the reason for both the lines on his face and his tiredness.

"Lace, could I have a word?"

Lacey opened her mouth—presumably to deny Gemma's request—but she looked at her friend's face and had a change of heart. She followed Gemma out of the room, leaving Chet and Levi behind.

Chet gave him an apologetic look. "I'm sorry. She was worried Gemma was hiding something."

Levi nodded. Seconds passed before he realized it was his turn to make small talk. "I guess she was right."

He wasn't talking about himself, but about Gemma's secret sister. He assumed no one else in her life knew about the situation, or he wouldn't be needed. Alternatively—and this seemed likely now that he'd met her friends—she had told them, and they simply hadn't been able to help.

Gemma and Lacey returned before he had to come up with anything else to say. Lacey seemed much more muted now.

"Chet, we should go." Lacey gave Levi a sweet, slightly saucy smile. "It was nice meeting you, Levi!"

Chet nodded at him, and they left the room. Levi waited a few minutes before he followed, in case they were still there and he was forced to attend another event he didn't want to go to. Gemma turned to him after she locked the door, and quirked a brow.

Now.

Usually, he wasn't the kind of guy who got turned on by attitude. Usually, he'd meet someone he thought attractive, pursue them, and once he got to know them, he'd get into the physical stuff. The relationships never lasted, the physical stuff the first to go, since he rarely had the time or energy that part of a relationship required.

It meant that he didn't have much experience being turned on by anything or anyone outside of a relationship. It meant that being turned on by a quirk of someone's brow—someone inappropriate, at that—took him by surprise.

His eyes swept over her. He wanted to wrap her long brown hair around his hand, tug her head back, kiss her. He wanted to taste those soft wide lips, feel them against his again, this time without an audience, so he could touch her the way her body deserved. He wanted to see her big eyes fill with desire and heat, wanted to see the flecks of gold and green sparkle with emotion.

None of it made *sense*.

"I have good news, and I have bad news," she said.

He nodded, hoping she'd take it as a sign to continue. He didn't trust himself to speak.

"I'll start with the good news: They left! And they probably won't be back for a while." She clapped her hands, applauding herself, and folded her arms behind her back. "The bad news is that they left because I told her I wanted to jump your bones, and she was interrupting." She winced. "Sorry."

His lips parted before he could help it, his throat suddenly dry. He had to clear it before he could speak, and even then, he needed a second.

"You told her we were dating."

"No." She frowned. "Those two things do not mean the same thing."

He didn't reply.

She studied him. "You're not from here, are you?"

He blinked. "I don't understand."

"You do," she assured him, "but since we're playing pretend, I meant that you're not from the world I'm from. This one."

"How could you possibly know that?"

"I'm right?"

He gave a slight nod.

"Oh, man. I knew there were other universes out there." She paused. "And to think, I'd have never known for sure if something about you didn't feel . . . right. Hmm," she hummed, "that might not be the best description. It's just . . . I can't put my finger on it. Maybe it has something to do with your antiquated views."

"My views are not antiquated."

"You said sex and dating are the same thing."

"I didn't say that," he said through gritted teeth. "I wouldn't have. I am a gentleman."

"Even gentlemen get freaky."

He stared. She bit the corner of her lip. When that clearly didn't hide her amusement, she laughed. "I'm sorry. It's your expression."

He could feel his frown deepen, was unsurprised by it. Because that apology was truly pathetic. As if *your expression* were an adequate excuse for laughing at someone.

"You are not a lady."

"Never claimed that I was," she informed him. "This is exactly what I'm talking about, by the way. Who talks about 'ladies and gentlemen' anymore? Those terms have lost their relevance."

"I do come from another time," he told her, "but I'm not sure I understand what you're talking about."

"Those terms are unnecessarily gendered, old-fashioned, and they imply breeding, which is gross." She paused. "Wait—did you say you were from a different time?"

He looked unsettled with his angry little frown, but he nodded.

"As in, a different decade? A different century? Obviously in the past, because you say things like 'ladies and gentlemen.'" She looked at him. "I'd ask you what it's like living in the past, but since you look like that—" She grimaced.

"Since I look like what?"

"You know . . ." She wrinkled her nose, waving her hand in a circle around his face.

"I *don't* know."

"You're getting irritated with me?"

"You're being vague."

"I'm not being vague! I just didn't think I'd need to tell you you're not white." She said the last word with a wry twist of her mouth.

"I'm not . . ." His frown deepened. "Gemma, why would you say that as if race mattered in the past? As if it matters now?"

There was a beat before they both started laughing.

It was the first time anything remotely easy had happened between them. Gemma hadn't expected it to be a result of race, but she'd bonded with enough people over the issue to not be surprised.

He had a nice laugh, deep and rumbling. It made her think about how she'd rolled down the hills near her grandmother's house when she'd been younger. That joyous, free feeling that only children could have, even when they were doing something dangerous.

It suited him, the joy and danger, the rumbling and freedom. She didn't know how, but there were many things she didn't understand about Levi. She almost welcomed it—until she remembered that she had to understand *some* things, or she would be in her current predicament forever.

"So you're here from the past?" she tried again, more tentatively than before.

"No." He seemed to be weighing his words. "The present. But an alternate reality."

He'd all but confirmed it earlier, but to hear him actually say it . . . She tried to act cool. "Like a multiverse?" she asked.

"I believe so."

"Gosh." Her eyes widened. "So there might be a version of me who didn't cut her own bangs when she was fifteen and had to hide it from her mother for years with a ton of gel? I don't even know why I did it, and I was terrified she would find out. It was my sole act of rebellion as a teenager, and I really regret—" She broke off at his stare. "Never mind. Not important."

"You're right." He paused. "Your relationship with your sister is important."

"I have no relationship with my sister."

"Not with that attitude." His face went blank. He met her eyes. "I was trying something. Didn't work."

"Depends on what your goal was." She smiled. "I enjoyed it."

He looked at her ceiling. "Gemma," he said slowly, "I'm here to help you with your sister."

"No, thank you."

"So you're happy?" he asked quietly. "With not having a relationship with your sister? With a strained relationship with your parents?"

She didn't bother asking him how he knew things were

strained with her parents. It was probably in that "presentation" They'd given him. She made an unintelligible sound to both his questions and the fact that there'd been a presentation on her, and went to drink her tea. It was cold now, but she didn't mind.

"I'm waiting."

"Of course I'm happy," she lied. "I have a job I enjoy. I have a great"—she ignored the hesitation—"family, and good friends. Why wouldn't I be happy?"

"You found out you have a sister. You've longed for one all your life, and you had one. And your parents knew about her. It's undermined the very foundation of your happiness. It's undermined the very foundation of the trust you have in your parents. Why would you be happy?"

"I . . ."

Speechless. She was speechless.

But there were words in her head. Things that couldn't make it out her mouth, because they would prove that he was right. She preferred not to admit that. It was uncomfortable enough to have him in her home, to have him meet her friends, to pretend she was sleeping with him. She didn't need him to be right, too.

"Please, leave."

It came out as a rasp. A plea. She saw him struggle with it. Struggled with it herself. She wasn't the kind of person who pleaded. She didn't know how that person looked or why it was bad, but it felt . . . it felt like she wasn't being herself.

It was strange that it was that same feeling that had spurred her into looking into her family. Her parents had always glossed over the details or maintained that they'd told her what she needed to know. But they hadn't. Either that, or they hadn't been honest with themselves about what she needed to know.

She needed context. To not be a black-and-white outline, but a colored picture. Then she had found out that the picture she thought existed wasn't the full thing. That someone had deliberately cut out parts of it. Was it any wonder that she regularly felt like she wasn't herself after discovering that? Hell, she didn't even know *who* she was.

"Gemma—"

He stopped when she lifted her head, looked at him. She didn't know what he saw, but he nodded and left.

She heaved a sigh and got out the emergency emergency ice cream that she hid behind the emergency ice cream. It was the most expensive snack she had ever bought, but if ever there was an emergency emergency, it was now.

CHAPTER 4

Levi was in a predicament. He had no money, no way of getting back to the hotel he had one more night in, and no human charge to take him in. There was a strong possibility he was going to end up sleeping on the street, and he was not a fan of that solution.

It didn't help that Gemma lived in the kind of place where neighbors would definitely call the cops on him. He gathered it was in the Helderberg area, based on the greenery and the mountains peaking in the distance, which was about thirty minutes from his old home of Kuils River.

He never thought he would miss Kuils River because the neighborhood wouldn't blink an eye at someone sleeping on the streets, yet here he was. But Gemma's neighbors would care. That tended to happen when people had money. They lost compassion, unable to understand that one misstep could mean they'd be the ones on the street.

Yeah, the people in his old neighborhood understood that.

"Jude," he said under his breath. He didn't know who was looking out their window, but he wasn't going to give them a chance to judge him for talking to himself, too. "Now would be a great time for you to do one of your guardian things."

He kept walking, the sidewalk illuminated by streetlights and the moon, casting shadows from his body and the trees above ahead of him. The air was full of sounds from the night. The song of crickets; the occasional siren in the distance; the almost static sound of silence. There was no answer from Jude; of course there wasn't. If there had been, Jude might actually be a guardian instead of a commentator on everything he said and did.

Jude reminded him of his father, actually. Heath Walker had a habit of making unhelpful observations about Levi's life. His inability to apply that talent to his own life was staggering. Case in point was when Heath blamed his wife entirely for their divorce, which even Levi, at sixteen years old, had known wasn't true.

What would have been a great observation to make was how Heath had spent a significant time working, not paying any attention to his wife and son, determined to prove the people who'd told him he wasn't worth anything wrong. His father should have observed how those people didn't matter, that his family did. He should have known that every success he'd made at work eroded his marriage. He should have seen that having another baby in an attempt to fix something he hadn't even known was broken would only make things worse.

His mother hadn't been innocent, of course. She could be vindictive and immature. Having another kid was the worst possible decision, but she had spearheaded it. She was desperate, Levi could see now, but he wasn't sure what she was desperate for. Reconciliation or driving the final nail into the coffin.

He exhaled. Shook his shoulders. None of that mattered. At least it wouldn't if he failed at this task. There was no chance of returning to his life if that happened. He would never see Haley again, and she'd live an entire lifetime thinking she was responsible for his death.

Is it a sex thing?

Thanks, he silently told that voice inside him. It was a great reminder of what did matter right now—and how spectacularly he was failing at it. What an unexpected bonus for his mind to offer him one of the many inappropriate things she said to him, too! One of the things that made him remember how plump her lips were, how soft, how her tongue could—

"Hey, need a ride?"

Levi turned at the voice. He studied the face in the car before he stopped walking. The car halted, too.

"Chet, right?"

"Yeah." The tired eyes were still tired, but for the first time, Levi noticed how sharp they were. "Do you want a ride?"

Levi opened his mouth to accept, but realized he didn't know where he'd take that ride to. The hotel he'd been staying in was on the other side of town. He couldn't expect a lift there. Perhaps he could borrow money to call a car service that operated this late at night? It would be a hefty fee, too, so that wasn't the best idea, either.

"It's not rocket science."

"Yeah, sorry." Levi rubbed his head. "I just don't know where I'd go."

"You homeless?"

He would have said yes if he didn't know Chet would immediately tell Lacey, who would give Gemma a hard time about it. Although, to be fair, it wouldn't surprise him if Gemma engaged with homeless people all the time.

"Nah. I live on the opposite side of town. Can't expect a ride there."

Chet studied him. "She kick you out?"

He nodded. Endured some more studying before Chet eventually said, "Get in."

"What?"

"Get in the car. You can stay in my spare room tonight."

He was about to protest, but he'd be shooting himself in the foot if he did. So he got in the car. Buckled his seat belt. Hoped that Chet wasn't a serial killer who picked up strangers late at night and took them back to his place to torture.

But hey, he was already dead.

"Thank you," Levi said. When Chet merely angled his head in reply, Levi asked, "Why?"

"Gemma's done a lot for me. The least I can do for her is take you in for a night."

"This wouldn't be for her. She kicked me out."

"It's for her," Chet assured him. He took a left, then another, before continuing. "She'll feel bad about it in the morning. She'll call you, and you'll be able to tell her you were safe."

Because he agreed, even if hope fueled that agreement more than logic, he said, "You know her well?"

The side of Chet's mouth lifted in an almost smile, but it was like the other half of it didn't have the energy to commit to a full one. "We've known each other a while."

Levi nodded and looked out the window. He wasn't looking at the scenery; he was trying to give Chet space. And when that wasn't possible physically, the next best thing was to look away.

He wasn't sure why he was giving Chet space, beyond the fact that the man seemed to need it. Levi couldn't put his finger on it, but Chet felt . . . fragile. Levi would put money on that being Lacey's fault, but he remembered the devotion on Chet's face when the man looked at his fiancée. He loved her. Adored her, really. But love and adoration wouldn't protect him from exhaustion. Mental and physical, as one would expect from planning a wedding.

To Lacey.

"My place is a mess," Chet said as he pulled through the gates of a security complex. "We're moving into a different house, so I've been packing. Actually came from dropping some stuff there when I saw you walking the streets." He stopped the car. "Come on. You probably want some sleep."

Levi followed him out of the car, up two flights of stairs, and waited as Chet unlocked the door and put off the alarm. He didn't care much about the mess, which was less of a mess and more untidiness. Closed boxes stood in stacks near the walls, half-packed boxes on the opposite side of the room next to a glass sliding door with others under cabinets in the kitchen they'd entered. The kitchen led to a living room that had a television mounted on the wall and two couches, one of which was already wrapped in plastic. The coffee table had a single empty coffee cup on it and what looked like a makeup bag.

"Bathroom's over there," Chet said, nodding at a door in the middle of a short passageway that had two rooms on either side. "Spare bedroom"—Chet pointed at one of the rooms—"my room. You can help yourself to anything you want in the kitchen."

Levi nodded again and tried to figure out how often he should say thank you. He wasn't used to needing help. Usually, people asked *him* for help. Hell, he was back on earth as a ghost because he was supposed to help Gemma. Yet here he was, being helped when he needed it, and he couldn't even figure out how to say thank you. A normal response in this situation. What did that say about him?

"Thank you," Levi said again, because he didn't know how to answer that question, but he for damn sure wasn't going to be bested by two words. "You didn't have to do this."

"I'm not doing this for you."

"So you said."

There was a long silence. Chet sighed. "That was rude, wasn't it? Sorry. It's been a hell of a long day. Long months," he clarified. "Do you want to . . ." He hesitated. Sighed again. "You wanna get a beer and sit out on the balcony?"

"Sure."

It was the least he could do. But even as he accepted the beer from Chet, he knew that wasn't the only reason he was doing it. He wanted normality. In the last seven days, he'd died, come back to life, and messed up the mission he'd come back to life for. He wanted a beer, he wanted to drink it with another human, and he wanted to sit on the balcony while he did.

The balcony looked out on another block of flats and the road separating the two buildings. It was oddly perfect, as was the silence he expected at 10:30 p.m. They drank in silence, too, but it wasn't uncomfortable. It wasn't even awkward.

Eventually, Chet said, "So you met Gemma at a bar?"

"Yeah."

"Kissed her, right?"

He nodded.

"Hmm." A beat. "Lacey was still talking about it when I said goodbye to her. She's convinced you're a serial killer."

Levi smiled. "I thought the same thing about you."

Chet laughed. Sobered. "I have a sense about these things."

"Serial killers?"

"I guess, yeah." He looked over. "You seem like an okay guy. Have to see how you treat Gemma before I commit to that judgment, but I can help an okay guy out when he needs it. Besides," he said, taking a swig of his beer, "I'm pretty sure I can take you."

Levi drank from his beer, too. "Sure."

"That doesn't sound sincere."

"I'd still be walking down that road if it weren't for you. It's sincere as shit."

Chet laughed again, patted him on the back. "Yeah, you're okay. Just don't steal any of my stuff and prove me wrong."

He grunted in agreement, but chuckled.

Gemma tried not to think about the ghost who appeared in her house and made her lose her mind. Instead, she focused on her job. She had a new client, a friend of Lacey's who had heard Gemma was an interior designer and wanted to meet on Saturday to run through some of Gemma's ideas for designing her office.

Gemma hadn't needed to jump through any hoops to get the job, either. She supposed that was because of her link to Lacey. Since Lacey was a criminal lawyer, Gemma didn't want to know what had inspired such loyalty.

The office in question was a large container building in the garden of the client's house. Lacey's professional circles included people who could afford container offices. People who had yards big enough to house those container offices.

The container wasn't a boring square box, either. It was a two-story structure painted an unassuming green with massive glass windows that allowed for a view of the stunning garden. Tall trees, a pool that spread the entire length of the yard, and perfectly maintained hedges and flower bushes.

"This is beautiful."

"Thank you," Meg said, her pants flowing behind her. She was the kind of person whose pants flowed behind her. As did her hair, her top, and—Gemma was certain, though not of the technicalities—her shoes. "We've been so blessed with this property. I've done my best to honor the space."

Gemma wasn't a landscape designer, but she could appreciate the artful arrangement. "You've done a wonderful job. I hope I can continue that by giving you exactly what you want with your office."

She had already seen pictures of the space and had given Meg a preliminary idea of what she would do. But it was always different in the space itself. She allowed herself to envision what Meg wanted: something that felt like a continuation of the garden. Which would be relatively easy with all the windows and the light streaming in.

Gemma could already see the paintings she'd put up, the colors bright and sharp like in the garden itself. The floors would be grounded, natural shades like brown and charcoal, although the latter may be too harsh. Not in the bathrooms, though, she mused, running her fingers over the white marbling. There was a piece by a local artist that would work wonderfully to tie the two rooms together. She wondered if she could get Meg to pay the artist what she deserved . . .

"I can see your mind's already on the job," Meg said.

Gemma winced. "Sorry—that was rude! I didn't mean to ignore you. This space is . . ." She shook her head. "The pictures didn't do it justice. Look at this!" She walked to where she'd imagined putting the sculpture. "This is the perfect place to put something to merge this area with this one. I was thinking of—"

She broke off. She was sure she could find the picture of the sculpture she had in mind. She dug into her handbag, offering Meg an apologetic smile when her phone wasn't in the side pocket she usually put it in.

"Sorry."

It was a huff. She had a huge bag that she threw everything in. Most days, she loved it. Unless she was looking for something important, in front of a client, especially, and she couldn't find it. It was so embarrassing and unprofessional.

"Why don't I give you some time to find what you need to," Meg said, stretching out her hand. "I'm sure you need time here by yourself, anyway, and I have a conference call in ten minutes. Email me your ideas. I'll have Lydia come out and bring you some coffee. She can show you out when you're done."

With a small smile, Meg walked away.

"Bye," Gemma said weakly, though Meg was long gone.

"That was the politest brush-off I've ever seen."

Gemma whirled around at the voice, her fingers curling around the first thing she could get in her bag and bring out, ready to defend herself. She couldn't explain the reaction. Ghosts regularly did this to her, and she almost never startled anymore. Perhaps it had something to do with who the ghost was.

"What are you doing here?" she hissed, checking behind her to make sure Meg hadn't doubled back. She hadn't. Some of the tension loosened in her stomach. "I thought you couldn't *poof*?"

He grimaced. "It seems I can do it when it's . . ." He looked almost pained. "I can do it when I need to be with you."

She wanted to say something sarcastic, like "well, I'm honored," but he shrugged and leaned against the wall, and she was distracted by his sexiness.

He wore a black T-shirt with denim shorts and sneakers. It was the plainest outfit, except for those little buttons on his T-shirt. And those would have been plain, too, but on him, they said, *Hey, Gemma! Did you know that if you undo me, you'll see approximately five centimeters of Levi's chest? Come on! I know you want to . . .*

Urgh.

Not to mention that now she was looking at his *bare legs*. They were awful! Just two *tree trunks* sprouting from the ground and blooming into the *most tempting tree* she had ever seen. How *dare* Mother Nature?

"I thought I was pretty clear last night," she said quietly, her tone not matching her thoughts at all. Her thoughts were caught by how he made her skin feel like it had taken a trip to the beach and rolled around in the sand. "What do I have to do to get rid of you? Hose you down? Is that the key to sending you back to the Otherside or wherever?"

He straightened. "You will not hose me."

"'Will not' sounds like a challenge."

A storm brewed on his face.

She wanted to stand under the clouds and wait for the rain.

She wanted to dance in the rain.

She wanted to shout in praise because the drought was finally over and—

What the *hell* was she thinking?

But the storm on his face broke, and he smiled.

He *smiled.*

"What is that?" she asked, taking a step back.

"What?"

"That." She pointed at his face.

The smile waned. "I'm smiling."

"Yeah. Why? Why are you smiling?"

It disappeared completely now, and he glowered at her.

Much better.

"I was trying to be nice," he growled.

"Why would you try to be nice? You either are nice or you're not. Niceness isn't something you should fake."

"Fine." He took a deep breath. She knew because his chest lifted and fell, and she thought about laying her head there so she could hear his heartbeat and trace her fingers over the muscles of his chest.

Gemma.

She needed to get a grip.

But it wasn't her fault. Her sister's romance novels were having this effect on her. She'd finally built up the courage to start reading one the night everything had happened with Levi, when she hadn't been able to sleep because she'd been worried. Once she started reading it, she couldn't stop. In the very first chapter, the hero had the heroine on the bed! He'd kissed her! Touched her! It was so hot that Gemma had had to fetch herself a glass of water.

So this wanton behavior of hers? It was all her sister's fault.

"You kicked me out of your house."

Levi's words brought her attention back to their conversation. To him. There was no part of her that could be defiant about kicking him out. She felt bad, and her initial reaction to seeing him and pretending like she hadn't spent all night thinking about how bad she felt had taken a surprising amount of energy.

"About that . . . I didn't mean to. What I mean is . . . I *did* mean to kick you out. I wanted you to go, but in hindsight, maybe that wasn't the best way to do it. I'm sorry." She bit the inside of her lip. "Did you get home okay? And where is home for a ghost, anyway?"

"Look, Gemma—" Why did he say her name like that? Like it was honey coating his tongue? "I . . . I have to help you. I have no choice."

"Didn't you choose to take this assignment?"

"I have no choice anymore," he said with a sigh. "So you need to let me—" He stopped when she turned around. "What are you doing?"

"Not looking at you. If I look at you, I'm going to agree to something I don't want to agree to."

"Gemma." It was less honey now, more lemon. "This situation isn't going to disappear because you pretend I'm not standing here."

She knew he was right, but the worst thing would be admitting he was right, mentally or out loud, so she started to sing to block it out.

She wasn't going to win any competitions, but she had an okay voice. Maybe even more than okay. The kind of voice that could make her *want* to audition for a competition—*if* she didn't have people in her life to tell her she was never going to be good enough to win.

But she didn't have to be good enough to win anything. She didn't even have to be good. She just wanted to be distracted from the offensively sexy ghost who wanted her to deal with her problems.

Did anyone even do that these days? Deal with their problems?

Well, not her. She was happy living in denial. She would live in denial until the end of time, amen.

He silently counted to twenty, then back, and then repeated it when none of it brought him the calm he desired.

There was a little kid inside of him that wanted to throw a tantrum.

Please, please listen to me. It'll be so much easier if we got along. I could tell you how to fix your problems, you fix them, and

I go back to my life and keep my sister from feeling guilty for the rest of hers.

He was about to say some of it when he saw a woman with a tray heading their way. His mind offered an unconventional strategy. And he considered it, because things hadn't once gone the way he thought they would when he started this thing. That very morning, he'd had to lie about having to go to a job that started later than Chet's job. Chet had repeated the line about stealing, but there was no real concern behind it. He'd told Levi to leave the keys with security and even offered a spare set of clothing. Levi couldn't have predicted that. So maybe unconventional was the way to go.

"I wonder," he said over the singing, "how your new client will feel about you bringing your boyfriend to see the place?"

The singing stopped.

"Don't think that would make a good impression," he continued. His gaze shifted to the woman outside, who had dropped something and was now walking back to the patio table. He had time. "At first you seem scatterbrained. Now, you've brought a friend. No—your boyfriend." Warming up to it now, he pulled off his shirt. "A boyfriend you intended on making out with in your new client's space."

"Oh, please," she said, spinning around. "She would never—"

She stopped when she saw him. Her eyes widened, sweeping over his shoulders, chest, lingering over his torso, before resting on his face. Well, no. They didn't rest on his face. They looked at his face, and her gaze dropped down and kind of . . . stayed on his body.

He did his best not to flex. Hated that he had to think about it. He'd never been a self-conscious person, but he wouldn't call what he wanted to do now self-consciousness. It was more . . . preening. He wanted to preen.

What was this woman doing to him?

His life was at stake.

His death was at stake.

Preening wasn't an option.

So of course, he said, "Do you need another minute? Because that woman is on her way. And while I don't mind you eyeing me—"

"—I am not *eyeing* you—"

"—you need to make a decision."

"What decision?" she asked incredulously. "You haven't given me a choice!"

But behind that incredulity, he could see she was genuinely panicked. He wanted to think about the stakes, about Haley, but he couldn't bring himself to disregard Gemma's feelings that way. He settled.

"A cup of coffee. So we can talk."

Someone knocked on the door.

"Okay, fine. Fine! Now go."

"And you have to listen to me," he added, putting his shirt back on.

"I said yes," she hissed. "Go on. *Poof.*" When they both realized that wasn't going to be possible, her eyes widened. "Why was I even negotiating with you?"

"I'm willing to hide."

"Do it!"

He looked around, saw a tree in the pot, looked at Gemma. Looked back at the tree. Looked at Gemma.

"You are the *worst* at hiding!" She threw up her hands. "Go to the bathroom. Lock the door. I'll make something up if she wants to go in there."

"Anything for you."

That was unnecessary, he could admit, but being glared at had never felt so satisfactory.

CHAPTER 5

She ignored him for the entire drive back to her house.

It was a problem. Without her talking to him, Levi was distracted by things. Things like the air-conditioning blowing through her hair. Like how she wiggled her nose, pursed her lips, huffed when she was annoyed at another driver or pretending not to notice him. Her smell was the worst. A smell of whimsical wishes and floral delights. How was that even a description? How did it fit her perfectly, even though it shouldn't have been a description?

Now he felt the need to break the silence, to stop being distracted by her. It was an urge he'd felt more while dead than he ever had alive. But before he could act on it—thank goodness—she pulled in front of her house.

He hadn't been able to see it in the dark the night before, but it looked exactly as he'd imagined it would. White paint, yellow frames around the windows, a yellow door, flowers of all colors sprouting in the garden next to the driveway. She had a white pebbled pathway that crunched under their feet as they walked to the house, and a mat that said WELCOME HOME, SUNSHINE! on her porch.

He waited as she unlocked the door, and followed her inside. She continued to ignore him. Wait—no, she didn't. She took off her coat, threw it behind her onto his head, and walked toward a small passage on their left.

"Really?" he asked, taking the coat off. "Can't we be more mature?"

"Me being mature is a privilege you have yet to earn," she called over her shoulder and disappeared into a room. Seconds later, he heard the shower run.

And caught himself smiling.

He was still standing in her living room, where every single design choice felt deliberate. The peach, almost golden curtains; the floral throw pillows on her stone-colored couches; the wooden flooring; the shelves; the paintings. He couldn't figure out why it made him feel so strange until he realized it was art. The skill it took to put together a room like this . . . it took talent he'd never considered before.

When he felt an unreasonable surge of pride, he walked through a small archway to her kitchen. Coffee. He'd make coffee. It would give him something to focus on, even though he didn't want it. An added bonus was that coffee had a strong smell. He would shove his nose into the grounds if it meant her scent would finally leave him alone.

First he was smiling because of her; now he had her smell following him around. What was next? Fathering her child?

"Not something you should be worrying about right now," a voice said from beside him.

Levi's hand tightened on the mug, but he continued stirring. Jude had ignored him when he needed his guardian. Levi would do the same now.

"You're upset with me," Jude said. "Why?"

At the genuine confusion, Levi glanced over. Today, Jude was young, early twenties probably, with long blond hair and soft, unobtrusive features. Levi wondered if Jude did this deliberately. If she chose a seemingly innocent form to appear in when she was trying to get in his good graces.

"You can't read my mind, huh?" Levi said.

"I'm reading your facial expression. Usually, yours says 'don't talk to me,' but today it says, 'don't talk to me because I'm upset with you.'"

Levi drank his coffee, even though it was scorching hot.

Great. Now he'd burnt his tongue.

Jude reached out and patted him on the hand, her fingernails painted in cute colorful swirls to match her cute colorful top. Immediately, his tongue felt normal again. Jude grinned when Levi stared.

"I can only do that with minor complaints." Jude took Levi's cup and hopped onto the kitchen island. "Burnt tongue, splinters, stubbed toe. Anything more serious, and I have to get approval."

Levi didn't reply immediately. "There are things I'm fine with not knowing."

"You would wonder, though, wouldn't you? Now," she went on, "shall we talk about what's upsetting you so we can move past it?"

"You left me stranded when Gemma kicked me out," he said without preamble.

She frowned. "No."

"Yes. I had to stay at Gemma's friend's fiancé's place."

"Exactly."

"What does 'exactly' mean?"

"If you had a place to stay, you were not stranded."

He took a deep breath. A part of him hoped the air was comprised of patience, too, so he could inhale some. "Fine," he said on an exhale. "Let's move on."

"Levi, I don't have to be present to help." She spoke softly, placatingly, as if she were speaking to a child. "Did you think Chet happened to be driving past you last night?"

Yes, he had.

"I . . . was mistaken." He forced out the next words. "I'm sorry."

"Don't be." She waved a hand. "He did just happen to be driving by. Joking!" She lifted her hands at the look he gave her, grinning. "I couldn't resist."

He looked up, mentally asking whomever was in charge of these things why he'd been given two impossible beings to deal with on this mission.

"Okay, so what's the plan?" Jude asked.

Levi looked at Jude. "Plan?"

"Yes, your plan." She paused. Sighed. "What do you intend on saying at this coffee date that is going to convince Gemma to accept your help?"

"Honesty." He didn't like the way his voice went up, like he was asking a question. "I'm going to explain that I need to help her so I can go back to my life."

"Ah." She nodded sagely. "The emotional blackmail route."

"How is that emotional blackmail?"

"You don't see how telling her what you have on the line might make her feel responsible for your existence continuing?"

"It sounds bad when you say it like that."

"Yes, it's the way I've *said* it that's bad."

"Is there a rule that says I can't tell her?" he asked sharply.

He felt as if *he* were being blackmailed, though he probably wasn't, and he did not like it one bit.

"Not at all. I'm simply asking you whether you're sure you'd like to add to the emotional burden she's already carrying."

Jude hopped off the counter, miraculously not spilling the coffee, before handing the mug back to Levi. She hadn't drunk any, it seemed. She'd merely taken it to annoy him.

"She's on her way! Good luck!"

She disappeared with a soft *pop*.

"Oh, yes, please do help yourself to whatever you find in my kitchen," Gemma said as she entered the room. "I have muffins in the cupboard if you like." She paused. "What? Why are you standing there like you've seen a ghost?" She laughed.

"You'd be an awful comedian," Levi informed her.

He hadn't realized he'd been staring into space until she came into the room. Staring into space and thinking about what Jude had said. Now his conscience was nagging him.

Great.

"I'd be an amazing comedian," Gemma countered. "People love bright and sunny comedians."

"Name one bright and sunny comedian." He waited, but when a long enough silence passed that it became clear he'd made his point, he smiled. "Besides, I wouldn't call you bright and sunny."

She opened her mouth, but stalked out of the kitchen before she said anything. When she returned a few minutes later, she was carrying a stack of papers. She set them down on the table, spread them out.

"My school report cards." She picked one up and began to read. "'Gemma is a happy addition to the classroom.' 'Gemma is a popular student who often encourages her fellow students to do their best and makes them laugh.' 'Gemma has an infectious smile and can-do attitude.'"

"You kept all these?"

"Of course." She sniffed. "How else would I have won this argument?"

"We were not arguing."

"Besides," she said, ignoring him, "you can't tell me you didn't keep yours?"

He shrugged. "Wouldn't know where they were if someone paid me."

"So what would you use to defend yourself if someone defamed you?"

"Defamed . . . Gemma, I have no idea what you're referring to."

She narrowed her eyes. Seconds later, she shook it off and smiled, as if wanting to prove him wrong. "Would you like to go out for that coffee, or are you happy drinking that?"

"I'm happy drinking this."

"Out it is." She smiled brightly. "There's an adorable coffee shop around the corner. They know me quite well there, and it doesn't get too busy. We can sit outside."

Biting back a smile, he followed her to the door and tried not to notice the way her dress swirled around her thighs. He didn't succeed, which is why he ended up wondering about that dress. Why on earth would she wear something that short? Something that noticeable?

It ended mid-thigh and was yellow, giving him an eyeful of brown skin made even more visible by the bright color. It immediately drew his eyes, simply because of that fact. It had nothing to do with how soft those thighs looked, how they shook with each step, how they appeared to be designed to draw someone's gaze and force that person to imagine what they would feel like. They weren't just thighs; weren't just a way for her to move forward. They were temptation, a path to a destination that he would—

No. No, he wasn't going there. He would never be able to return from that particular trip.

He forced his eyes up, but they settled on her shoulders. On the shapely curve of them, the easy way they moved under the blanket of her hair.

And that hair. Thick and long, pulled up from the back of her neck by a headband. He wanted to draw it around his wrist and tug it, so her chin lifted and she looked up at him with those big brown eyes. He wanted to see her eyes cloud with confusion before realization entered, and both were eclipsed by desire. He wanted—

"Why are you staring at me like that?" Gemma asked. Was that a catch in her voice? Had she somehow managed to read his thoughts?

"Like what?"

His voice was gruff, but that didn't matter. His real problem was that he was attracted to her. With an intensity he hadn't felt when he was alive.

But maybe he was experiencing life in a new way. He'd died, and now he was alive again, kind of, and he was living in an alternate universe.

Yes, that made perfect sense. He didn't even need to ask Jude about it.

"You're looking at me like you're thinking about a really delicious dinner and can't wait to eat it." She said the words completely unironically. "Are you hungry?"

He almost choked. "No. Yes."

It was easier to take her lead.

"You know, I've never spent enough time with a ghost to wonder about things like this." She looked at him. "Do ghosts get hungry?"

"I can't speak for all ghosts."

"I'm not asking you to. I'm asking you whether *you* get hungry. As a ghost."

"I said yes."

"Yeah, but it looked like you were lying."

"You can't tell when I'm lying."

"I don't have to," she said smugly. "You give yourself away with your grumpiness."

He gave her a stony look.

She gave him a wide smile.

"Whenever I think you're lying now, I'm going to tell you, and wait to see whether you get grumpier to determine the answer."

"Gemma," he replied, fighting for patience. "Are we going to get coffee or what?"

Her laugh made his skin prickle.

No. There was not a single thing he liked about this.

Not one at all.

* * *

It was strange being in a car with Levi. He didn't speak much, and sometimes Gemma could feel him looking at her. During those times, she tried not to do something embarrassing. Like wink at him. Or the much stronger temptation: push out her chest.

"You should think of me as a normal human being with normal human functions," he said as they got out of the car and started walking toward the café.

"Why would I want to think about your human functions?" she asked, wrinkling her nose.

He frowned. "You asked me whether I get hungry."

"Oh." She'd forgotten about that. "Well, that's the only human function I'd like to know about, okay?"

She was lying. She wanted to know how he felt after their kiss. If his human functions had responded like her human functions had.

Gemma.

Thank goodness for her common sense. It always kept her from jumping off the cliff into insanity.

When they got to the café door, Gemma pulled it. She felt some resistance, but sometimes it got stuck, and she needed to yank—

"Oh my gosh!" Gemma exclaimed, staring at the woman and her spilled drinks that the door revealed. "I am *so* sorry."

"No," the woman said, the hand that wasn't carrying the cardboard holder for her drinks palm up, fingers open, as if she could somehow catch the dripping liquid. "I put too much of my weight against the door when I was trying to open it. When you pulled it, I lost my balance and . . ." She gestured to the mess.

"Let me get you something to clean up with," Gemma said. She went inside, got a stack of napkins, and returned outside to where Levi was holding the empty cups.

"I should have asked for help," the woman muttered. "Now I have to go back and get another round."

"No, you don't!" Gemma said quickly. "I'm going to get you a refill, on me, because it was my fault."

"It wasn't—"

"You're being kind, which I appreciate, but it's not necessary." Briskly, Gemma asked for the woman's order. When she had it, she went back inside, ordered and paid for it, and went back out. "Here you go. I'm sorry for the inconvenience."

"It wasn't that much of an inconvenience. At least not for me."

"Your clothes are dirty," Gemma pointed out. "I can give you money for the dry cleaning if you like."

"No! I'll throw them in the wash."

"If you're sure."

"I am. Thank you."

Gemma waited as the woman walked off with a slight wave, and turned to Levi. "Ready?"

He stared. "What was that?"

"What do you mean?"

"Your response to an accident."

She waved her hand. "It was fine. Shall we go in?"

This time, she didn't wait for Levi to reply. She opened the door—gently—and walked into the café. She waved to the staff, pointed to the outside, and led Levi to her usual table.

Part of what she loved about the café, aside from it being nearby, was the veranda. Vines crawled over the wooden railings, sprouting white flowers Gemma had never thought to identify, merely enjoyed. Small round tables filled the area, few enough that it didn't feel crowded, and the waiters had ample space to move around. Her favorite table was in the corner, her favorite seat facing the outside so she could people watch.

The café was situated near a park, and there were almost always people walking their dogs, going for a jog, taking a stroll. It was the kind of place people weren't guarded at. No one felt the need to pretend when walking in the park. Gemma got to see hand-holding and smiles, kisses and guffaws. Often, watching had become a way for her to unwind.

"I hope you don't mind if I get something to eat," she said as she sat, her eyes scanning the park. "It's been a long day, and I spent most of it afraid my new client would find a boyfriend I don't have."

He didn't reply, but his body blocked her view as he settled into the chair opposite her. She opened her mouth to ask him why he'd done that, but shut it when she realized it was an impossible question. The table was small; there was only one other seat.

"What?" he asked.

"Nothing."

He gave her a look.

She shrugged. "I was going to say something unreasonable. So I didn't say it."

He was still looking at her, his expression stoic, though most of his expressions were. But there was something in the way he looked at her now that made her feel . . . unsettled.

A thrill skipped down her spine, and she was thankful when Cory, one of the servers, came to take their order. She had her usual—lasagna and an iced tea—and waited as Levi gave his. Or while he decided. He scanned the menu before he asked for the same as her.

When Cory left, Gemma asked, "What happened there?"

"I . . ." He paused, as if deciding what to say. "I had a moment."

"I know. That's why I was asking."

The silence extended past polite, but eventually, he said, "I didn't know what to order. I thought about what I would usually have, but I realized that . . ." He exhaled. "That I relied on what my family was having. If they ordered something for the table, I'd eat that."

"I understand."

He blinked. "You understand what?"

"What it's like to mold yourself to your family's needs." He kept staring at her, confusion and defiance a strange combination in his expression. She shook her head. "It's okay. We don't have to talk about that. Tell me why you wanted to have coffee so badly."

His dark eyes swept across her face, and her cheeks heated. She felt like a specimen in a lab. Like he was trying to see what the effects of an experiment he was conducting on her were.

Yes, that was what she felt.

"I've offended you," he said softly, surprising her.

Okay, so not an experiment. Genuine confusion.

"No," she answered honestly. "But it is strange trying to figure out why, out of every single ghost"—she lowered her voice on that one—"I've encountered, I suddenly have one assigned to me. The last time this happened was twelve years ago, and it was only because I didn't know I had this ability. Since then, there's been nothing. And this isn't the first time I've been in a situation. Nor is it the first time I've been unhappy. So why now?"

"I don't have an answer for that," he replied. "All I know is that I died, this was offered to me, and I . . . I want to help."

"What if I don't want your help?"

"I guess I haunt you forever."

CHAPTER 6

"That was a stupid joke to make," Levi said quickly, because she was blinking at him, her eyes uncomfortably serious. He'd never noticed that they sparkled until now, when the sparkle wasn't there. "I don't know what happens if you don't want my help."

"They didn't have that discussion with you?" Her tone went from cool to curious. "Why would They offer you this and not tell you what happens if I refuse? Why would you accept?"

Because if I succeed, I go back to my life like none of this ever happened.

And if he failed, he would cease to exist. Forever.

Maybe he did know what happened if she didn't want his help.

"It feels cruel," she said with a laugh. There was no more seriousness, that sparkle back in her eyes, taunting him. "They assigned you to someone who hasn't spoken to her parents since she found out they knew she had a twin sister and chose to adopt only her, and not that sister." She eyed him suspiciously. "What did you do to deserve this? Were you a criminal?"

"They wouldn't offer a guardianship to a criminal."

"That's what you're calling yourself? My guardian?"

He opened his mouth to make it sound less strange, but it was what it was. "Yes."

"Okay, Mr. Guardian. Give it a go. Help me."

She lifted her palm, waved it in front of herself to emphasize her words.

It would have been a really great time for him to give the answer he'd practiced the entire time he'd been a ghost. He would give her an impassioned plea, spell out why and how they would do this, why it was important for her to do this, and how he was going to support her through it.

Pity he didn't have any of it.

Why the hell didn't he have an answer, a plea, a *plan*?

"I . . . I have not thought this through."

Her features twitched. Just . . . twitched. All of them. The skin between her eyes, her eyebrows, the tip of her nose, her lips.

"You haven't thought about what?"

He fidgeted. "I haven't thought about how to convince you."

"But you . . . you asked me for this coffee date?" It was half question, half statement. "What was your plan?" When he didn't answer, she prodded. "You were going to tell me . . . what exactly?"

"I don't know," he said, exasperated. "This is the first time I've ever done anything like this. And I'm not only talking about being a ghost. I'm talking about . . ." He took a deep breath. "I'm talking about this." He gestured between them.

She tilted her head, considering him. "What is this?"

"This," he repeated, more insistently.

"Levi." She leaned forward. "I need more."

Of course she did. He sighed. "I've never spent time trying to get someone to face their feelings."

"You weren't a therapist in your past life?"

He gave a bark of laughter. "No. I was a store manager."

"What kind of store?"

"Clothing."

"And you didn't have to manage conflicts at work?"

"I . . ." He stopped. She was right. Not that it seemed to help. "It's not the same as this."

"Probably not," she agreed.

She smiled.

There had once been a storm so bad back home that he and his father had boarded all the windows shut, set out plastic containers to catch the rain, and played white noise so his sister wouldn't get frightened of the thunder. It had been a long night. Haley had cried a lot, and they'd had to distract her with play and eventually bribe her with song and bedtime stories to get her to calm down.

The storm was gone by the early morning, and the sun was coming out by the time Haley woke up. They'd taken down the boards, threw out the water in the plastic containers, and went to check out the damage outside. There had been nothing but some rubbish from their turned-over bin, some branches that had flown into the yard, and a piece of fence that had broken off. But considering the kind of storm, that damage was minimal. All in all, it had been a relief, and they'd watched the sun take its place in the sky with a kind of ease and happiness that could only come after a rough night.

He thought about that day often. Not so much what they'd had to do, but more that feeling. That intense relief. The way he'd felt when he'd seen the sun after a hellish night. He wouldn't ever want to go through it again, but sometimes he thought it might be worth it if he could have that feeling again. That lightness, that happiness.

And here it was.

Because this woman, this frustrating woman, *smiled.*

"Now, now, there's no need to get upset," she chided him gently, responding to the frown on his face. "I liked that you were being honest. Plus, it's nice to know you don't know everything."

"I don't."

Her eyes softened. "Yes, I got that." She stilled. "You help-ing me . . . is it some kind of penance? For your misdeeds on earth? Are you being tested before you can move on to the next part of your existence?"

It was alarmingly close to the truth, and it would have been so easy to say yes. Let her make her own assumptions about it, let it be enough so she'd be willing to work with him, and move on. Move forward.

He couldn't do it.

"Helping you is part of my existence. A stop before the next phase, I suppose." The words spilled from his mouth. "It isn't a test, nor will the outcome of it affect anything." He leaned forward. "But . . . I can see you're unhappy. It would . . . please me, to try and help you."

Please you? Really?

He tried not to wince.

"You're a strange man, Levi."

He allowed himself a small smile.

"Strangest I've ever met," she emphasized. "At first, you're not remotely interested in being sincere. Now, you're giving me a sitcom-worthy inspirational talk. How do I even process that?"

"With a simple yes or no."

She laughed. Time did a record scratch. Like the universe was determined for him to see her face and hear her voice. Her eyes went light and twinkled. Her mouth spread, her cheeks lifted, her nose wrinkled. The sound of it was like wind chimes, and it *confused* him. When had he ever been this . . . this . . . he didn't even know the word for it. Corny? Idiotic?

Enamored.

No, that couldn't be right. He couldn't be enamored. That implied an emotional connection, and there was none of that.

"See, strange."

He only then realized that time hadn't stuttered at all, that he'd merely been lost in her laugh, and that now she was staring at him with the remnants of that smile on her face, as if he amused her somehow.

"I have some questions before I agree to this," she said, not pressing. He silently thanked her.

"What?"

"Are you going to answer them?"

"It depends on what they are," he told her.

"Simple, unobtrusive questions." Her eyes twinkled.

He exhaled but nodded. He might as well get it over with. He braced himself for questions about his life, his family. She seemed like the sort who wanted to know things like that. So he was surprised when she said, "What's it like being a ghost?"

Gemma had always wanted to know, but she hadn't thought it polite to ask the ghosts she helped. They had other priorities. They didn't have time to answer her questions.

But if this one was going to interfere in her life, the least he could do was answer her questions.

"What does it feel like when you *poof*? Before you were in that bar and kissing me essentially made you human again, did you walk through walls?" She leaned forward, her whisper conspiratorial. "Could you claim people's bodies? Like, walk into them and become them, like in the movies? I've spent a long time wondering about that. Is it ethical? Well, obviously it isn't," she answered her own question, sitting back in her chair, "but how would you resist the temptation when no one can see you?"

He stared.

She blushed. Annoyed herself by doing so. There was something about him that made her feel embarrassed for saying what was on her mind. She hated situations like that. It was why she hadn't talked to her parents since finding out about her sister. She knew she couldn't speak her mind. Knew that if she did, they'd say something that would make her feel embarrassed.

No—it was more likely that they'd invalidate the anger

and judgment she felt about the fact that they'd kept so much from her.

By all rights, she should have hated this situation. Maybe she should have even hated Levi. She should have wanted to avoid spending time with him. Instead, it was like each cell of her body came alive at his voice, clamoring at the surface of her skin, trying to get to him. What an odd feeling.

"Imagine a balloon popping in your face," he spoke suddenly. "That's what it's like to appear and disappear, except it happens all over your body. You recover quickly, but it's a shock." He paused. "I can only do it when I think of you, as you know."

She tried not to feel anything at that. It was probably only because he was her guardian.

Why did *that* sound so weird?

"How did you get back to your place last night? Wait—where is your place?"

He looked away, but it felt more like he was avoiding her gaze out of . . . was that guilt? Why would he feel guilty?

"Are you living in my backyard or something?"

His head whipped back. "What? No."

"Then why do you look like you're hiding something?"

"I'm not—" He blew out a breath. "I don't have a place."

"What do you mean?"

"I mean, I don't have a place."

"Repeating it doesn't answer my question."

"The answer remains the same."

Did this man not know how to have a conversation?

"Fine. Where have you been sleeping this past week?"

"In a hotel."

"Oh," she said with a sigh of relief. "Which hotel?"

"It's in town."

"Levi, give me more information."

It all rushed out of his mouth.

"The day we met was the day I became a ghost. I *appeared* at that bar. No one noticed. I can't answer your questions about walking through walls or possessing someone's body because we kissed and . . ." He trailed off; shrugged. "After it happened, my guardian took me to a hotel room where I've been staying for the past week. I didn't leave the room until I was told to take a car to that bookstore where you met Gaia. After that, I thought about you and appeared in your house."

He paused for a brief moment to take a breath; then he was talking again, and it was *fascinating.*

"When you kicked me out, I didn't know how to get back to the hotel—I had one more night there—but before I got desperate, Chet picked me up, and I stayed at his place for the night."

The pause was longer now, his gaze lifting as if he were running through the events in his mind. When he nodded, she thought that was exactly what he'd been doing.

"And now you know everything."

"No," she said immediately. "There are a number of things I don't know, starting with—you were *at* the bookstore?"

"Yes."

"So you saw what happened?"

"Unfortunately."

She lifted her eyebrows. "If I were the one stalking someone, I'd be careful with my *unfortunately*s."

His lips twitched. "It won't happen again."

"I'm not saying you're not right," she added. "It was mortifying. I . . . I didn't expect to see her, you know? And then she was *there*, and every single thing I knew how to do—like have a normal conversation—went out the window." She shook her head, remembering. "And that window was at the top of a very high building. The fall to the ground was just"—she stared off in the distance, imagining it—"*splat.*"

"I understood most of that," he said, angling his head. "The solution here is to try again."

"Did you hear what I said?" she demanded. "*Splat*."

"Does *splat* mean you're never going to meet with your sister again?"

"*Splat* means I need to be prepared the next time I do."

"So prepare."

"Easy for you to say."

"Yes," he agreed. "Preparation is something I do well."

"Yes, your plan of action once you got me here illustrates that real well," she said dryly. "Not to mention your accommodation."

He winced. "The accommodation is not my fault. I would have preferred—" He stopped, eyes flickering over her, telling her that what he said next wasn't what he was going to say. "I'd rather not be in this position."

"Why did you only book a week at the hotel?"

"It wasn't me," he replied, pained. "Jude, my guardian, told me I only had a week."

"Then what?" When he didn't answer, Gemma continued. "Doesn't seem like much of a guardian."

"They're alright."

"A glowing recommendation."

He made a face that was similar to sticking out his tongue, although she was sure he would never do something so undignified.

They sat in their silence. Gemma felt like she was waiting, but she wasn't sure for what. She spoke, and realized she was waiting on herself. Reasons as to why were unclear. She chose to ignore the contribution those piercing eyes watching her had on the situation, intense beneath those intense brows.

"Two things?" she asked. He nodded. "You slept at Chet's last night?"

His eyes flitted from hers. "I did. He offered."

"Yeah, he would." She paused, watching his expression with interest. "Do you feel guilty about that?"

"No."

But he was avoiding her gaze again. She gave a small laugh. "My goodness, you *do* feel guilty."

"He's your friend," Levi said defensively. Adorably. "I didn't want you to think I was imposing."

"More than you already have, you mean."

He grunted. She didn't speak guttural Levi, but she was pretty sure he was acquiescing.

"You don't have to feel guilty," she told him. "Chet's a good person. He would have done it for anyone."

Levi threaded his fingers together and rested them on the table. "He did it for you."

"How do you—" She broke off at his look. "He said that? Ha! Guess we're even for Lacey coming over last night."

"You don't mind?"

"Why would I mind?"

He shrugged, but she wasn't sure whether it was in answer to her question or at her response. She didn't have time to ponder it. Levi distracted her with a significant miscalculation. He reached for the water jug, his eyes still on her, and he missed. Knocked it; spilled the water all over the table and onto their thighs.

Gemma jumped up, grabbed a cloth napkin from one of the other tables, and used each of her hands to pat them dry.

"Gemma."

Oh, the water had spilled *all* over her thighs. It was uncomfortably close to her underwear. She probably needed to dry higher up, but that would look uncouth. Maybe she should—

"Gemma," Levi said again, in a voice that sounded strained.

"What?"

"Please stop patting my penis."

Her hand froze. Hell, everything froze. Everything but her eyes. Those lowered to his crotch area, where her hand did, indeed, seem to be resting on his penis.

She moved it. Of course she moved it. She was *touching* his *penis*.

Except moving it didn't take away the memory of how it felt. It was delayed, that memory, but it was etched in her brain. Forever. Because what she'd felt had been impressive, and maybe that had been because of the patting, but she didn't think so, and now she was kind of afraid of what would happen if he was actually responding to something.

Or someone.

"Gemma," he said slowly now. "Would you stop looking at my penis?"

She straightened, which was the first time she realized she'd been staring at his pants while thinking her thoughts, and that her head had started to tilt to the side because of her ruminations, and she was absolutely, one hundred percent going to hell.

"I'm . . . that was . . . I'm so sorry."

She met his eyes for the first time since all of this had begun, and blinked. Usually, he had Resting Grump Face. And sure, his RGF was intact. But there was also a flicker of heat in his eyes. Suddenly, there was a part of her that wanted to take off all her clothes and dance naked around the fire.

She cleared her throat. "I'm sorry. I'm sorry. Did you . . . um . . . did you want this?" She offered him the cloth. "It probably didn't do much good. I'm still wet." She gestured to her legs and their new friends, the water droplets.

"Let's stop talking about this."

"What?"

"You being wet." He coughed. "Because of the water, I mean. The water that made you wet."

She was confused for a second. Her brain caught up, and she grinned. "The water, huh?"

"Gemma."

"You know, I think you've said my name more in the last five minutes than you have since we met."

He grunted.

"I like the way you say it," she said teasingly. "You have this weird way of saying the G, somewhere between the hard G and, like, a J, and it's very sexy." She shortened the distance between them. "You said you were human, right? In every way except the whole popping thing?"

He made a strangled noise.

She couldn't help it; she laughed. She had to look away, because his death glare made her laugh harder. When Cory arrived with a new tablecloth, Levi asked for his food as takeaway and started walking toward the door.

"Hey. Hey, wait," she said. He didn't. It made pausing to tell Cory to put her food in a takeaway as well less polite than it should have been, but she needed to catch up.

"Levi!" she called when they were outside in the parking lot.

"We have an audience," he said.

"Okay? What do you think I was going to do? Jump your bones?"

"Please leave my bones out of this."

It was such a ridiculous phrase to utter so seriously, but somehow, he managed.

"I'm sorry," she said. "I shouldn't have teased you about that. It was inappropriate."

"It was."

He didn't say anything else. She didn't, either. Because now she was feeling terrible about teasing him when he had clearly been uncomfortable. She felt even worse about ogling him.

"Stop that," he all but barked.

She startled. "Stop what?"

"Blaming yourself."

"Am I not to blame for what happened?"

"No." He left it at that.

She sighed. "I'm going back in to pay. Are you coming?"

"No," he said again, more sullenly. She had no idea how he

managed it. "I acted like a kid in there. I'm too embarrassed to go back."

I will not laugh, I will not laugh, I will not laugh.

She bit her lip.

"If you laugh . . ." he warned, and she threw her hands up in surrender as she walked away.

But she allowed herself a giggle when she got far enough away.

CHAPTER 7

Levi wasn't proud of the way he'd reacted. Not so much his initial reaction—there was little he could do about that. She *had* been rubbing the cloth vigorously over his shorts. It was what had come after. When he'd been watching her rub the cloth over her thighs, inching her dress up and allowing him a glimpse of the soft flesh of her inner legs. When he'd been wondering about what he could do to get her to part those legs so he could see even more . . .

He shifted when the thought, the memory, had his blood heating.

No, he wasn't proud; he was *desperate.* And it pissed him off that she'd seen it and narrowed in on it.

The polite thing to do would have been to ignore it. But no, she'd stared at his erection—which at that point had already decided it didn't care that any reaction to Gemma was inappropriate—and she'd teased him about it. She didn't even have the decency to tease him the way he wanted to be teased.

Desperate, a voice in his head said again, and he turned, kicking the duvet, somehow tangling it even further.

He needed to get it together. He couldn't think about Gemma teasing him when she was one door away.

One door.

He kicked the blanket again. It had zero effect on his body. Not on his brain, either, which was currently calculating how many steps it would take to get to her bedroom. As it had for the past week.

To think, he'd been happy when she offered him her guest bedroom that first night. She hadn't even made it weird, just offered him the room until he could find something else and told him she had spare clothing and toiletries for him. He hadn't asked where she got the clothing from, though they fit him well. Which of course meant he couldn't stop thinking about who they belonged to and whether it was unethical to plot the murder of someone whose clothes he was wearing.

See, this was the type of shit he thought when he was under the same roof as her. He'd spent a full day with her after their failure of a coffee date—could he even call it that?—and he'd barely survived. She just took up so much *space*. He'd caught himself smiling once, simply watching her, which was ridiculous. As ridiculous as the relief he'd felt when Monday had rolled around and she'd told him she'd be working late for a new client that week. Often, she returned after he'd gone to bed.

Purposefully, he was sure.

Not that he'd slept, thinking about her being so close. And he was dead tired.

Ha. Guess he made stupid jokes now, too.

There was a knock on the door. He checked the time on the alarm clock beside him. 8:00. He hadn't checked the time in ages, and somehow it had magically jumped to a reasonable time to be awake, even on a Saturday morning.

Carefully, he made his way out the jungle of his bed and opened the door.

"I'm going out," Gemma announced.

His eyes swept over her. She wore a black sleeveless halter

top that fit into black high-waisted trousers, with large earrings that sparkled blue and matched the delicate bands of her sandals. Her handbag—blue as well—was already strung across her body, her fingers tight around the band, and she wore rings. Lots of them. Different designs, but most of them silver. Only one had a stone in it. It was the same shade of blue as the rest of her accessories. He was oddly impressed.

"Great. I'll be ready in a second."

"No," she said quickly. "No, this is . . . it's a private thing." She leaned against the door, folded her arms. She was trying so hard to act nonchalant, and she was failing miserably. "You know, one of those . . . private things." She straightened.

"I *don't* know." But he was suspicious. "Why don't you explain?"

She looked lost for a second. "A date. It's a date. With a person. A man. A human man."

He stilled. His entire body went dead. Yet another joke, considering he was already dead, and it certainly hadn't felt like this when he'd died. This feeling lasted for about thirty seconds before his brain started working again and he realized that she must be lying. She *was* lying. Everything about the way she couldn't meet his eyes, her shifting feet, told him she was lying.

But the image of her dating someone . . . it sat in his mind. No, worse, it sat in his body. He suddenly had the overwhelming urge to punch someone.

He cleared his throat. "I'll put on some clothes and get out your way."

"You don't have anywhere to go."

"I don't want to be here when you get back, in case you bring him home." He lifted his brows, purposefully taunting her. "From your breakfast date."

She studied him. Narrowed her eyes. "You don't think he's real."

He couldn't help it: He smiled.

She was glaring now. "Yes, please get out of my house. I might want to have sex with my date. Hard. On my kitchen table. Hell, the coffee table. I'd love to have to buy a new one because of *all* the sex!"

She spun on her heel, the air swirling with her perfume. Something light that reminded him of butterflies flitting from one flower to the next. It tightened his gut, had his chest constricting, too.

He went after her. "Tell me what you're doing."

"I did!"

"You're obviously lying!"

"I am *not*!" She stomped her foot.

Stomped. Her. Foot.

"You're acting like my little sister when I won't let her go to a party. She's sixteen."

"Guess you're a wet blanket for everyone!" She grabbed her keys, stormed to the door, but turned before she could go through it. "Okay—that was . . ." She shook her head. "That was out of line. Your sister should not be going to parties you don't approve of, especially at sixteen. That was a good move. But"—she pointed a finger at him—"I am *not* your sister!"

No shit, he thought, staring after her as she slammed the door. Of course she wasn't his sister. If she were, he wouldn't be sinking in quicksand. The more he fought, the deeper he sank, and yet standing made things worse, too. There was no winning.

He clenched and unclenched his fists as he listened to her car start, as she drove away. He knew she wasn't going on a date, but he was hyped nevertheless.

But.

If there was anything he'd learned from co-parenting with his father, it was that bottling up his emotions was the most productive. So he did. He kept calm as he made the bed, as he went to the bathroom and got ready for the day.

Then, he tried to figure out how he was going to get to Gemma.

With that thought came a subtle twinge right before he felt that hurricane again. He went with it, welcoming the nausea and dizziness, because it meant he'd *poofed*. And *poofing* meant Gemma. Apparently, thinking about her was all it took.

Shut it, he commanded his inner voice, before it even had a chance to point out what else thinking about her did to him.

He looked around. He was in a bathroom. It was dimly lit, with a large mirror above a basin on one side of the room and huge potted plant on the other in front of two stalls. A man stood in the doorway of one of them, watching Levi with strange eyes.

Levi tensed, but the man smiled. "It's only me."

"Jude." He exhaled. "What are you doing here?"

"I'd like to know your plan."

"I don't have a plan." He used to have plans. The Levi who used to have plans was a good man. A sane man. He missed that man. "I'll have to see the situation first."

"You mean check whether or not she has a date."

"No. No," he said more firmly. "I know she doesn't."

Jude raised his eyebrows, gaze steady. Suddenly, Levi wasn't so sure Gemma didn't have a date.

"Be careful," Jude said in a voice so soft and gentle, Levi didn't recognize it as a warning at first. "To answer your question," Jude continued in a normal tone of voice, "she's not going on a date. But she is outside the café, preparing to properly introduce herself to her sister."

He hadn't known what to expect, but it certainly wasn't this. "Does *she* have a plan?"

"Good question. Perhaps something you should have asked her this morning."

Levi frowned at the disapproval. "Is there something you'd like to say, Jude?"

"I already have."

"No, you haven't." Feeling the emotion he had bottled up start to bubble, he took a deep breath. Spoke through clenched teeth. "There are many things you could have said that you haven't. For example, you could have explained how *poofing*"— still so annoying to say—"works. You could have warned me that interacting with Gemma in a public space would mean I'd become human again." He couldn't let that fact go.

Jude's expression was somber, his eyes harder than Levi had ever seen them. "You agreed to this assignment, Levi. I didn't make that decision for you."

"You have the power to make it easier, though, don't you?"

"Yes," he agreed, "but what would that teach you?" Jude stepped closer. "You have things to learn, and that requires engagement. From *you*," he emphasized, in case Levi didn't get the point. "You can't ignore the way you're feeling. Not anymore."

"Not anymore? What's that supposed to mean?"

"Figure it out," Jude said simply, and disappeared.

"Thanks for that," Levi muttered, knowing he'd spend whatever free time he had coming thinking about it. But he couldn't dwell on it now.

He walked out of the bathroom and scanned the room, but Gemma was still outside. She paced back and forth, lips moving, as if she were practicing. She stopped, squared her shoulders, and moved toward the door.

If he were a better man, he would have intercepted her, asked her what her plan was, tried to help her. That was the entire purpose of his existence as a ghost, after all. But he was still bitter about the way she'd left him behind that morning, about the conversation with Jude. So he looked around, found Gaia, and took a seat at the empty table behind her.

Gemma walked in at the same time. Her eyes rested on his, and her jaw locked. Determinedly, she walked to his table. When she passed Gaia's table, she hesitated, but her sister didn't notice. Gaia's attention was split between a laptop and notebook. She didn't even notice she was getting her coffee refilled.

"You shouldn't be here," Gemma hissed, slipping into the seat opposite him.

"On your date?" he replied easily. "Pretend I'm a ghost."

Gemma clucked her teeth at him, which was probably meant to be offensive, but only came across as nervous. So did the tapping she was doing on the table. Because of her rings, the sound was almost rhythmic. He felt a pang somewhere inside him, but stuffed it into the bottle along with everything else.

"Fine." Gemma stood with a huff and went to her sister's table. "You probably don't remember me," she said to Gaia.

Levi tilted his head. It wasn't the worst introduction, but *hello* would have been better.

If only you'd told her that instead of playing games.

He ignored the thought. Focused on Gaia's response instead.

"I remember you." There was a slight pause. "Are you stalking me?"

Levi shifted so he could see Gemma's face as she said, "What? No."

He snickered. He couldn't help it. Her expression was part guilt, part insult, part indignant, part how-did-you-figure-it-out. But while he hadn't helped her before the conversation had started, he shouldn't do this. Sabotage her. He shook his head and tried to pretend he wasn't eavesdropping.

"I'm Gemma, by the way. I don't think I introduced myself last week. And okay, yes, I am stalking you." *Oh, for heaven's sake, Gemma.* "I swear it's not for creepy reasons. Or maybe it is? I'm not sure."

Okay, so this was how it would go.

He leaned back. Accepted it.

"Do you know him?" Gaia gestured to Levi.

"Who?" Gemma asked brightly.

"The man behind you. The one who keeps making noises through his nose."

Shit.

He clearly needed to work harder at being a neutral third party.

"Oh. Well," Gemma said, and left it at that. Gaia didn't push, so he supposed it wasn't the worst answer.

"Who are you?" Gaia asked.

"I'm your . . . I'm your biggest fan," Gemma answered.

"And you've been stalking me? I don't know how I should feel about you doing it, or admitting it."

"I'm not dangerous," Gemma assured her. "I promise. I just . . . I really love your, um . . . your books, and I wanted to meet you. Properly. And I know you work here sometimes. Not a lot, because I've been in here—" She broke off with a smile. "Well, you're here now."

Levi listened to the rest of the conversation with his eyes closed.

This was his fault. He hadn't helped her, though he didn't think he could have anticipated this level of destruction. Gemma was elaborating on her lie, even with Gaia poking holes in her argument, and it was hard to listen to. Not because he was embarrassed on her behalf—not *only* because he was embarrassed on her behalf—but because he could hear the need in Gemma's voice.

Suddenly the pang no longer wanted to be contained. It pushed the cork out of the bottle, and all the emotions he'd been ignoring, successfully, stormed his body. He tuned back into the conversation out of desperation, hoping that Gemma's train wreck would distract him in the same way wrecks did for people who slowed down on a highway to watch them.

"It was unfortunate that we met on the night I got your books before I could read them," Gemma said.

"You were giving my books away."

"The second set of books, yes. I bought two sets. One for me and one to, um . . . donate."

Gaia tilted her head. "Why?"

"Don't sales matter to your career?"

"They do," Gaia said slowly. "But it's unusual for someone to buy all of an author's books when they haven't read one yet. It's even more unusual for that person to buy two sets of those books and donate one set."

"Oh," Gemma replied. "Well, I wanted to support you."

"You don't even know me."

"Maybe I feel as if we have a bond of some sort."

Gaia blew out her breath. "So you're going to keep leaning into the weirdness, then." There was a pause. Levi didn't have to see her face to know why. He was cringing, and those words weren't even directed toward him. "You seem like a very nice woman," Gaia continued eventually, "but we don't have a bond. We're not connected in *any* way. I would really appreciate it if you stopped, um, stalking me, and maybe—"

"We might be." The words were quiet. "Connected, or—"

"Right-o," he said, the word leaving his mouth before he fully had a chance to process it. Suddenly, he was standing, his hand resting on Gemma's shoulder before he had a chance to process that, either. "We're done here. Very nice to meet you," he told Gaia. To Gemma, he said, "We need to leave. Now."

"Hey!" Gaia said, her eyes wide. "You can't touch her like that. What the hell?"

That was the problem with things happening before he fully realized them. He didn't think them through. He didn't consider how they would look. The people at the table next to Gaia's were looking at them. He dropped his hand.

"We're in a relationship," he assured her. It was the first thing that came to mind.

Gaia narrowed her eyes. "Are you sure? Because she didn't even admit to knowing you earlier."

Levi looked down at Gemma; Gemma looked up at him.

Her expression knocked the breath out him. He'd never seen pain, never seen need so intense before. It reached inside him, touched a part of him it recognized, and there went his breath again.

He blamed that for what he did next. For being unable to resist squeezing her shoulder. Comforting her. The spark of appreciation he got in return turned his throat thick, and he dropped his hand, afraid of what might happen if he didn't.

Gemma turned to face Gaia. "Yes, he is my . . . partner. Levi." She swallowed on the last word.

Gaia gave them both a look. "You two have a really weird dynamic."

"I know," Gemma said at the same time Levi said, "Yes."

Her eyebrows rose. "Maybe you are in a relationship then. Who am I to judge?" But her eyes rested on Gemma, and something on her face changed. "Do you mind giving me a second here?" she said to him. "I'd like to talk to my biggest fan."

"We have to leave," he replied, giving Gemma a look.

"And you will." Gaia offered a fake but polite smile. "In a short while."

She wasn't going to back down. He could already see it on her face.

With a sigh, he walked out.

CHAPTER 8

Levi was waiting when Gemma walked out of the café. She'd expected it, but even that couldn't spoil her mood.

It had gone well! She had *talked* to her *sister*. They'd had *a proper conversation*. Her sister had shown *concern*. Sure, it was because Gaia was worried Levi was abusive, but Gemma had dissuaded her of that notion. She couldn't throw him under the bus, especially after that moment they'd shared inside.

But that wasn't important. What was important was that she and her sister had bonded! She was almost bouncing when she stopped at Levi's side.

"It clearly went better after I left than while I was there," he noted dryly.

"What? No. It went pretty well while you were there, too."

He lifted a brow. She had the oddest urge to lift her top, too, and flash him. Luckily, she was an adult who didn't give in to her baser whims.

"You and I have different definitions of 'pretty well.'"

"I imagine that's true," she agreed. "Anyway, we should get out of here. You know how awkward it is when you say goodbye to someone and end up seeing them again. And I don't want to tempt fate by sticking around." She grabbed his hand. "If she comes out, I don't want her to think I'm waiting for her."

"Why not?" he muttered. "You already told her you were stalking her."

"Don't say it like that. You make it sound ridiculous."

"It *is* ridiculous."

"Levi—"

She stopped short when she saw Lacey, Pearl, and Onu walking toward them.

Her brain told her this was a logical development. They all lived in this area, tried to get lunch together at least once a week, and they enjoyed trying new places. The problem was that she should have been with them. She'd ditched every meal for the last month, telling them her parents had needed her help to pack, since they were moving.

Her parents were not moving.

She was a liar.

And she hated it.

She'd never lied to her friends about anything important before. The occasional white lie was acceptable, of course. Lacey did not have to know Gemma had once caught Chet stuffing his face with a burger during one of his and Lacey's "No Meat Novembers." And Pearl adored a jersey that her grandmother had knitted her, that they had, as a friend group, collectively decided not to tell her was extraordinarily ugly because she adored it so much.

But this was not a small white lie.

She knew that if she went to lunch with her friends, which was more social than the times she saw them for Lacey's wedding, she would tell them everything. That she'd discovered she had a sister that her parents had hidden from her and that she felt angry and at the same time so guilty. Lying about her parents moving to avoid lunch was a medium lie obfuscating a big lie of omission. A big, *important* lie of omission.

She wanted to tell her friends the truth. But she was afraid . . . she was afraid that telling them what had happened, and how she felt about it, would make them look at her differently. Her stomach churned thinking about it.

Can you blame the universe for sending you a ghost to help you figure your life out?

Indeed, she could not.

The fact remained: She could not let her friends see her out, let alone with Levi. And what if they saw her sister? They wouldn't recognize her, but what if they thought she looked familiar? What if *Gaia* saw Gemma and came over and Lacey thought Gemma was friend-cheating on her and kicked her out of her wedding and—

"What? What is it?" Levi demanded.

Oh. She'd forgotten about him. She was still holding his hand, so she dragged him into an alleyway. It was nowhere near big enough to fit them both, but she didn't care. For this, she was willing to press herself against his body.

"It's Lacey! And two of my other friends who I'm supposed to be meeting right now. They can't see me!"

Levi blinked, as if something were distracting him. Honestly— what the hell did he have to be distracted by right now?

"What?" Levi asked when he saw her face.

"My friends," she hissed. "Those women walking towards us? They will not be happy if they see me with you."

Slowly, he looked to where she was pointing. His eyes widened. "Lacey," he breathed, as if she were his archnemesis. "Do you think Chet told her you kicked me out and I stayed at his place the other night?"

"Yes."

"Why are we hiding?" he demanded, shifting. Or attempting to. She pressed herself more firmly against him so he couldn't leave. "We need to run."

"It's too late! This is where we live now."

"This isn't even a good hiding place," he complained. "It's the smallest alley I've had the misfortune of being in. You can't call it an alley. It's a gap."

"But it's concealing us, which—"

She stopped when Pearl's head turned in their direction. Without thinking, she buried her face in Levi's chest so that if Pearl saw them, she wouldn't recognize Gemma.

"Gemma."

"Just do this one thing for me. Please?"

Her words were muffled, but based on his sigh, she assumed he'd heard and accepted her request.

The seconds ticked on.

At first, she was able to ignore the position they were in. But he shifted. It was an innocent shift. A slight change in position. Except it brought his lips to her ear. His breath tickled the side of her neck. She tried to keep from shuddering, but the effort only resulted in a tremble.

Like when Grey pressed a kiss below Ilona's ear in *Swept Away,* the second of Gaia's books Gemma was reading. She never thought her sister's books would predict her future, and yet, here they were.

"You okay?" Levi whispered.

"Of course," she replied automatically, except she trembled again, because he'd spoken directly into her ear, moved his hand to her waist, and now, somehow, they were in this intimate embrace, and it felt . . .

It felt good.

She made a sound, a protest, really, except it left her lips in a moan. She was even more aware of him now. His body was . . . firm. Steady under her. Muscular, but not in a way that made her think he spent hours in the gym. But she remembered how he looked when he took his shirt off at her client's house. He definitely spent hours in the gym. Usually, that type of man would annoy her. She didn't need someone who spent all their time focusing on their body; she needed someone who would invest time in focusing on *her* body.

But she didn't think that would be a problem for Levi.

She looked at him, their eyes meeting, as if he'd heard her thoughts and wanted to weigh in. He didn't have to say a word to do so. She could feel in his gaze, hot and intense, that he'd spend ample time focusing on her pleasure. As it was, his hand was moving, up, up over the indent of her waist, the curve of her breast. It was an investigation, an inquiry, and she lifted her arm to give him more access, showing him she was willing to cooperate.

Their gazes locked as he continued his exploration. She shivered when his hand cupped her breast, when his thumb found her nipple, when he brushed the finger over the spot again and again, sending heat to her core. Her hips shifted, pressing forward, pressing against the hardness of his erection, seeking to soothe the ache that was between her legs.

As she did, she realized that *soothe* wasn't the right word for it. She didn't find the result remotely soothing. But it didn't matter. Not when it felt good.

Later, she might tell herself that thought came from a long dry spell. From the fact that she hadn't been interested in anything remotely sexual with anyone since she'd become obsessed with finding out more about her family. She would blame it on a physical reaction; on a need or desire that was simple.

Later, she'd be lying to herself.

Because in that moment, it wasn't only physical. It couldn't have been when she was still staring at him. When she couldn't tear her gaze away from him. When she was thinking about how he was trying to help her for reasons she didn't quite know, but didn't seem to matter. She knew there was something about his motives that he wasn't telling her, but that didn't seem to matter, either. The only thing that mattered was that he was staring at her, too. That his dark, soulful eyes hadn't moved once, not *once*, since they'd started whatever this was.

He inched forward, as if in response to her thoughts. As if he wanted to clarify what this was. She sucked in her breath. Parted her lips. Oh, man, she could already taste him. She'd spent every minute since their last kiss pretending as if she didn't care that they'd kissed. As if she were content to leave it at a dare, a scientific experiment.

The truth was that it was seared into her brain. The truth was that she had never had a kiss so hot, so intense, as that one. And now she could have a repeat if she wanted to.

She wanted to.

She wanted to very badly.

So she leaned in and—

"Gemma?"

Startled, she jumped back, but there was no space to jump back to, so she ended up knocking her head. Hard. It took a second for the pain to subside, and she tried to edge out of the small space. Levi did the same thing at the same time—what had he even been *doing* in that second she was in pain?—so their bodies bumped. Including certain body parts that apparently didn't care they'd been caught fraternizing, since they both seemed very eager to continue what they'd started.

Get it together! she told her vagina, and directed her next words to Levi. "You should go first."

"No," he said, his voice deep and rough, and man oh man did she want him to say something other than *no* to her. "You go first."

"Levi—"

"Gemma." His voice sounded strangled. "If you don't go, I'm going speak to your friends with an erection. I'm sure it will disappear as soon as Lacey starts talking, but while I still have you against me—" He broke off, locked his jaw. *"You. Go. First."*

That had to be the bluntest, sexiest thing anyone had ever said to her.

"So what you're saying is that's *my* erection?"

He made a noise. If sounds could kill, her friends would have found her dead on the floor, not horny in an alley.

"You guys!" she said as her friends came closer, and she shifted so she stood in front of Levi when he joined her. "What a surprise."

"Yes," Lacey agreed. Her gaze flitted to Levi and back to Gemma, dropped. Lacey had the uncanny ability to see things people didn't want her to see, which made her a ruthless and successful lawyer. Now, Gemma was concerned Lacey could see right through Gemma's body to Levi's erection.

Currently resting against her butt.

Still undeniably impressive.

She shook her head. "What . . . um . . . what are you doing here?"

"Lunch," Pearl answered, tone amused. "Did you ditch us to spend time with your new man, Gemma?"

"No, of course not." She swallowed. "We were . . . I was—"

"Ditching us to dry-hump a man in public!"

"Lacey!" Gemma said at the same time as Pearl and Onu, though theirs was more amusement than Gemma's shock.

"Why are you pretending like that isn't what we witnessed?"

"Because we're being polite," Onu told her.

"Do you want us to be polite, Gem?" Lacey asked Gemma, voice sharp but expression gentle. Like she knew something more important was going on.

Did Lacey know something more important was going on?

"Yes." Gemma's voice was prim. "I would like polite very much."

"Too bad. We're your friends!" Lacey lifted her hands at Gemma's glare. "Polite isn't what we do."

"What Gemma does in the privacy of an alleyway is her and the police's business," Onu intervened. "What *is* our business, is why she's been missing for the last month?" She directed that last question to Gemma.

"I told you—"

"Your parents need you," Onu said. "I'm sure that's true."

"It is true!" Gemma exclaimed, extremely offended that they hadn't believed her lie.

"Why don't you introduce us to your friend?" Pearl interrupted. She was second-in-command when it came to peacekeeping in their group, and Gemma was once again *offended* that she, commander in chief, had been turned against.

Levi gently pushed Gemma to the side. "Levi Walker."

Gemma's eyes lifted—they had inappropriately dipped to his jeans for some reason—at that. A full name. It suited him. An aggressively sexy man like him should have an aggressively sexy name like that.

Walk her? Yes, please.

Gemma, you're having a breakdown.

It was entirely possible that was true, but Gemma preferred not to think about that, or the causes of it, for the moment. It had been a long moment, basically since she'd found out about her sister, but the time would come when she could focus on it.

Maybe it already had.

But not right at this very second.

She waited for the introductions to finish. When they had, they all looked at her.

"Yes, this is Levi," she confirmed, as if he hadn't told them that. "He's . . . a friend." She wrinkled her nose.

"Yeah, Pearl and I were that kind of friends before we started dating," Onu said with a smirk.

"Maybe if Chet and I had been that kind of friends, doing that kind of thing in public, we would already be married." Lacey gave a dreamy sigh. "Doing time together for public indecency."

"It wasn't what you thought it was," Gemma said, compelled to defend herself. "We just . . . um . . . you see, Levi had something stuck in his—"

"Okay, look, I know we were giving you a hard time," Lacey interrupted, "but we don't really want to know the details."

"Speak for yourself." Onu grinned when Lacey shot her a look. "Okay, fine. We don't want to know. But you didn't have to lie to us about it. You could have said you had a date."

Levi gave a quiet chuckle, and she knew he was thinking about that morning, when she *had* lied about having a date. The irony wasn't lost on her. Nor was the fact that the Gaia situation—and the resulting Levi situation—meant she had been lying more than usual. To herself, too, she realized.

But her lies weren't only to protect herself; she was also protecting her parents. She was afraid her friends would see them differently now. That looking at her parents through her friends' eyes would be even worse than what she'd already been through.

Jasmine and Simon Daniels had taken her in, raised her, loved her like their own. But they had also kept her away from her biological sister. *Separated* them, for goodness' sake. Her and her *twin* sister. Who would do that?

Despite that, despite her anger, despite the fact that she wanted distance, she didn't want anyone to think poorly of them. She felt an uncontrollable need to protect her parents, to shield them. Perhaps because once, they had done that for her.

She didn't know how to handle any of that. How to balance it, how to work through it. That was why she'd been avoiding any situation that might force her to pay attention to it, including starting a relationship with her sister. It was why she had ordered books instead of reaching out. It was why she was pretending to be a fan instead of telling Gaia the truth. Because how could she tell Gaia the truth when even she didn't want to face it?

"We're still figuring stuff out," she said, aware that her voice had gotten dimmer, heavier, but unable to do anything about it. "Telling you guys makes it really official, you know?" She swallowed when pressure began to grow in her chest. "I should have told you the truth, though. You're right. I'm sorry."

She turned on her heel, walking away from them as fast as she could. When she turned the corner, she ran. In her mind, it was graceful, like she was running through fields and fields of flowers. In reality, she bumped into a couple of people. Someone swore at her. She felt something wet on her back and realized one of the people who'd sworn at her had spilled water—she really hoped it was water—on her.

Finally, she got far enough away to have privacy. It was a car lot that served as parking for a nearby office. On weekends, they offered paid parking, but the rates were so expensive that people only parked there when they had no other choice. It was funny it was so expensive, too, considering it was essentially a gravel-filled square with no covering. People even had to figure out the parking spaces themselves, since the owners couldn't be bothered to paint some lines on the floor.

Today, Gemma was thankful for its unpopularity. There were only a few cars in the lot, and the security guard manning the gates hadn't seen her sneaking in through the trees.

She'd gone to the university that claimed most of the small town of Stellenbosch. Back then, she had snuck into the car lot countless times to do something her parents hadn't approved of—all while thinking about how her parents wouldn't approve of it.

When she'd done it, it had felt like a rite of passage. She had to get drunk at university because that's what people did. She was people! She definitely wasn't the orphan who got adopted and was struggling with her identity for as long as she could remember. Hell, no! Kids like that did not do what people did!

But it was always spoiled when she remembered that she was an orphan. Sure, she had been adopted at a young age, but there was a sense of displacement that she'd never been able to silence, no matter how hard she tried. There was also that gratitude. That deep, undying gratitude that she had been the kid her parents had picked.

Out of everyone there.

Between her and her sister.

"Oh, no," she moaned when the tears began to fall. She slid down to the floor, obscured from the guard by a car, and gave a little hiccup.

CHAPTER 9

There were many things Levi didn't like. Fish, because it was impractical for something to smell that bad. How was he supposed to eat it at work? Dead branches at the top of a tree. He couldn't help the tree thrive if it insisted on dying at the most inconvenient point. And crying. Anyone crying, but particularly people he cared about crying.

He stared down at Gemma, hating the prickling sensation at the back of his neck as he watched her sob. It was the helpless feeling he despised, honestly. Witnessing someone feel their emotions was terrible, because he couldn't do anything about it. Couldn't fix it, couldn't help with it. Haley would often do this to him. Sit there and cry. A punishment for all his sins, he thought every time, and sat through it, listening to her teenage woes as she blubbered all over him.

It was worse with Gemma. Because she *was* bright and sunny, no matter what he admitted out loud. She was the kind of person who went out of her way to make up for a silly mistake like contributing to someone spilling their coffee. She thought a fairly disastrous meeting with her sister went well, practically bloomed with joy because of it, and he couldn't . . . he couldn't just watch her cry.

He lowered down next to her, gritting his teeth when the gravel poked his ass. Her head shot up. When she saw him, she rolled her eyes.

"Why did you follow me if you're going to be mad about it?" she asked.

"I'm not mad."

"You're frowning."

"You chose an uncomfortable place to sit."

"I wasn't exactly thinking about comfort when I sat."

The words lacked the bite he imagined she was going for, and he looked to the sky. To the heavens. To whomever the hell had put him in this situation.

When he'd accepted this assignment, he'd expected emotion. But less *involved* emotion. Denial, or resentment, or something other than hurt and betrayal, and now that he thought about it, he realized he hadn't thought about it at all. What did less involved emotion even mean?

Oh, right. It was the way *he* dealt with his emotions. Bottling them up, ignoring them. Calling denial and resentment "less involved" as if somehow, that lessened their impact.

"You're still frowning," she accused.

"It's not because of you."

"Liar."

"Fine, it is. But not for the reasons you think."

She turned her head and rested her cheek on her knees. "Tell me."

"This isn't about me."

"It could be . . . if you told me. *Distracted* me." She pushed her bottom lip out, looked up at him with big brown eyes. "Please."

It shouldn't have worked.

It did.

"I wasn't prepared for this." He met her gaze. "For you."

She blinked. "Maybe I shouldn't have asked."

"No, I don't mean—" He exhaled. "You've challenged the way I think about things."

"Oh." She went quiet. "I think that's a good thing, maybe. But it's not fair to blame me for it."

"No, it's not," he agreed. "But I *can* blame you for what's happening to my body."

The last part came out without permission and got raised eyebrows for its efforts. She laughed—slow, deep, voice husky from her tears. True to his admission, his body responded. His blood felt heavy as it flowed downward; his fingers itched to touch her hair; his tongue slipped through his lips, hoping to somehow taste her there.

"You have that hungry look again," she noted. She'd stopped laughing and was watching him with interest. Suddenly, her eyes brightened. "That's what it is! You *want* me! Ha!"

The last word was surprise more than arrogance. She was making this moment endearing instead of mortifying.

No—it was still mortifying.

"I don't want you," he said on principle.

"Well, you should tell your penis that."

He frowned, refusing to look down. He didn't need to see it; he knew what was happening. "Inappropriate."

"You were pressing your body against mine earlier. It's not my fault I felt it."

She was talking about the alley. Of course. Thank goodness he hadn't looked down.

He did shift, though, lifting the leg closest to her and lowering the other so he looked casual, but was actually obscuring her view of his erection in case she noticed it.

"Was it bad?" she asked quietly.

"What? Why would you ask me that?" When she only frowned, he sighed again. "No, it wasn't bad. It might have been if we'd done more in that alley, but—"

"What are you talking about, Levi?" she interrupted. "I meant when I left."

He closed his eyes. Opened them. "You're doing this on purpose."

"Doing what?"

"Getting me to admit things I don't want to admit."

"It's a you thing that it's turning out to be so easy. But," she continued, "I'm talking about my friends. Was it bad when I left? I'm too afraid to look at my phone in case they've all broken up with me."

"It wasn't bad," he said after a moment's consideration. "They asked me too many questions, none of which I could answer, but it all came from concern." He paused. "They're worried about you."

Gemma nodded, set her chin on her knees and stared at the car in front of her. "I should have known that. They're decent people. Of course they're worried about their friend running away from them. Even if she doesn't deserve their concern."

"Why don't you deserve concern?"

"I've been lying to them."

"They've already figured that out."

"No," she said with a snort. "They have not. They would have called me out on it."

"Were you not listening to what they said back there?" he asked. "They did call you out on it."

She frowned. "Oh. Yeah."

"Oh, yeah," he repeated dryly. "It sounded like they've known you haven't been honest with them. They seem to be giving you your space."

"Why?"

"You're asking me?" When she shot him a pleading look, he shook his head. "I don't know, Gemma. If I had to guess, I'd say they love you."

She opened her mouth, but nothing came out. Silence sat between them for a moment as Levi replayed the last minutes of their conversation.

He turned to her. "You don't believe me." She made a noncommittal sound. He stared in disbelief. "You don't believe your friends love you?" he demanded. She still didn't answer. "Gemma!" His voice was sharp this time.

She folded her arms around her legs, the position so contrary to her fierce frown that he could almost ignore the vulnerability it revealed.

"It's not that I don't believe you. It's . . ." She trailed off. Didn't speak for a long time. "Okay, fine. It might be that I don't believe you."

"Why not?"

She didn't answer.

He locked his jaw. "Gemma, how the hell can you not believe people love you?"

"Maybe because they talk to me in stern tones of voices, like they're reprimanding me!"

He blinked. She was talking about him. He had been stern and reprimanding, and he hadn't even known he was doing it. She had officially infiltrated his mind and brainwashed him.

"I did not mean that," he said in a similar tone of voice, but he couldn't help it.

She looked at him. The frown on her face softened, as did the line of her lips, and she almost looked like the Gemma he'd gotten to know. The one who didn't sob, who was happy and confident, who didn't doubt that people loved her.

Although now, of course, he was wondering if that version of her was real, or merely one she wanted him to believe.

"Of course you did," she replied softly. Reached out and squeezed his hand. "But I know it comes from a good place."

She took back her hand too quickly, and cradled it on her knees. Did she know she was doing it? As if their contact had been special to her?

"I think," she started, saving him from having to answer those unwelcome questions, "I don't believe I deserve it because I've been lying to them. Keeping secrets." She ran her tongue over the top row of her teeth. "That doesn't seem worthy of love."

"Yeah, but lying to them because you're trying to process something personal isn't bad. It's not great," he acknowledged, "but it doesn't negate that you've been a good friend to them in every other way."

"You don't know that."

"I do," he said flatly. "I've spent less than a week with you, and I know that. They've probably spent years with you, so they sure as hell know it. One mistake doesn't make you unworthy of love, Gemma."

She didn't reply, but her head fell forward, and her hair curtained her face. After a while, her shoulders started to shake. It took him a second, but he realized what was happening. He swore under his breath.

She looked up at him, confirming his fears with her tear-streaked face. There was a beat; she was waiting on something. From him.

Oh, shit.

He lifted his hand, awkwardly placed it on her back, and patted.

One, two, three.

There.

That should be enough.

When he met her eyes again, they were sparkling, but not from tears. From amusement. Relief filled his body, as if it had been behind a dam wall and the wall had finally burst. He didn't even mind that it was because she was laughing at him. Laughing was better than crying, even if it was at his expense.

"You're such an idiot," she told him, but it sounded affectionate, so he merely rolled his eyes.

"That's what I get for supporting you."

"No," she disagreed. "You get this."

He didn't see it coming, because he didn't expect it. When she leaned forward, he thought she was going to hug him. Or touch him in some other way, because that's what people like her—people who were accustomed to giving and receiving affection—did. So when she leaned all the way forward, hovering a breath away from his lips, he almost pulled back. To ask if she was sure, if this was the right thing to do when she was clearly emotional and vulnerable.

Instead, he found himself closing the distance. He told himself it would be rude to refuse. Hell, she would probably interpret it as rejection if he didn't accept. That would be worse for her emotional state.

He bought that excuse for all of ten seconds. In those ten seconds, he relished the feel of her lips against his. Soft, a little wet from her tears, and warm. It felt like he'd had a rough day outside in winter and was finally coming home, where the fire was on.

He pulled back. "Gem, I don't think—"

"Shh," she said, putting a finger on his lips. "You'll spoil it."

She rested her head on his shoulder. After a moment's hesitation, he put his arm around her waist and pulled her closer.

And that's how they sat until she wanted to go home.

CHAPTER 10

Jude was sprawled over the couch when Levi came out of the bathroom.

He didn't acknowledge her presence—she was lazily twirling her hair, now curly, as it fanned out on the armrest—which was good, since he'd glimpsed that she was wearing a skirt, and there were some things he didn't have to see.

He helped himself to some coffee, opened the fridge to peruse his breakfast options.

"Don't you look right at home," Jude commented.

Levi was uncomfortably aware that she was right. Since Gemma had invited him to stay at her place, he'd felt as relaxed as he had at his own place. Perhaps even more. He wasn't thinking about Haley's schedule, work, or any of the things that usually distracted him. He wasn't even concerned that he should have been looking for somewhere else to stay.

"We both know this can't be a long-term arrangement," Gemma had told him when the topic had come up. She'd given him a look, too. That look had said, *We're barely keeping our hands off each other as it is. Living together is tempting fate.* He agreed, so he was choosing not to think about practicalities like money or length of stay. He was aware that it was a stupid approach, but he wasn't sure what else to do.

"In all the years I've spent helping charges, this has to be the most entertaining," Jude spoke again, resting her chin on the back of the couch, watching him.

"Why do I feel like that's a lie?"

Jude thought about it. "You're right, although not an intentional lie. I merely forgot about the time one of my charge's charges decided to rob him." She pulled her mouth to the side. "Crimes are obviously against the Laws, so I had to intervene. She was spirited. It was certainly an interesting experience."

"You forgot that?"

"It was a long time ago. Horses were still the main mode of transport." She rose to her knees, elbows over the back of the couch now. "But this . . . a *relationship*."

"It's not a relationship."

"You've kissed, had an adventure in an alley, and shared another kiss."

"A thank-you kiss," Levi qualified.

"Sure, sure," Jude said easily. Levi didn't believe it for a second. "What are your next steps?"

"I'm looking for a short-term rental."

"Really? Where?"

"I . . . er . . . I haven't officially started looking. But I haven't had a chance to—"

"Levi," Jude interrupted. "We both know you've had ample time."

Levi stared.

Jude was right, but there had to be a rule against pointing it out.

Jude sighed. "Fine. Does she know you're looking for a place close to her?"

"She knows."

"But she doesn't know you only have three months—sorry, two months and two weeks—here."

Levi drank from his coffee, scorching his tongue. *Nice little taste of what you can expect in the next phase of your existence,* an unpleasant voice said in his head. An unpleasant voice outside his head started speaking, too.

"What is the best-case scenario here?" Jude's question was soft. "You're a ghost from an alternate reality."

"I know that," he said through his teeth. "Of course I know that."

He knew that he was dead. He knew that helping Gemma should be his priority, because it would get him back to his life. That was the *only* reason helping Gemma should be his priority.

But it wasn't. He knew it; Jude knew it. So was there even a point in pretending that what happened in that alley had simply been his body reacting to her? That when he'd followed her as she ran from her friends, his heart pounding, he'd been thinking about his mission and not that she wasn't in the right state of mind to be alone?

That wasn't even the most alarming part. The most alarming part was that getting back to his life didn't seem as appealing as it once did.

Guilt, resentment, anger spun in the bottle he kept it in. He only just managed to keep the cork in place, afraid of what might happen if it popped. It already had, once, with Gemma, and it had gotten him to this very point.

No—his emotions would stay exactly where they belonged, and he'd remind himself of his priorities.

Haley. His family. His life.

He looked at Jude. "I can't live here."

"No," Jude agreed.

Since Jude had been the one to suggest he move in with Gemma at first, the agreement emphasized how much of a mess he'd made.

"How do I get enough money to find a place of my own?"

"I can help."

Levi set down his coffee. "Let's do it."

* * *

"Levi?" Gemma called as she walked into her house Friday night. She could smell dinner cooking in the kitchen, some delicious mix of spices that transported her to a home she never had. Her mother was the principal of a private school, her father a doctor, and dinner was usually what whoever was home first could throw together. Gemma had eaten a lot of toasted sandwiches and pastas in her day, made healthier—according to her parents—by the spinach they snuck into every meal.

She didn't want to think it—which meant that she invariably thought it—but she could get used to coming home to dinner, as she had every night this week.

Levi wasn't in the kitchen, so she snuck a look into the pot. It was spaghetti Bolognese! Her *favorite*. Had it been in that presentation he'd watched on her? It was less disturbing now for reasons she didn't want to examine. Instead, she scooped some up into a spoon, blew on it, and put it into her mouth as Levi walked in.

With nothing but a towel around his waist.

She was a *very* proper person. She knew and appreciated boundaries, was polite, and was *absolutely* not forward. The one exception to this was when she'd kissed Levi in the bar, but she had more than atoned for her sins by graciously allowing him to live with her. And while he lived with her, she had avoided any situation where things could become improper.

When she heard he was in the shower, she put her earphones in and played music loudly while also doing some form of exercise. That way, her brain was kept busy with a constant refrain of affirmations as she exercised, and her body was too tired for horniness.

When he cooked, she pretended to work at the dining room table, facing her back to him, so she didn't ogle him and plan their wedding.

When he reached in the cupboard for a dish, she looked

away, out of respect for that strip of skin she absolutely didn't sneak a peek at.

So this . . . this was *rude*.

Levi was frowning at her. "I'm sorry, I didn't realize you were home already."

"I called your name."

Was that her voice that sounded so faint? She better move to the carpet in case her body decided to go the same way.

"What?" he said.

"What what?"

He smirked—*smirked*—and mimed something that had to do with his mouth.

Her jaw dropped.

How could he ask her to do *that* when they barely know each other? Sure, they'd been living together for a bit. Yes, it was nice. But they were nowhere near—

A clatter interrupted her thoughts. She looked down. Saw the spoon on the floor. Oh. She'd been talking with the spoon in her mouth. That's what he was saying—he couldn't hear her.

She cleared her throat. "I said, I called your name." Discreetly, she stretched out a foot and slid the spoon to the kitchen island. It made a screeching noise. She ignored it.

"I didn't hear it."

"Clearly." Deciding the spoon would have to be a casualty in this situation, Gemma walked out of the kitchen. "I'm going to shower," she called over her shoulder.

She hoped someone was keeping score, and she hoped they made a big old tick in the *resisted temptation by walking away instead of jumping bones* column. She sighed when she got in the bathroom, until she heard a voice behind her.

"I was still busy," Levi said.

She jumped, spun around, and stared straight at his chest. He had a sprinkling of hair in between his pecs, so faint that she hadn't seen it when he'd been at Meg's house trying to bribe her. She hadn't noticed it in the kitchen, either, because she was *proper* and trying to do the *proper* thing.

"Why are you here?" she demanded.

Levi looked at her as if she'd suggested he jump out of a window. "I told you I was still busy. Let me grab my stuff."

Please grab my *stuff.*

She took a second to check she hadn't said it out loud, swallowed and pressed herself against the bathroom wall. "Sure."

He reached to grab his clothing hanging over the shower railing. She looked up, so she didn't see his muscles ripple as he did. Patted herself on the back mentally when he turned and walked to the door. Nearly groaned when he turned back.

"Can I borrow your lotion?"

"Yep!" she replied, not asking where the lotion she'd bought him was; not even caring that he was going to smell like cocoa, and it would torture her whenever he walked past her.

She should have asked, should have cared. If she had, she would have thought about how her lotion was in the cabinet behind her. That he was going to come toward her and *bend* to get to the lotion. And then she wouldn't have had to see the towel fall delicately over the curve of his butt, or stop herself from reaching out and yanking the towel off so she could see it properly.

"You know what?" she said, frightened of how strong the urge to give in to temptation was becoming. "You finish up in here. I'll get my stuff in my room"—*where I can close the door and be sure you won't follow*—"and you can call me when you're done!"

"No, Gemma—"

She didn't want to hear the rest of what he was saying. She got to the sanctuary of her bedroom as fast as she could, shut the door, and breathed a sigh of relief. Why did her top feel so tight? Her fingers found the edge of it, and she pulled it over her head. Oh, that was better. Now she had cool air on her skin, and if she got out of this damn skirt, she'd feel all the way better. It was high-waisted and required shapewear, but she knew what made her look good and—

A knock on the door.

When she was younger, one of her teachers had been doing her PhD in psychology. She had been not-so-gently urged by her principal mother to take part in her teacher's study, the parameters—or ethics, for that matter—of which were still not clear to Gemma to this day. She was given a chocolate, told she could eat it now and only have one, or eat it later and get two. She'd managed that easily. But they kept adding chocolates, and delaying the time, and after a while, the temptation had been too much and really, how many chocolates could she even eat?

Besides—she'd wanted to eat the damn chocolate.

Just like now.

She walked to the door, pulled it open wildly. He opened his mouth, but his eyes immediately lowered to her breasts, which were still shaking. She'd known that would happen, so she let him have his moment. When he dragged his eyes up to hers, she lifted a brow.

"Can I help you?" she asked.

"I . . ."

She waited, but he didn't finish. His gaze kept lowering to her chest, the strip of skin above her skirt. It would get all the way to her hips before he seemed to realize he was ogling, and snap up. Then he would do it again. And again. She allowed it about five times before she snapped her fingers.

"Hey! My face is up here."

At a different time, she would think back to this moment and enjoy that Mr. Stoic was blushing. Right now, she was too focused on keeping her limbs exactly where they were, so she didn't do something foolish like jump on him.

Not without his consent, anyway.

"Why did you do this?" he asked, his eyes meeting hers. Staying there.

"Open my door? You knocked."

"That's not what I meant, and you know it."

"Did you think you were the only one who could walk around topless?" she asked carelessly. Truly carelessly. This wasn't only wanting to eat the chocolate. This was tearing off the wrapper before putting it in her mouth.

Even that comparison was dirty. She was in *trouble*.

"I didn't mean to—"

"Didn't you?" she asked. "I've been running away from you since the moment I saw you in that towel. Hell—I've been running away from you since you moved in. And I was doing a pretty great job at it until tonight. I was doing a good job until you came to my bedroom door. For—what? For what, Levi?" she repeated when he didn't answer. "Tell me you came to my door for some innocent reason, and we'll forget this even happened."

He stared at her, his eyes becoming darker with each passing second. What caused it, she couldn't tell. It seemed a mixture of emotion and desire. There might have been confusion, or uncertainty, but it all disappeared when he relaxed the fingers that were curled into balls at his side and said, "It wasn't innocent."

She was kissing him seconds after. It was a mess of lips and tongue, of no longer resisting after an endless period of wanting. He had her skirt off in an impressive amount of time, and he stepped back, his eyes moving over her hungrily.

"If you're going to look at me like that," she said, aware of how husky her voice sounded, "you better follow through."

His lips curved. "Oh, baby, I plan to."

There was a time in her life when she thought the term *baby* was terribly clichéd.

That time was literally the second before he said *baby* in that gravelly voice, with the clear intention of ravishing her.

They both closed the distance at the same time. Her hands ran over his back, his shoulders, gripped his biceps when his mouth found that spot in her neck and she needed something to steady herself with. His body felt as impressive as it looked, though there was a new level now that she had free access to it. A possessiveness that she shouldn't feel, not when this was . . . whatever it was. Uncertain. Unreal. Two descriptions that meant there should only be one layer, one purely physical layer, to what they were doing.

But of course there wasn't. Of course every touch felt like it was embedded in her heart. Of course the stroke of his tongue over hers, the caress of his fingers over her breasts, the pressure of his body, hard and strong and comforting, felt like it was filling her soul.

She pulled back, chest heaving. He stilled, his hands sunk into the generous flesh at her hips, his own chest a mirror of her own. *In, out, in, out*, in this rapid, almost alarming pace. She placed a hand over his heart so she could feel it for herself. So she could calm it, even though she was half-enthralled by the fact that she had done this to him.

That they'd done this to each other.

She lifted her eyes to his. Something heavy sat in her chest. Emotion that was wrapped in confusion. But she appreciated that it was wrapped, confined, since she was sure exposing it would destroy a vital part of her.

He looked at her warmly. Not only with the heat of desire, but of . . . of kindness. She couldn't remember ever making out with someone who'd looked at her with kindness in the peak of passion. Her breath shuddered out her lungs as she used her free hand to trace his lips, his hairline, and slid her fingers through his hair. She stopped at his shoulder, thought she would keep it there, but soon her hand was moving and it was cupping his neck and she was standing on her toes, pressing her lips to his in a tone that was so different to what had come before.

He seemed to feel the shift, because his hands left her hips and slid around her waist, pulling her to him in a hug that was warm and tight and made her feel safe. His tongue against hers was easy, a summer holiday kind of kiss where there was no rush, only time. Where exploration and depth was the goal, and her mouth was suddenly connected to her vagina, and she was wondering what it would be like for his tongue to move somewhere else.

But no—his tongue stayed exactly where it was while his hands moved. One hand cupped her butt; the other slid along the waistband of her shapewear. It stayed there for longer than she would have liked. She realized he was waiting for her to give him the go-ahead, and she made an impatient sound in her throat.

He chuckled and pulled down the tights. Slid his hand into her panties. She inhaled deeply, pulling away from him so she could breathe through her mouth, since she didn't trust her nose to be adequate. She was kind of right. Neither her nose nor her mouth was adequate when he began to play with her. Softly at first. Tentatively.

No, that wasn't it. It wasn't tentative; it was explorative. He was teaching himself about what she liked. She knew it because he was looking at her face, taking in every subtle breath, every harsh exhale, every little moan.

When his finger dipped inside her, she thought she stopped breathing altogether.

"Gemma," he whispered. "Look at me."

She opened her eyes, looked at him. She didn't know what he wanted her to see. The gentleness etched into the lines of his face? The desire burning in his eyes? Or did he want her to see what she felt was hidden beneath that wrapping of confusion? A mirror of the intensity, the overwhelmingness of this moment? Clear and loud on his face, in his voice.

She should run.

She should kick him out of her room, out of her house. *Run.*

Yes, she told herself. Opened her mouth to tell him to leave and instead, heard herself say, "More. I want more."

She could hardly be upset when he obeyed.

CHAPTER 11

"I'm moving out."

Levi could have kicked himself when he heard the words—coming from *him*. But he'd been staring at her for at least ten minutes now. He'd left to get his pants, and now he was standing in the doorway, *staring*. She still had her bra on, her panties had been replaced since he'd taken them off, and she looked so content on the bed that he felt content, too.

It wasn't a word he'd ever used to describe himself. It implied a deep satisfaction, a deep peace, and he'd never had that. Realizing that now, when he was dead and had just about made love to the charge he was meant to be helping so he could live again . . . that's why the words had fallen out of his mouth.

Gemma pushed up to her elbows, studied him. "You thought now was the best time to tell me that?"

He ran a hand over his neck, which suddenly felt prickly. "Thought you'd want to know sooner rather than later."

"Did you?" she asked sarcastically. She pushed all the way up, curled her legs to the side, and rested her weight on a hand she placed on the bed.

Despite the content of the conversation, not to mention the fact that he'd brought it up after they'd been intimate, she didn't make a single move to cover herself. She sat there in her underwear, letting him see every perfect curve of her body, every single flaw. His eyes swept over her. The light was still off and only the moon shone through her windows, but she looked like a goddess under that light, surrounded by the plants in her room. Some nature goddess that had compelled him to give her an orgasm and to accept one in return.

"Levi."

He blinked. She quirked a brow. He wanted to lower her down to that bed and do what they'd stopped themselves from doing, citing *we should probably take a breath* as the reason they didn't go all the way.

All the way. Listen to him sounding like a teenager.

He shook his head. "What?"

"I asked when you were leaving."

"Next Wednesday."

She nodded, took a breath. "Where are you going?"

"A little place a couple of roads down. Nothing to write home about."

"Nothing to tell me about, either."

There was soft accusation in her voice. It hit him harder than if she'd screamed and shouted, if she'd thrown a tantrum or made demands. Maybe he'd wanted that instead of her softness. Her obvious understanding, even when it was clear he had hurt her.

"I only signed the papers today."

"Which meant that you found a place you liked, went to look at it, and arranged to live there, all without mentioning a single thing to me."

She got up now, gathered the clothes that had been strewn around the room, and threw them in her laundry basket. She chose new clothing from her cupboard, lay them over her arm, and walked to the door. He was still blocking it, but he didn't move. He wasn't sure what his goal was here, but he stayed.

"Please move."

"Look at me," he commanded.

She did, lifting her chin with such insolence that he wanted to bite her lip. "Now what?"

Yes, Levi. Now what?

"I didn't tell you . . ." He paused, trying to figure out what he should say. "I thought you were busy."

"Bullshit."

"Yes." He frowned. "I'm sorry." He paused again. Hesitated. "I don't know what the truth is."

She studied him, her expression hurt and yet somehow, still understanding. It made him feel worse.

"When you figure it out," she said softly, "let me know."

She needled her way past him, poking him in the ribs with her elbow in the process.

"Was that necessary?" he called after her as she disappeared into the bathroom.

"Yes!" she shouted back.

He laughed and felt another part of him fall into contentment. He didn't think anything was funny then, so he stumbled back into his bedroom and pulled on more clothes. They were all new, his T-shirts and pants, because Gemma had insisted on getting him clothing when he moved in.

"You can't keep wearing my ex's clothing!" she'd informed him, and laughed at the look on his face. "I'm kidding! I always keep a spare pair of men's clothing in my house. You never know."

He'd stared at her, and rolled his eyes. "You'd never succeed as a comedian."

"Probably not," she agreed, "but I'm not joking about that."

She had disappeared from the room before he could figure out if that was another joke, and he was forced to trail behind her to the car, to the shop. When he'd told her he didn't have money, she waved it off with an "I've always wondered what it would be like to be a sugar mommy" and winked at him every time she whipped out her card.

It made no sense that he was worried he'd messed something up by telling her he was moving out. He hadn't done anything wrong. This was their agreement. His stay was always meant to be temporary.

Fine—he could have timed it better.

But at the core of it, he hadn't done anything they hadn't agreed to. Why did he feel like he *had* done something wrong? And why hadn't he told her about his plans while they were in play?

"It almost seems like you were sabotaging yourself," Jude said, appearing in the same form she had before, although this time, she was sprawled over the bed.

"What are you doing here?" Levi checked the door to make sure Gemma wasn't there. It was highly unlikely—he could still hear the shower running—but he needed to make sure. "Gemma's home."

"I know that. Don't worry, she's not going to walk in and think you're cheating on her."

"Cheating would be impossible," Levi said slowly, "since she and I are not in a relationship."

Jude narrowed her eyes. "I'm omniscient, Levi. I know what happened between you and Gemma. In fact, I'm impressed with the way you—"

"Aren't there rules about this kind of thing?" Levi demanded. "You can't watch me while I—"

"Relax," she interrupted. "I didn't watch. I read a summary."

"A summary? What are you *doing* up there?"

"You're not my only responsibility," Jude said. "You are my most troublesome responsibility, which is unfortunate, because I like you. Plus, I thought you and I were on the same page about how your relationship with Gemma should progress."

"We are." He sank down on the bed next to Jude. "I made a mistake."

Jude didn't say anything immediately. "It's mature of you to admit that."

"Thanks."

"Why did you do it?"

"Didn't get the idea with the summary?" he asked dryly.

She snorted. "I didn't mean it that way. I want to know what was going on in your head. Or your heart."

He took a long time to formulate a reply. But even then, nothing he came up with felt adequate. "I thought about how she offered me a place to stay when she realized I didn't have one. And how she bought me clothes, toiletries, gave me free rein to eat what I wanted. She even started bringing back a certain brand of chocolate on her way home from work, because she realized I liked it." He paused. "I thought about all those things, how they made me feel, and how . . . how beautiful she looked. I lost myself."

He tried to shake the emotions loose, the memories. Tried to resist the embarrassment that he'd admitted to all that. He succeeded with neither.

"Still, you sabotaged it?" Jude enquired. "Why?"

"I did not sabotage it."

"You brought up moving out at a less-than-good time. What would you call it?"

Fear, his subconscious answered, but he couldn't say it out loud. It would probably lead to more whys that he couldn't answer. He couldn't even wrap his head around fear.

"You might want to ask yourself why what you're feeling for Gemma makes you so uncomfortable."

"You're turning it into something—"

He broke off when he heard a soft *poof.* He clenched his jaw, but forced himself to relax and got dressed properly. He wouldn't think about it. He wasn't going to indulge Jude's unnecessary questions.

But as he finished up the food, dishing two plates despite

not knowing if Gemma would join him, he kept thinking about what Jude said.

He did not appreciate that turn of events. For a number of reasons, the first being Jude had specifically warned him against getting involved with Gemma. That was what Levi was doing. He wasn't sabotaging; he was facing reality. He was a ghost, his existence depended on her, and his family . . . his family depended on him. If he didn't go back, his sister would forever believe she was responsible for his death. His father wouldn't know how to manage that. The man couldn't have the period conversation with his daughter, for heaven's sake. What the hell would he do about grief?

He had to go back. For his sister's sake, if not for his own.

Which is exactly the point. It wouldn't be for your own sake, would it?

"Thanks," Gemma said, entering the kitchen and preventing him from thinking about what his subconscious had once again offered. "Do you want something to drink?"

"Um, yeah." He threw the dish cloth over his shoulder. Studied her to try and figure out her mood. "What's going on?" he asked when he couldn't and didn't feel like guessing.

"What do you mean?"

She took two glasses out of the cupboard. She wasn't wearing her usual pajamas of an oversized nightshirt and leggings. Instead, she wore a thin-strapped top and loose pants, both a soft pink color that made her look deceptively innocent. The top rode up when she reached for the glasses. Obeying the command, his eyes greedily took in the skin she revealed. He had to force them away, which was ridiculous, since only minutes before he'd had her trembling in his arms, much more of her skin exposed.

Much more of her soul exposed.

He swallowed at that thought, at the guilt it came with. She had been beautifully vulnerable with him earlier. And he'd repaid her by closing up, pushing her away. He didn't know if that was sabotage, but he knew it was a dick move.

"I shouldn't have told you about moving the way I did earlier."

"No, you shouldn't have," she agreed.

"You were right to chew me out about it."

"Yes, I was."

"Why are you being nice to me?"

"I spent my shower thinking about how you died," she said cheerily. "Fantasizing about how I'd do it. How, you ask?" He hadn't asked, but he let her continue. "Well, there's this guy I know. The kind you don't want to give your personal details to, because he'd definitely steal your identity. Anyway, I'm pretty sure he'd give me the contact details to someone who could take care of you. You wouldn't have suspected a thing." She sighed a little too happily for his liking. "And that gave me closure."

"Thinking about my death gave you closure?"

"Well, something felt closed after I thought about it." She cocked a brow. He shouldn't have found it funny—she was fantasizing about his *death*—but he did. "Are you ever going to tell me about it?" she asked casually, offering him the glass of cooldrink she had poured.

"Yeah. Sorry. I thought what I told you was enough. I think the listing is still up. You can see the flat, if you want."

"No, I meant your death."

She took one of the bowls of spaghetti, sat down at the kitchen island, and stared at him expectantly. He followed her lead, sitting down at the chair next to her because there weren't any others. If there had been, he would have taken it. They needed space, not knees almost touching. Not hands within reaching distance.

He started talking to get away from the thought, from the temptation. "I discovered I had an adult-onset allergy too late."

She put a forkful in her mouth and waited.

He sighed. "Hazelnuts."

"You ate a hazelnut and you died?"

"My sister made a chocolate hazelnut cheesecake." Why was this so hard? He was already dead. This shouldn't be affecting him this much. "I had a slice. I went into shock a few minutes later. We were alone at home. She didn't know what to do. I died."

He heard how stilted the words were. He didn't know how cold they made him until Gemma put her hand over his.

"That's awful. I'm sorry."

"Why?" he asked with a wry twist of his mouth. "Because it's such a stupid way to die?"

"Hardly stupid, Levi," she chided with a click of her tongue. "I blame myself for my sister not being adopted. Something I had nothing to do with. If you're anything like me, I'm sure you feel like your death is your fault. At least your sister's part in it."

She'd gotten it exactly right, which shouldn't have surprised him but did. Maybe because she'd put into words the driving force behind his decision to take on this mission. It was why he felt so guilty about getting distracted.

Haley was back in their timeline, thinking that she had killed him. She would blame herself; her life would be shaped by it. By this accident. She didn't deserve it. And if he could go back and resume their lives, it wouldn't haunt her. She'd be able to move on without the death of her brother following her. If he could save her from that burden, he would.

It was highly inconvenient, then, that Gemma was making him realize how little he wanted to go back to his life. He felt the same way about the situation with his sister, but now it was weighed up against . . . well, freedom, he supposed.

But there was no freedom. He was dead. His options were to help Gemma and go back to Haley, or to fail and cease to exist. It was an impossible choice; neither gave him the option of staying with the person who was making him feel things he'd never felt before.

Highly inconvenient.

What a terrible way to describe the end of his life.

"You take care of her, don't you?" Gemma interrupted his thoughts.

It took him a second, but he frowned. "How did you know?"

"You cooked dinner every single night this week, and every meal was delicious. You did my laundry—which I thought was weird at first, but you saved me a lot of time." She paused to take another bite, and continued. "You brought me tea and a snack when I was working late the other night, and you did the dishes with only a small sigh when you realized I didn't intend to do them immediately. You"—she pointed her fork at him—"were either extremely well-trained, or you were doing something you're used to. I figured it was the latter. You're not the trainable type."

Her eyes sparkled at that, but beneath the teasing was sincerity.

"How did I not know you were that observant?" he asked.

"Because *you* aren't," she retorted. Her voice took on a softer tone. "How old were you when you had to start taking care of her?"

"Sixteen."

"And your sister?"

"Two."

"Wow."

"My parents were stupid," he said simply. "Their relationship hadn't been good for a long time, and they decided to have another baby. Desperation," he added. "Taking care of me had bonded them once upon a time."

He'd known it was a stupid idea even at fourteen, when they'd told him they were pregnant. It had taken them *much* longer to see that. Haley had been a year old before they even acknowledged that having a baby who needed them twenty-four seven didn't leave them time to fix their relationship. It had been another year before they called it quits. A year of arguments, of passive-aggressiveness, of vague threats and no communication.

"They divorced."

She was stating a fact, her eyes on him now. There was concern on her face. Pity.

If he were an egotistical man, he would have been bothered by the pity. But he wasn't. Not when it mattered, anyway. To him, the pity was sympathy, empathy. Hell, he felt it for the sixteen-year-old boy who had been torn between two parents, neither of whom could set aside their feelings and put him first.

"My mom moved out the day after they told me. She wanted me to come with her, but she wasn't the kind of mom who could take care of us by herself. She was forgetful. Liked spending time outside the house. Didn't care about silly things like making sure we were fed." He folded his arms. "My dad was a lot better at stuff like that, even though he worked a lot, so I stayed. Had to tell the court I wanted to stay, too. My mother didn't like that."

"What happened?"

"She got visitation rights, but she never visited." An old pain slithered around his heart, tightening. He might have lost his breath, but he wouldn't give her that power. "I understood that she didn't want to see me. I betrayed her. But Haley . . ." Maybe he *had* lost his breath. It was the only reason he could think of for the quick inhale he did. "She didn't deserve it," he finished after too much time had passed.

"Neither did you," Gemma said. "A sixteen-year-old who had to think about who would take care of him and his sister better, his mom or his dad?" She shook her head. "I think that's the real person betrayed here. And no kid," she continued, not giving him the chance to process, "should have to think about who was going to take care of their basic needs better. The fact that you did, that you thought about what would be best for yourself and your sister . . . it's pretty damn strong, if you ask me. Haley's lucky to have a brother like you."

And there went his breath again.

She seemed to know it, because she patted him on the hand and finished her supper. She took her bowl to the sink, washed it, and placed it on the drying rack. Then she turned around, leaning against the counter with folded arms.

"Is that what the earring's about?" she asked.

He pulled at the earlobe out of habit. "Yeah." There was silence as she waited for more. He grunted, but said, "Haley wanted to get her ears pierced, but she was scared. So, I got mine pierced first, and told her it was only a second of pain, and she did hers."

Gemma inhaled, puffed out her cheeks, blew out the air. "I thought it was something like that. You bastard."

He was too astonished to respond.

She continued. "A man who does that . . ." She shook her head. "You don't deserve to be killed by a friend of some guy I know. You deserve . . ." She trailed off, lifted a shoulder. "You deserve everything."

Pleasure burst inside him. But she didn't give him a chance to enjoy it—or question it.

"Hey, do you think there's a version of me who exists in your timeline?" Her expression was pensive. "Do you think we would have met there? Do you think I would have annoyed you as much?"

"You don't annoy me."

"I annoy you," she said, in the same way he'd heard people say, *you complete me.*

"You don't annoy me," he repeated, meaning it. And she didn't. Not when it mattered. What she did, though, was confuse him. "Why do you think that? We've been getting along perfectly well."

"I think you're saying that because of what happened in there." She tilted her head to the bedroom. "But fundamentally, we're different people, right? I'm all rainbows and brightness, and you're all rain and darkness."

"Rainbows come after rain," he replied defensively. Why did he feel so defensive?

"In my experience, rainbows never come after rain. Either the rainbows come first, or they don't come at all."

He stared at her. She stared at him.

"I . . . um . . . I didn't mean for that to sound as dirty as it did," she said after a moment.

The color deepening on her cheeks was *fascinating.*

"How did you mean it to sound?" he asked.

"I don't know! Like it sounded. Normal. You have a dirty mind."

"That can happen after you share an orgasm with a person."

"Levi!" Somehow, her blush became even darker. "Settle down!"

"It embarrasses you." When she didn't reply, he grinned. "Sexual intimacy *embarrasses* you?"

"It does not *embarrass* me." She frowned. "We've talked about sex before. We all but had it earlier. Because I'm an open, free, sexual being." She waved a hand. "Whatever. I'm going to bed."

"Would you like me to come with you?"

"No!"

"I honestly didn't expect you to be this way."

"It was one orgasm, Levi." She rolled her eyes. "Start expecting things when you're regularly—" She broke off with a shake of her head. "No. No, I'm not going to let you lure me into this conversation."

"Lure you?" he repeated. The longer this conversation went on, the more amusingly perplexing it became. "That sounds like I have criminal intentions. I meant that you'd be uncomfortable talking about sex."

"I'm not. *You* are," she accused. "We both are, because the moment we talk about sex comfortably, we're going to think about having it. Tell me I'm wrong?" she dared him.

He couldn't.

"Your intentions might not be criminal, Levi, but they're definitely dubious."

She turned to leave.

He couldn't help it. He put a hand over hers.

She looked down at it. Looked up at him. And suddenly, he was reminded of every single feeling he'd had in that bedroom. The desire and flames he'd felt when she lowered down to her knees in front of him. The fire he was burned by when she took him into her mouth. The way she shuddered when she orgasmed in his arms, eyes open, hands cupping his face.

She'd looked at him with trust, with vulnerability, and no matter what he did to try and deny it, that memory would always undermine that he felt nothing for her. Hell, he couldn't even make it an hour without thinking about her body. Even worse was that her heart was just as tempting.

He lifted his hand. Her eyes followed the movement. When she looked back up at him, they were sad.

"It's not going to work," she whispered.

"I know."

But he pressed his thumb to the slight indent in her chin, brushed it over her lips. They parted beneath his touch, her warm breath grazing his skin.

It would be so easy to slide his fingers into her hair. To cup the back of her scalp and press his lips against hers and repeat what they'd done inside that bedroom.

Then what? a voice in his head asked. He couldn't answer. Because what they'd done inside that bedroom had been a mistake. It had already seared itself into his body. Into his soul. He could never repeat it. *They* could never repeat it. Where would it leave him if they did?

Still dead.

Still trapped in a reality where his sister and father didn't exist.

Still bound to help Gemma with her family situation.

She held his life, his existence, in her hands, and she didn't know it. If she did, she would almost certainly do what he needed her to do. She wasn't ready for that yet, but he knew he could get her there. He had about two months to do it. That was enough time.

And he *would* do it. He wouldn't throw his life away for Gemma. He couldn't do that to his family. It didn't matter what he wanted.

In truth, when had it ever?

CHAPTER 12

Gemma had never been as grateful for the distraction of Lacey's wedding as she was the week before the big event.

It started Saturday, a day after The Thing had happened with Levi. Well, The *Things*, if she counted that he'd shared personal information about his life and told her that they would never repeat the orgasm situation via a very gentle touch on her chin.

After she'd stayed up all night thinking about it—it was hard not to, when she was sleeping in the bed where It happened, and she could smell him on her sheets—she knew she needed a distraction. It came in message form at about 6:00 a.m.

> **Killing your sister-in-law the week before getting married . . . Yay or nay?**

> **Depends on her crimes.**

> **Refusing to wear the bridesmaid dress because it "isn't the shade of green we agreed on."**

Definitely yay then.
She really said that?

She really said that.
Oh, and she's bringing a plus one now.
Apparently, the man she's been seeing
for a month is "the one."

Do you have space for him?

One of my aunts got sick and can't
make it, so yeah. But still.

Want me to take care of it?

What are you going to do?

Didn't we always talk about this?
Murdering someone and plotting to hide the
body together?

Gemma, I'm a lawyer. I would never
entertain this . . .
Without telling you that pigs eat dead
bodies.
But chop them up in small enough
pieces first.

The fact that you know this is highly concerning.

Criminal. Lawyer.

I'm going to stop entertaining this now because I like living in a world where you aren't defending murderers.

I mostly do financial crimes.

"Mostly."
Anyway, I'm serious about the Izzy thing.
I can handle the dress and the plus one.

I love you for that, but it's fine.
She'll wear the damn dress if she can bring the plus one.

Did you suggest that or did she?

I'm a lawyer, Gemma. Who do you think?

Gemma grinned and was about to type back when Lacey called her. "Let's do a girls' day. Just you and me."

"Don't you have wedding stuff to do?"

"Yes, and you'll help me do it. While we're at the spa, getting our massage on."

She was concerned about spending time alone with Lacey— she was clearly risking her secrets by doing so—but the truth was, she missed her friend. Even that short text exchange had reminded her of how easy things were between them. Or had been between them, since Gemma's actions had caused a chasm that she now knew Lacey was aware of.

Maybe that was why she'd agreed to the spa date, which led to a sleepover at Lacey's house. Gemma filled gift baskets and put name tags on wedding favors, while Lacey vented about everything and everyone involved with the wedding. She got home on Sunday to find both Levi and a meal waiting for her. He didn't seem the slightest bit upset that she'd stayed out all weekend. He hadn't on the phone when she'd called to tell him earlier, either. It shouldn't have bothered her, but it did. As did the fact that she loved coming home to find him there.

That she'd started waking up earlier in the morning to have breakfast with him.

Who *was* she?

It won't last. Even if he wasn't a ghost, even if the literal universe deemed it impossible, you have too many issues to try and focus on the relationship.

That voice in her head was real sage when it wanted to be.

Her days were filled with work. Meg had turned out to be quite the trying client. Gemma had had to revisit a number of her initial ideas, run every single one past Meg, who had lost her cool attitude from their initial meeting. Now, Gemma got emails early in the morning, late at night, with the clear expectation that they be answered immediately.

She didn't have to deal with it. She wasn't at the beginning of her career anymore, and could afford to choose whom she wanted to work with. But it took her focus. Gave her a necessary distraction. Besides, Gemma was all about leaving doors open.

If she put up with Meg's nonsense, there was a chance Meg would refer her to her other rich friends. Sure, they'd probably be as demanding as Meg, but at least she would have the option.

She spent her evenings with Lacey. Occasionally, Pearl and Onu would join them, but since she was the maid of honor, most of the responsibilities fell on her. She pretended not to see the concerned glances the couple shot her way, and Lacey . . . well, Lacey was distracted enough not to bring up how Gemma had run away from them. But she knew Lacey was worried. All these things her friend kept finding for Gemma to do wasn't only because she needed them done for the wedding. It was a way to keep an eye on Gemma.

Gemma found it oddly comforting.

As with the weekend, Levi didn't say anything about her not being around. He greeted her in the mornings, far more pleasantly than she would have expected from him, and served her dinner no matter how late she came home. When Wednesday morning rolled around, she found him in the kitchen as usual. This time, he was significantly less pleasant.

"What's wrong?" she asked, jumping to get the cereal from the top of the fridge. She had no idea why Levi kept putting it there—she supposed the top of the fridge was more like the countertop for someone as tall as him—but since he did the tidying up, she didn't complain.

"The pipes in the place I've rented have burst."

She turned. Idly, she thought about how she had never seen a frown so deep. Nor had she ever been attracted to a frown.

A lot of firsts today.

"How?"

He gave her a surly look. She just about got shivers down her spine. "The landlord chose not to share that information with me."

She picked up her glass of water and pressed it to her cheek. "What now?"

"Now I have to find another place to live."

"Hmm."

"What does that mean?"

"Can't a girl 'hmm' in her own home?"

"Not when the girl is you."

She hid her smile by drinking from her water, and set the glass on the table. "You can stay here. While you look, I mean."

He quirked a brow. "Are you sure?"

"Of course. Why wouldn't I be?"

He lifted the other brow now, and suddenly, she was having flashes to when his head was between her legs, and she got it very quickly.

"Yeah, okay," she said, "that could be a problem. But I won't be here much until the Sunday after the wedding. You'll pretty much have the place to yourself, and since you found the first place so quickly, I'm sure that's plenty of time."

"How did you make a kind offer sound accusatory?"

"It's a gift," she answered dryly. "Look, it's up to you. Take the offer, don't."

She shrugged to emphasize how little she cared about his decision, all while holding her breath, because she didn't care so little at all.

It was so messed up. Whoever was in charge of ghosts thought she needed one to guide her through her emotional turmoil, only for that ghost to add to that emotional turmoil. Had They thought about that? Had They chosen someone she'd fall for so that she could run from yet another thing in her life? Or was this Their way of forcing her to face her problems? A person could only handle so much before they cracked and handled their business—or cracked and spilled onto the floor. And she wasn't the spilled-onto-the-floor type.

Apart from that day she'd met Gaia for the first time and ended up eating ice cream on the floor that evening because the meeting had been so disastrous.

But that was a one-time thing, she was sure.

The doorbell rang before she could prompt him for an answer. She frowned, checking her watch. "I'm not expecting . . ." she trailed off. Closed her eyes to prepare. "Okay," she said to Levi. "That's going to be Lacey. There will be some emergency, and she will be more than usual. You okay with that?"

He looked to the sky, took a breath, and said, "Why not? It's apparently meant to be one of those mornings."

She didn't respond, torn between defending her best friend's honor and accepting that he was right. The doorbell rang again, followed by urgent knocking. She patted him on the arm as she passed him and opened the door.

"Edward is sick," Lacey said as she stormed into the house. "*Sick,* Gem. With a flu so bad he can't get out of bed. The doctor has booked him off for two weeks."

"Can't Justin step in?" she asked, not bothering with niceties.

"If Justin steps in, Chet's mom won't like it. She wanted Bradley from the beginning, and the only reason we managed to calm her down about it was saying that we didn't want to choose family because we don't want to cause any drama. The real reason is of course that Bradley is an absolute dick and Justin isn't, so we explained the situation to Justin, and he was fine about it."

"Lace, take a breath." Gemma took her friend's arm and led her to the couch. Lacey's eyes flickered to Levi, who was still in the kitchen, but her current situation was too important to get distracted. "Chet has other friends."

"None of whom he has a good enough relationship with to step into his *wedding*," Lacey cried. "He has two cousins he could use as a substitute, *if* he didn't care what his mother had to say."

"But he cares what his mother has to say."

Lacey responded with a look. "So we're in a situation, right?"

"Yeah," Gemma said, even though it really wasn't as bad as

Lacey was making it seem. She would never tell her friend that, though, because it was the week of her wedding, and she was stressed, and everything felt like the end of the world when stress was involved. "If Chet doesn't feel comfortable asking his friends, let's hire someone." Gemma shrugged when Lacey looked at her in surprise. "It'll be a great story to tell. Chet's friend from overseas—Britain, because that's an easy accent to replicate—who surprised him a few days before the wedding and graciously stepped in when Chet's best friend got ill."

"That could work," Lacey said slowly. "It could work," she said again, and moved her head in Levi's direction.

When Gemma looked at this moment in the future, she was sure she would see the terror on her own face as acutely as she did Levi's. It probably happened at the same time, too. When they both realized what Lacey was going to suggest before she even opened her mouth.

"Levi could do it," Lacey said, predictably.

"No, he wouldn't work," Gemma replied immediately.

"Why not?"

"Because he's"—oh, no—"my boyfriend."

"Boyfriend?" Lacey gave it a second, likely because she wanted Gemma to sweat, but she let it slide. "It makes him perfect, actually."

Gemma was shaking her head, but Lacey continued.

"He doesn't have to do the whole 'I'm a friend of Chet's' thing. He can literally be your boyfriend, and we'll say that he and Chet became close in a relatively short time—"

"*Weeks?*"

"We'll fudge that." Lacey waved her hand. "You've been dating for six months."

"Lace—"

"They've already had a sleepover!"

"I don't know if I would call it that," Levi said.

Gemma looked at him. "*That's* what you're commenting on?"

Levi shrugged and went back to staring at them. She knew he had an opinion on this, but he generally retreated into his Shell of Misery and Silence around people.

Oh. That meant that he wasn't miserable or silent around her anymore.

Hmm.

"Great, it's sorted!"

Crap, she'd gotten distracted. Rookie move. Lacey could smell weakness.

"No, no, it's not sorted." Gemma stood, hurrying after Lacey, who was already halfway to the door. "You can't expect Levi to step into this . . . this huge role!"

"If he's your boyfriend, he's already stepped into a pretty big role. Besides, I trust your judgment. He'll be fine." She kissed Gemma's cheek. "You're the best, Gem. I'll see you tomorrow night at the rehearsal dinner. You, too!"

She directed those words at Levi. With a finger wave, she was gone.

Neither she nor Levi said anything for a while.

"Was this her plan all along?" Levi asked.

"No," Gemma replied, turning to him with a sigh. "I know why you'd think that, but no. She came up with that now, and it was my fault for suggesting we get a neutral party to fill in." She waited a beat, but he didn't say anything. "You're not going to deny that it's my fault?"

"It's the truth."

"That doesn't make me feel better."

"Would you like me to say something that would make you feel better?"

"It would have been nice, yes, but not now, after I've pointed it out. I want you to *want* to make me feel better. You know what? It doesn't matter." She grabbed the coffeepot and poured herself a generous cup. "We need to talk about this situation."

He was studying her when she looked at him. She lifted her

eyebrows but didn't interrupt. In fact, she used the time to study him right back. Maybe doing that would prevent having more unhelpful observations at less-than-ideal times.

She already knew his frown had nothing to do with her. It was as part of his face as his nose was, his mouth, and as appealing. Finding a frown, a nose, a mouth appealing was still new to her. But that described so much of her experience with Levi.

When that first ghost appeared in her bedroom, she thought it was the universe's way of asking her to show her gratitude. Her parents had helped her by adopting her, and in return, Gemma had to help ghosts with their unfinished business.

She didn't mind it. It was a real, concrete way of saying thank you to whomever had designed her life plan. But she could never have imagined this. Having a ghost living in her home; being attracted to him; being intimate with him.

She had been *intimate* with a *ghost*!

She'd cried out his name, and he'd cried out hers.

Surely it broke the rules. Surely it meant she'd done something wrong and would be punished for it.

And yet, her fingers curled at the memory of being with Levi, and she struggled to keep a straight face. She would, though. She couldn't let him see that he had this effect on her.

And that was another new thing about this experience. He made her stubborn. He challenged her sunny approach to life. Or had that happened because she'd discovered her parents, the foundation of her very being, weren't the people she thought they were? No, that couldn't be it. It was almost certainly him, with the silence he gave in answer when she asked him questions, or the grunts she got when he felt silence didn't adequately describe how little he wanted to answer her.

"We need to talk about the wedding," she said again, because continuing to study him might have led to more observations, but she wasn't sure she was ready for them.

"What do you want to do about it?"

"I . . . I don't know." She walked across the kitchen and sat at the island, dragging her coffee over the table. "This relation-ship lie has taken a turn I wasn't expecting."

"It's a lie," he replied, as if that explained it all.

"Yes, but it was supposed to be a simple lie," she said, like the expert she now was, who could distinguish between white lies, simple lies, and medium lies that obscured big lies.

She didn't like that she'd become an expert. But if anything revealed the desperation of the situation she was in—the reason she needed a ghost to fix her life in the first place—it was that.

"You told your sister and your friends about it," Levi said, oblivious to her turmoil.

"My sister was going to call the cops on you if I didn't lie," she pointed out. "As for my friends . . . well, you know what they saw. Could hardly tell them I was dry-humping a ghost in the alley by accident." His mouth opened, lips curving up, and she grabbed the spoon out of the coffee and pointed it at him. "Don't you dare smile at that."

"I was only going to say the description was accurate."

"Yeah, sure."

"Why does it bother you so much?"

Levi was leaning against the counter now, regarding her with eyes that reminded her of a lion's. Did that make her prey? She wished she paid more attention to nature shows. If she did, she'd know if prey ever played dead so they could get caught. If they got caught, they'd get eaten. She had some experience with that, and him, and it was extremely tempting.

"You're a ghost," she said, to remind herself as much as him. "You live in an alternate reality. But I . . . I live here. Now. This is my life, Levi. When you leave, I'm going to have to explain where you went and what went wrong. You can't be in my best friend's wedding photos. I'll never live it down."

He rubbed his jaw. It was the first time she'd seen him do it. It was already etched into memory and would definitely visit her at some inopportune time, like when she wanted to sleep.

"If we're lucky, I won't appear in the photos."

"You're a ghost, not a vampire."

"How do you know?" he asked, and she had a flash of his teeth grazing her neck. "Have you ever tried taking a photo of a ghost?"

Oh, that's what he meant.

"I have, actually. Long story," she said at the question in his eyes, "but there was a ghost who wanted me to give his wife a picture of his—" She stopped. "Anyway, it came out perfectly."

He stared. "You took a dick pic for one of your ghosts?"

"Anything to help them move on."

His features twitched. Eyebrows, nose, mouth.

She didn't smile. She refused to allow his brain short-circuiting to amuse her.

"If you don't want me to do this," Levi said after a moment, "I won't."

"I appreciate that." She ran her finger over the rim of her mug. "But this isn't really a choice. Lacey wants you to do it, so you're going to do it."

"You sound like a hostage."

"I know."

She pushed her mug away, lay her head on the table, and blew out a breath. Everything she had said to Levi was true, but it was venting. She knew she had no choice. She couldn't disappoint Lacey by putting her foot down. It was her friend's wedding, and she deserved that everything go well. If that meant Gemma had to suck it up and pretend Levi was her boyfriend, that's what would happen.

Heat spread on her back. It took a second to realize it was because he'd put his hand there. She didn't know what to do. If she stayed where she was, he would probably keep touching her, however reluctantly. And maybe it was because she knew it was reluctant, because she knew touching, comforting didn't come naturally to him, that she didn't want to lift her head. If she lifted her head, he would stop. And he *should* stop. She'd already been over why.

But she could give herself a few more seconds.

Seconds turned into minutes, but when she eventually lifted her head, he moved his hand as she expected. He didn't move his body, though, staying close enough for her to smell him. Strong and bold, she thought, and familiar.

"What?" he asked, taking a step back now.

"Nothing," she replied dutifully. "I know that wasn't easy for you."

He shifted. "You looked like you needed it."

"I did. Thank you."

He nodded, folded his arms, leaning against the fridge. He must have known how it made him look. Why else would he keep leaning? No human being leaned that much.

"We'll make it as easy as possible, Gem," he said quietly. "I'll be in as few of the pictures as Lacey will allow. We'll stick as close to the truth as we can."

"We're playing fake relationship inception," she replied. "A fake relationship within a fake relationship."

"Doesn't mean we stray from the truth. We met at a club six months ago. Kissed. It was so great that you and I couldn't help but continue with our relationship."

"That's your truth, huh?"

His mouth quirked up. "It's a version of the truth."

"And when you leave?"

The answer came after too long a silence to pretend that he hadn't thought about it. Perhaps that was because she'd infused some of her real feelings into that question, too. What happened to them when he left? What happened to whatever was blossoming between them, even with their attempts to starve it of water and sunshine?

"It didn't work," he said softly. "The relationship burned too hot too fast, and it fizzled out."

She searched his face, desperate to check whether he believed what he'd said. But true to form, his face revealed nothing. It was deliberate; she'd gotten better at reading him over the weeks. If he hadn't been trying to hide his feelings, she would have seen them.

That was answer enough, she supposed.

"I'd still like to stay until I find another place."

"Yeah, of course," she said. "It'll give me a chance to explain who's going to terrorize you at the wedding."

"Can't wait," he responded dryly.

CHAPTER 13

The rehearsal dinner was a nightmare. According to Levi, at least. Gemma had patted him on the knee on the drive back to her place and told him he'd done a great job. He half expected her to give him a treat for being so obedient.

It was unfair to think that, but everything about the way she'd approached him the last few days had been so . . . so *platonic*. Did she not remember that she'd cried out his name barely a week ago? That he'd *tasted* her, that she'd tasted *him*, that they'd *shared* something, damn it.

It was possible that socializing had soured his mood.

Lacey had made a big production of him joining the wedding party. He'd gritted his teeth, but smiled when Gemma elbowed him. She'd elbowed him again.

"Stop," she'd hissed under her breath.

"You wanted me to smile."

"Yeah, that was before I knew you were going to smile like a mass murderer."

He'd done his best to prove her right after that. Because he was pissed off that she was treating him so amiably. So *politely*. Not to mention that he couldn't believe he was in this situation. Chet had pulled him aside, thanked him profusely, promised to make it up to him, but it didn't really matter what Chet said. Levi was doing this for Gemma, and she didn't seem to care. Not even when he growled at Lacey's mother, who peppered him with questions he didn't feel like answering.

How could she tell him he had done a great job?

Now he didn't know what came first. Was it the socializing that put him in this mood, or the way Gemma was treating him? Had he been a grouch at the rehearsal dinner because of Gemma, or was he being a grouch after *because* of the rehearsal dinner? It was confusing, and he fully expected Jude to descend and tell him to get a grip.

But of course, he hadn't seen Jude since before his flat had fallen through. He'd gotten the deposit money back, as well as the first month of rent he'd been required to pay when he'd signed the contract. It had gone into the bank account Jude had created for him. It was the only money in the account, so he hoped whatever flat he found next was less than that. Especially since he was using some of it to help pay for Gemma's expenses.

Honestly, was anything going right on this mission?

"You okay?" Gemma asked as they went inside the house.

She had thrown her handbag on the couch, and was now regarding him curiously, her hands in her back pockets. He followed the movement, noticing how tightly her jeans hugged her thighs. How she could only slip her fingers in and not her whole hand.

She probably had to jump to get those pants on.

He swallowed the moan. Stuffed the desire the image had exploding inside him into that handy little bottle. He could barely fit it in.

And *why* had he thought *that*?

"Levi."

Now he was thinking about her love handles, how they probably jiggled as she pulled her jeans over her hips, and he was glad he was dead, because he would have almost certainly died at that image.

"Levi!" she said, louder this time. He blinked. "What's going on with you?"

"You," he barked. "I'm going to bed."

"Oh, no," she said, following him as he stormed to his room. "No, no, no. You're not going to say that and go to—"

He didn't hear the rest, because he slammed the door in her face. He immediately regretted it and opened his door to apologize.

She was still standing there.

"I'm sorry," he growled, "I shouldn't have done that."

She narrowed her eyes but didn't say anything. Instead, she reached out and pulled the door closed again.

He could hardly be mad. He'd done it first, in a much ruder fashion. Though her reaction . . . it was exactly why he was so dumbfounded by this situation. Everything about it had gone in the exact wrong direction.

His plan had been to come to earth, help Gemma sort through her life, and leave. When they'd told him he would get three months to do it, he'd scoffed. How hard would it be to come to earth, help someone, leave? Now he understood.

But surely not everyone's assignments were this hard? Gemma spoke a lot about the ghosts she'd helped in the past. Not once did she mention that she'd gotten involved with them in the same way she had with him. Were the situations different when the ghost came to earth to help a human rather than the other way around? If Jude ever returned, was that something he could ask? Would Jude even answer?

He probably wasn't the only guardian to find himself tempted by his charge, but he couldn't imagine that any situation of a similar nature had turned out well. His wouldn't, either, which was why he couldn't think about Gemma in her jeans. He couldn't keep thinking about how she looked out of them, either. Of her brown skin, its gentle shake around her belly, her thighs. Remembering the way she moved against his hand, his mouth; of that little sound she made in her throat before it escaped and became a moan . . . it would do him no good. It hadn't, in the days since that night, and so he'd found things to do.

He cooked and baked a lot, because that was what he'd done for Haley back home, and it made him feel connected to her. Reminded him of the stakes. He didn't want Gemma to know about it, though—she would inevitably ask questions he didn't want to answer—so he gave away his baked goods to her neighbors. Sometimes, they'd ask for his help with other stuff, and he'd do that, too. He was there; he might as well. It kept him busy—as did the wedding.

The rehearsal dinner had merely been one of the commitments he hadn't realized he'd agreed to with the wedding. The days after the dinner had been filled with suit fittings and wedding briefings. Lacey was as scary a bride as she was a friend, but she was efficient, calm. When she wasn't, Gemma stepped in almost seamlessly, said or did a few things, and Lacey would go back to being efficient and calm again.

He was still distracted by Gemma, especially when they were home alone, but he succeeded in indulging his distractions only when they went to bed. Then he'd spare a second to think of her perfume, or the dress she wore that day, or how the wind fluttered through her hair. It was a relief to not be caught in it every other moment, though it took immense control. And, like the night of the rehearsal dinner, sometimes that control slipped. But most of the time, the strategies he'd developed to distract himself worked.

There was counting—he'd gotten to a thousand once. He recited the periodic table—he didn't remember anything beyond the first line, but trying usually kept him distracted until Gemma left the room.

There were also the observations. *That* had started innocently. He'd look at the color of a wall in Lacey's house or scan every book she had in her bookshelf. After looking at the paintings, the color scheme, the pillows, he realized Gemma must have had a hand in decorating, because it felt like her. That made him think too much about what she felt like, so he moved on to people. He now knew that Lacey tapped her foot whenever she was feeling frustrated; Chet smoothed a hand over his thigh; his sister Izzy folded her arms; and Gemma twisted her rings.

She never wore those rings to work, but whenever she went out, she'd slip them on. Sometimes, she put them all on; other times, she wore only the one with the stone in it. That was the one she twisted. And she didn't only do it when she was frustrated. She did it whenever someone around her was frustrated, too.

That's when he noticed that when she stopped twisting, she would step in. Smooth things over. Had Lacey's mother-in-law ordered a bouquet of flowers to add to the main table? Well, why didn't they put it at the photo booth instead, where it would be memorialized with everyone's pictures? The cake wasn't going to be delivered on time because of the baker's car troubles? Why didn't Gemma and Levi fetch it the morning of? And so it went, even when it was to her detriment.

Like this cake thing. The last thing Gemma needed the morning of the wedding was to fetch a cake. She was already responsible for taking flowers to the church, making sure the confetti baskets were where they were supposed to be, and a bunch of other things Levi hadn't even tried to remember. Plus, she had to get ready for the day.

"It seems unfair that you have to do all of this," he said as they drove to fetch the cake. "Aren't there other members of the bridal party?"

"There are," Gemma replied, focusing on the road ahead of her. "They have their own responsibilities."

"As many as you do?"

She shrugged. "I'm the maid of honor."

"Sounds like you're just a maid."

"Yeah. Where do you think the term came from?"

He thought about it for a moment. "Is that true?"

She huffed out a laugh. "Feels pretty true now."

His lips quirked up before he could help it. He remembered he wasn't supposed to engage with her, and he frowned again. "I don't think it's honorable to treat your friends as if they're maids."

"The honor is in serving. I'm not saying I believe it," she said as he opened his mouth to argue, "I'm saying that's how it's been framed over the years."

He grunted.

She angled a look at him. "Accurate."

They drove a while longer without speaking, with Gemma making convoluted turns following her GPS's suggestion of how to avoid the traffic into town.

"Why did Lacey choose a baker on the other side of the world?"

"Because she's Lacey. And before you say it, yes, the baker intended on finding another way to deliver the cake, but I know Lacey would feel better if someone she knows got it, so I offered." Her brow furrowed. "I offered to do a lot to make Lacey feel better."

He almost pointed out that she did that for more than Lacey, but he didn't think now was the best time. He would have that conversation with her, though. He had to. She was spreading herself thin to try and make everyone happy, and the only way she could avoid cracking was by prioritizing herself sometimes. He didn't think she knew what she was doing, or that she wasn't thinking about herself, and she needed to know. She would probably be angry that he'd pointed it out, but he was leaving soon, anyway.

"What?"

He looked over. Didn't reply because he wasn't sure what she was asking.

"You sighed," she elaborated. "I don't even know if I can call it that. It was more a mangled sound that made me worry about your breathing abilities."

"Doesn't sound like me."

"Why do you think I was asking about it?"

She was frowning, and genuinely seemed concerned. Warmth crept into his chest. He tried to shut the door on it, but there was no point. It crept under the doorframe, over the top. Pressed its hand on the door so he couldn't shut it, even if he wanted to. He dropped his head against the headrest, harder than he intended to, so it landed with a soft thud.

"It's the wedding, isn't it?" Gemma asked. "You're worried about standing in front of all those people."

"No," he replied. "I'm used to that." But he realized it was a handy excuse and said, "Yeah, it's that."

She gave him a suspicious look. "What do you mean, you're used to it?"

"I told you I was a retail store manager back in my time."

"Oh, yeah."

"Why do you sound so surprised?"

"I'm not surprised."

"Gemma."

"Fine, I was surprised. Am, still. But it's rude to be, so I was trying to save face."

"I think we're past that," he said, allowing the smile now. Even allowing the warmth. *No, don't,* the voice in his head dedicated to self-preservation said. Since he apparently had no interest in self-preservation, he ignored it. "What's so surprising about me being a manager?"

"Nothing. You're very capable."

"Gemma."

It didn't even take much prodding. "Isn't it a very hands-on job?"

"It is."

"And the hands-on part has to do with people, yes?" At his

agreement, she gave him a look. "See where I'm going with this?"

"I do."

"Tell me how a man who is not a fan of interacting with people got a job where he's required to interact with people all the time?"

"I worked my way up," he answered honestly. "I started in a grocery store when I was seventeen. We needed the extra money around the house—my dad took a knock with the divorce—so I figured I could help. It wasn't much, but it did help. Plus, I could buy Haley a toy every now and then."

"That must have been nice."

"Yeah, it was. She would get this look on her face. Smile wide, eyes big. And she'd say, 'thank you, Leev,' because the double syllable thing was too much for her when it came to my name."

A different warmth entered his chest as he spoke. A familiar warmth that coated his heart and spread through his body with every beat. He loved Haley so damn much. She was the only thing that made what he'd gone through after his parents' divorce worth it. If it had only been him and his dad . . . if his father had been the surly, work-obsessed person he'd been the year after his mother had left . . . who knows who Levi would have turned out to be? Angry, he knew that much. Much angrier than he was now. And his relationship with his father would probably have been nonexistent.

It was good now. Well, as good as it could be between them. They did a decent job of raising Haley together. They had dinner together, talked about work, venting their frustrations about their workmates. Sometimes, they'd go out for a beer when Haley was away at a friend's. Their conversations didn't often turn personal. When they did, it was usually in terms of the most basic information. His father would be going out on a date that night. Levi was staying over at his girlfriend's. And it was always in light of Haley. Would the other be able to take care of her?

He missed his father, but it didn't compare to the way he missed Haley. He didn't think anything would.

"You adore her." Gemma's soft voice brought him back to the present.

"Yes."

She waited a beat. "You must be devastated that you won't see her again."

"I'll see her again," he replied without thinking. Only realized what he'd done when he heard the vow in his voice. He hoped she didn't read into it. But she was Gemma, so of course she did.

"You mean when she dies, you guys will be reunited in heaven or something?" She was asking, but she was also nodding sagely. "Well, that's a nice thought. I'm glad it brings you comfort."

He didn't correct her. She was offering him another easy way out—as she was intending to this time—and he was happy to take it. Only in this instance, he felt a pang of guilt. But why? He hadn't done anything wrong. Keeping this piece of information from her wasn't wrong. In fact, it was the one thing he was sure wasn't wrong in all of this. If he told her, she'd feel responsible for getting him back to his family. It would interfere with the natural progression of his assignment, of her healing.

Except . . . maybe he was keeping it in his back pocket. Maybe that was why it felt so wrong. When it got closer to the time he had to leave, and no progress had been made, he'd tell her the truth, and she would scramble to help him. That's who she was, wasn't it? That was exactly who he had observed her to be when it came to the wedding.

He wasn't any better than any of those people who took advantage of her. Yes, they all cared about her, and he doubted any of them knew they were doing it. But they were all counting on Gemma. She would step in. She would make the peace. She would make everything easier for all of them.

He despised them for it, yet he was doing it, too.

"It's okay," she said. He almost thought she was addressing his thoughts, but she continued. "To miss your sister. To hope you're going to see her again."

"Thank you."

She pulled a face, as if to make it clear she didn't need to be thanked. "I know a lot about missing sisters. You can almost call me an expert." She winked.

"You miss your sister?"

"Silly, I know." She rolled her eyes. "How can I miss her when I don't even have a relationship with her?"

"How can you?"

She took some time before she answered.

"The logical answer is that I don't know. The illogical answer is that . . . I feel like I've known about her my entire life. There was always something inside me that wanted a sibling. I would plead with my parents, but they came up with every reason as to why that wasn't happening." She paused. "As an adult, I see now that a sibling isn't a 'want one, get one' situation. I know that they couldn't have children, hence adopting me. Adopting someone else . . . I suppose it was an experience they simply didn't want to repeat."

"That's your view on it?" he asked when she fell silent.

"You're asking me that because when I say yes, you're going to tell me to ask them for their view." She glanced over. "I don't want to know their view."

"That's not fair."

"Neither is adopting me, but not my sister," she pointed out. "I've felt her for most, if not all, of my life, Levi. There was a part of myself that was missing, and when I found out about her, it slotted into place. That feeling was exactly why I looked into my family in the first place. I needed to know why I felt so . . ."

She trailed off, her grip tightening on the wheel. The GPS spoke, telling them their destination was on the left, and they pulled in front of the house. Neither of them got out.

He needed to know. "How did you feel?"

"Empty," she said simply. "What kind of terrible person says that?"

The wedding day passed in a blur. Gemma found herself doing tasks she'd agreed to and some she hadn't. The latter tasks were to keep Lacey from finding out things weren't exactly going according to plan. Her friend had been tightly wound for most of the day, occasionally distracted by her new husband. Now that the alcohol was flowing and the formalities done, Lacey was enjoying her wedding. That's what made the running around worth it.

Didn't make Gemma any less tired, though.

"I need your help," a soft voice said from beside her.

She was sitting in the reception area of the wedding venue. The lights had been dimmed as the action was happening in the main hall, with doors that led directly outside, where most of the guests now were. When she'd found the privacy of the reception area, she'd been grateful for the reprieve. But as soon as she'd lowered herself to a couch in the corner, she should have known it was tempting fate.

She'd never had to handle more than one ghost before. But then, she'd never had to handle a ghost sent *for* her, not to her, either.

The voice belonged to a young woman. Her head was bald, smooth like the rest of her dark skin, adorned with the most beautiful crown Gemma had seen in her life. She wore a simple white gown that made the crown all the more striking, and had on a pair of glass heels that reminded Gemma of a fairy-tale character.

She was going to get married. But something had happened, and now she was dead.

Despite her fatigue, Gemma said, "Anything."

The woman smiled. "I need to get a letter to my boyfriend."

"Of course." Gemma paused. "Your boyfriend?"

"Yes." She rattled off an address before handing Gemma the letter.

"You can come with me," Gemma told her. "You can be there and make sure I do it."

"I shouldn't be there when you give it to him."

That was . . . odd.

"Why not?"

"Well." The ghost took a few seconds. "I guess it would be fine for me to be there if you're giving him the letter. She'd think it was from you and wouldn't connect it to me, since I'm, you know . . ." She gestured to herself.

"She?" Gemma straightened. "Maybe you should tell me what I'm getting into."

"You don't need that information, do you?"

"If it involves my safety? Yes, I do."

"I'm sure she won't try to hurt you." The ghost waved her hand. "Not physically, anyway." She paused. "Well, no, wait. She didn't technically kill me, but I fell off the balcony because I was afraid of what she would do to me. Her eyes were *wild*. I thought maybe she saw a ghost."

She chuckled at her joke.

Things were becoming clearer.

"Your boyfriend's married."

"No. Yes. Well, he is now," the ghost said, playing with the skirt of her gown. "The week before his wedding, he told me that he was getting married. He was so nice about it that I thought he was proposing, but . . ." She trailed off. "I got really mad, and he was all, 'we can still have our relationship.' A real prize." She rolled her eyes, but somehow, the gesture felt fond. "I told him the only way we could continue was if he broke off his wedding, and he laughed and said he couldn't do that, what with all the deposits and everything. So I got myself a dress and crown"—she patted it—"and went up to the bridal suite before the wedding. He didn't have to marry *her* to get his money's worth."

Gemma resisted a sigh. It wasn't often that she got this kind of ghost, but when she did, it was really all the way out there. No mitigating circumstances beyond being foolishly in love.

Sounds familiar, a voice in her head said. She almost snorted. She wasn't foolish, nor was she in love. So that voice could suck it.

"Long story short, she knew about me, but she thought he'd broken it off, so when she saw me, she went a bit—" The woman gave Gemma a look, so Gemma knew how the poor bride-to-be had reacted. "I stepped back too many times and fell off the balcony. A couple of meters from here, actually."

Right. Gemma would have to make sure Lacey never found out about that fun fact.

"I think maybe she was upset that you'd pitched up at her wedding in a wedding dress."

The woman seemed to think about it. "I don't think so. I think it was because she thought her fiancé had broken up with me."

"Which he did."

She shrugged. "They got married anyway. My death didn't seem to bother them."

She sounded so sad that Gemma reached out and patted her knee. "He didn't deserve you."

"Really?"

No. It sounds like you deserved each other.

"Really," she said out loud. "I can't do this tonight for obvious reasons, but sometime soon will be good. Is that okay?"

"That's great!" The woman all but bounced up and down. "I'll come see you then!"

With a *poof,* she was gone.

CHAPTER 14

"You can't seriously be thinking of helping her," Levi said, lumbering out the shadows like some covert agent. Yet somehow, she wasn't surprised.

"Why not?"

"She's unstable."

"She's a ghost. Many of them are." She gave him a pointed look. He quirked a brow. "Fine. But I'm coming with you."

"I'd expect nothing else." When he lowered down to the floor in front of her, she frowned. "What are you doing?"

"This is the first time I've seen you sitting since this morning. Your feet must be killing you."

Gently, he took off her heels and began to rub her right foot. She stared at his hands. Before she could think about how he was *voluntarily* touching her, he started kneading at the ball, and moved to the arch and heel. She was convinced that at some point, she'd passed out, because when she came to again, her eyes were closed, she was making soft little noises through her nose, and he had a pained look on his face.

"Do they smell?" she asked, leaning forward. "They smell, don't they? It's the shoes. Well, no, it isn't. Sometimes, when I'm nervous, my feet sweat and—"

"They don't smell," he interrupted. "It's . . . never mind."

"No, tell me."

"I can't."

"Says who?"

"Me. And you, indirectly."

"Now you have to enlighten me."

He set her right foot down gently and took her left. "You were making sounds."

"I was . . . that upset you?"

"*Upset* isn't the word I'd use."

"Levi," she said when she still didn't understand, "I'm too tired to play a guessing game with you."

"It sounded like a moan," he answered through his teeth.

"I still don't—" She stopped. "Ah."

He grunted. She pursed her lips, leaned back and watched him massage her foot. He pressed against the arch, and she made a little sound.

"I'm sorry," she said when he shot her a dark look. "I can't help it." She considered her next words carefully. "Are we ever going to talk about it?"

"We have."

"No, you shut a door in my face."

"Not on the same night."

"Right. That night, you told me you were moving out."

"And you plotted my death."

"I did not plot your death. I *fantasized* about how you died. It's different."

"I'm beginning to think you're the best person to help that ghost cross over."

She kicked him with her other foot, but lightly. She didn't want to give him a reason to stop.

"You've been acting weird ever since that night," she said. "Was it bad?"

His hands stilled. So did her body. She hadn't meant to ask

him that. The words just came out of her mouth. She hadn't even known it was a concern until now.

Well, she might have considered it late at night, when she finally had a moment to herself. When her body chose to remind her about how clever his fingers were. How much cleverer his mouth and tongue were.

But he had been so closed off, so different since that night. No matter how much she told herself that it didn't affect her, it did. She threw herself into the wedding, because it was easier than contemplating whether she'd done something wrong. Whether he didn't like being physical with her or whether . . . whether he didn't like being with her.

"It wasn't bad," he said in a low, gruff voice, resuming the massage. He swapped feet again. Didn't offer anything else.

"Okay, so why have you been so weird? Because ever since that night, your energy has been all 'I'll slam the door in your face.' Which you've actually done."

"I apologized."

"Did you? Must not have heard it, what with all the steam coming out of my ears."

"Steam wouldn't prevent you from hearing," he answered.

She poked him with a toe.

"I'm sorry," he said. "That day . . ." His hands slowed. "It felt like you'd forgotten." He locked his jaw. Slowly relaxed it. "About what we'd shared."

"I didn't forget. I'll never forget."

His head lifted, his gaze met hers, and her breath left her body in one fell swoop. Only Levi had the ability to make her feel this way with only a look. And she didn't mind it. She *adored* it. It was special, sharing such an intense connection that something so simple could result in such a momentous reaction. She hadn't shared that with anyone else before.

It was scary.

It was wonderful.

After seconds—minutes, forever—had passed, he began to massage her again. Tired, content despite her concerning thoughts, she rested her head against the back of the couch and closed her eyes.

"It was good," he said softly. She opened one eye but didn't move. "It was amazing. But telling you that brings us no-where."

She lifted her head now, looked at him. His gaze was on her feet, but he knew she was looking. She could tell by the change in pressure of the massage.

"Nowhere?" Her voice was as soft as his. "Everywhere."

His head lifted at that, their eyes holding, telling the other more than they'd ever allow themselves to say out loud. A wave of longing so intense crashed over her heart, drawing it beneath the surface, making its beating seem dull, heavy. She had never felt anything like it before, not even when she had learned about her sister. She had felt desperation then. Desperation for a relationship, even though it seemed unlikely.

This was different. She didn't know how. Or maybe she did. Maybe it was the fear that accompanied this longing that made it different. Except the fear was dark; dark was dangerous. It was why she never allowed herself to dwell in it for too long. The moment she allowed the light to go out, she wouldn't rec-ognize herself.

With everything she had been through, the one thing she'd always had was herself. She wasn't going to allow anything to rob her of that.

Anything, or anyone.

"Come sit." Her voice was surprisingly steady, considering her insides were shaking. "You've done enough."

"Are you sure?" he asked dryly. "That didn't sound like a genuine offer."

"Don't give me a choice. I'd never allow you to stop other-wise."

His lips curved up at the side, as if that was all he would allow her. She drank it in greedily. Pathetically. Suddenly, she had much more sympathy for the ghost with the married boyfriend. Foolish was easier to come by than she'd thought.

For love?

She wasn't ready to answer the question her subconscious was posing, so she asked one of Levi instead. "How do you think today went?"

"Unsurprisingly well. You were involved," he elaborated at her look. "You went above and beyond to make everything perfect."

"She's my friend," Gemma said simply.

"Would she do the same for you?" he asked. "And I mean that literally. Was there anything you've done for her today, or leading up to the wedding, that she wouldn't do for you?"

Gemma thought about how she'd held Izzy's hair as she'd thrown up earlier, drunk from the free-flowing champagne. Izzy was supposed to do the toast, but she was in no condition to say the speech she'd prepared. Gemma had given her a bottle of water, instructed her to cry when they gave her the mic, and lift her glass and say, "To Lacey and Chet." It would seem like she was emotional instead of drunk, and since tears were generally the best friend of someone drunk—at least in her friend group—Gemma thought it a good solution. It went off without a hitch, and when Izzy had sobered up a bit more, she'd thanked Gemma stonily.

Lacey might have stepped in if someone had the potential of destroying Gemma's wedding, but she wouldn't have held anyone's hair while they threw up, let alone someone who caused drama unnecessarily.

"We're different people," Gemma said.

"That's an excuse."

"What good does the truth do?"

She was surprised by the bitterness imbued in those words.

She didn't *feel* bitter. It was a simple fact that there were people in her life who wouldn't reciprocate her level of commitment.

Is there anyone who would reciprocate that level of commitment?

She hadn't met anyone, but that was okay. She liked going above and beyond for people. Or she thought she had until this very moment, when she was suddenly feeling bitter.

"It's okay to feel like people don't care about you as much as you care about them."

"Is it?" she asked. "How do you know?"

"I've felt it. Often."

"Your sister?"

"Sometimes," he said, though she could tell it was a tough one to admit. "Sometimes my father. Always my mother. That one usually trips me up."

"It shouldn't," she replied kindly. "Your mother hurt you. You have a right to be angry about that while still wanting her to love you. She's your mother."

"I don't want her to—" He broke off, threading his hands together as he leaned forward. "What's the point?"

"Of wanting to be loved? Everything, I think."

He turned his head, eyes searching her face. "Is that why you do it? Why you go all out for everyone?"

She opened her mouth, but no answer formed. Not on her lips; not in her head. It was an odd feeling, to have no words, but it stayed like that for a long time. Slowly, words re-entered her mind, but they whirled around, so that when she tried to grasp at them, she only got one or two, but they would disintegrate in her palms before she could engage with them.

"I didn't mean to break you."

She blinked. "I think you have. Oh, no, wait. I can talk again." She blew out a breath. "I thought you had broken me. My head did something really weird."

"Mean something? That question?"

"Apparently. But obviously, I don't intend on figuring out

what now. I've already had too many revelations in this conversation alone." Finally noticing that he was still on the floor, she lifted a brow. "Are you ever going to sit with me?"

His lips curved, and slowly, way more slowly than was required, she was sure, he slipped her shoes back on. First the left, tying the thin strap around her ankle, looking up at her to check that he hadn't tied it too tightly.

It reminded her of how he'd looked at her when he'd been between her legs. How he'd lifted his gaze to make sure she liked what he was doing. How she'd nodded and pressed his head back down and wriggled in pleasure. In delight.

She nodded, only allowing herself to swallow when he turned his attention to her right leg. When he was done, he stood.

"Cold?" he asked.

"No." She cleared her throat when the word came out husky. "Why?"

"You have goose bumps." What a traitor her skin was! "You're also shivering," he pointed out.

Ah, so it wasn't only her skin that was a rat.

So what? her body asked her. *You tell me you don't want him anymore. I'll wait.*

Her eyes automatically scanned Levi. His hair was neat, freshly cut because Lacey didn't like the longer style his hair had grown into over the weeks. Gemma didn't mind it either way; it was hard to mind a haircut on someone as striking as him. She might have had something to say about his beard disappearing, but Lacey seemed to know that was a deal breaker for both Gemma and Levi, because she left it alone.

Since they'd started spending more time together, Gemma had noticed that beard hid a dimple. It felt like their secret now—the dimple and hers—and she often just looked at it in longing. What she longed for, she wasn't sure. It was somewhere between stroking it with a finger and licking it, so she thought it was for the best that she didn't try to pin it down.

His shoulders seemed made for the shirt and jacket he was wearing rather than the other way around. All broad and strong. That chest was pretty spectacular, too, and the narrower waist that she knew housed abs from the mental pictures she'd taken when she'd seen him with his shirt off. Below the waist . . . well, she knew *quite* well what he had going on there. If only she'd spent more time on figuring out what it could do.

I can't, she told her body. *You're forgiven.*

To Levi, she said, "Yeah, I'm cold."

He shrugged off his jacket and wrapped it around her. She caught his smell, reminding her of how he'd held her close when they'd danced. How he'd leaned over to whisper in her ear throughout the night. He'd been true to his word about their fake relationship, never telling any lie that wasn't absolutely necessary. But the way he treated her felt like a lie. Of course it did. He was acting like a man in love, and she knew that wasn't true. Knew it could never be true.

"You shouldn't do this," she said hoarsely as he settled down next to her.

"What?"

"Treat me this well. You've been doing it all day. I might get used to it."

His brow furrowed. "You *should* get used to it."

She snorted. "You must not know the men in this time. They don't do things like give you their jacket when you're cold. Or get food for you from the buffet, for that matter."

"Who have you been dating?"

"You don't want to know." She laughed at his look. "No, it's not that bad. I've dated perfectly fine men in the past. We had fun. But . . ." She spread her hands open on her lap, palms up. "I wasn't okay with caring about them more than they cared about me. I apparently drew the line there."

"Only with friends," he said with a firm nod, as if he knew all her secrets.

"I probably do it with family, too," she told him, because he did *not* know all her secrets. "Just not boyfriends."

"Why not?"

"I don't know, Levi. Maybe there's one space in my life where I'd actually like someone to go out of their way for my needs, too."

CHAPTER 15

Levi didn't know what to do about the intense desire he felt in response to those words. He didn't say anything; he'd already said too much by admitting that their sexual experience together had been good. He'd already done too much by massaging her feet, taking perverse pleasure in touching her, in making her moan, even if it was in such an innocent way. He'd put her shoes on and lingered. Lingered because it was tempting to slide his hands up her legs, past her thighs, and play between her legs.

If she knew what he'd been thinking, she'd run far away.

Or you'd be making love on this couch.

Neither option worked, so he ignored the thought and acted like an adult. Now he was thinking that he wanted to be *her* adult—her partner. A terrible, corny thought that didn't fit the Levi he had been when he was alive, but seemed pretty par for the course for the Levi he was dead.

"Should we go home, or do you want to sit here for a while?" he asked, when that revelation didn't bother him as much as he thought it would.

She sighed. "I should go check that everything's okay inside before we go home."

"So you want to sit here for a while longer, right?"

She nodded, giving him a beaming smile that went straight to his heart, filling a tank he hadn't known had been empty. He angled his head in acceptance. Stared ahead, because he was worried about looking at her. About talking with her.

He'd felt as if he'd knocked his head when he'd seen the way she looked in her bridesmaid gown. A mint dress that clung to every damn curve of her body. He had to believe that Lacey didn't think Gemma looked as good as she did, or she would have never allowed Gemma to wear it.

Lacey was wrong, and he'd never been more gleeful about anything else.

Talking to Gemma was more dangerous. He found himself admitting things he'd sometimes thought but never lingered on, too afraid of what conclusions they might bring. Like telling her about his mother. Where had *that* come from? Sure, he had his moments where he missed his mother. Where he thought about one of the few times they'd done something fun together or shared a pleasant experience. But he'd never linked it to wanting his mother's love. Except when Gemma forced him to.

It was easier to think she forced him than to admit he'd readily offered the information.

A weight hit his shoulder. He shifted his head to check, but his cheek hit something fuzzy before he could turn it completely. Gemma's hair. She'd rested her head on his shoulder.

His breath left his body in a smooth escape, a criminal well-versed in exits moving swiftly after hearing sirens. He waited for it to return, waited for his heart to go back to beating at a normal pace. He chided himself in the meantime.

This is ridiculous. You can't react this way to a woman laying her head on your shoulder.

"You know what I hated most about this wedding?" Gemma asked softly.

He forgot all about reprimanding himself. "What?"

"Her family. They were all assholes in some way or another." There was a pause. "And yet, I still wish I had it."

He was taking her hand before he fully thought about it. But the moment she threaded her fingers through his, gripping his hand tightly, he knew it was the right thing to do.

"You don't have a big family?"

"No," she said on a sigh. "My parents have one sibling each. My uncle on my dad's side lives in Australia with his family, and my mom's brother doesn't have a partner or kids. I grew up as an only child."

"Sounds like a lot of pressure."

"No." She shook her head, the movement rippling from his shoulder down to his arm. "I was lucky. My parents chose to raise me. They wanted me. I was lucky."

"How does that change that it was a lot of pressure?"

Her grip tightened in his hand again, but this time, he didn't think she realized it. He let her have the moment. When he thought it settled in her mind, he put his arm around her, shifting her head to his chest. He didn't move after that, waiting to see how she responded.

She snuggled into his body.

She snuggled into his body.

He had no choice but to draw her closer. And when she lifted her head, had no other option than to press his lips against hers.

It was the sweetest kiss. The softest kiss. He poured all his longing into it, letting his lips say what he couldn't, letting his tongue sweep against hers, letting her taste tangle with his until he didn't know what was her and what was him. It would be torture later, when he remembered this moment and found her to be a part of him. For now, it was pure pleasure. It was the knowledge that they were close enough to blur the lines between individuality.

He tightened his arm around her waist, pulling her in closer. She fell against him. He deepened the kiss. She slid her hand in his hair. Her other arm was trapped between their bodies. Neither of them cared. All that mattered was that they were as close as they could be. As connected as they could be. And that, for now, meant making sure their mouths never left each other's.

When they drew back, they were both panting.

"Why did you do that?" she asked, pushing away from him and standing.

"I . . . I thought you wanted to kiss me."

"Of course I wanted to kiss you!" she cried. "I always want to kiss you. I thought we'd already established that was the problem!"

An older couple came through the doors. The woman had a shawl drawn over her shoulders, and the man was carrying her purse. They stared at Gemma and Levi, obviously sensing the tension, but walked out quickly after, pretending like they hadn't seen a thing.

"This is not the place to have this discussion," Levi said.

"No, but I can't have this discussion with you at home. Because then we're alone. And when I say things like, 'I always want to kiss you,' you're going to oblige, and where are we going to be?"

He would oblige. And he would only remember all the reasons he shouldn't after. So he took a breath, begged his body to obey, and stood.

"We'll pretend this never happened," he said.

"Good."

With the look Gemma was giving him, Levi knew that neither of them believed that.

They gave it a good try.

In the week after the wedding, Gemma and Levi pretended they hadn't kissed—or done more, for that matter. They went back to the routine they'd established before the wedding. Before the subtle shift that happened at the wedding, which they were both determined to ignore.

"What do you do when I'm not around?" she asked him one evening.

He gave her a look. He didn't think it was enough, though, because he pointedly placed her dinner in front of her.

"I'm sorry for not acknowledging your hard work, honey," she said in a singsong voice. "I should be more appreciative of your efforts."

He reached out and pulled the plate away.

"Nooo," she moaned. "Don't take away my chicken!" He quirked a brow. "I'm sorry. I was only teasing. I really do appreciate everything you've been doing in the house. The cleaning, but especially the cooking. It's so delicious and fresh"—her eyes dropped to the plate he was still holding hostage—"with such exciting flavors, and—"

"Please, stop," he said, pushing the plate back in front of her.

She wriggled her shoulders. "What an angel."

"Ghost, actually."

They shared a smile. His was small and didn't show his teeth, but it was there.

"You know I didn't mean this, though," she said, cutting through the chicken and adding some of the salad to her fork. "You can't always be cooking."

"No," he agreed. "I . . . hang around. Do stuff."

"Do *stuff*?" she repeated. "Like what?"

He looked around, eyes resting on the television. "I watch TV."

"Real convincing, Levi."

"It's true," he said, stone-faced.

"What are your favorite shows?"

His face blanked. "Er . . . the one . . . with the superheroes."

"Hmm?" She put her fork in her mouth. Chewed. All while looking at him. "Which superhero?"

"The one who's strong."

"Oh, yeah? What color does he wear?"

"Blue."

"Can he fly?"

"Yes."

"Shoot lasers from his eyes?"

He nodded.

"Spin fast and disappear."

"Exactly."

"Liar!" she exclaimed. "There's no such hero here."

"There is in my life."

"Liar!" She accompanied this second accusation by pointing her fork at him. "You're lying! There hasn't been a single thing in this time that's been different from yours."

"There has been! Those chocolate bars."

"Okay, fine, but you're still lying." She eyed him. "What are you really doing, Levi? Watching porn?"

"I did *not* say that."

"Why else are you acting so sketchy?"

"Not because I was watching porn! I was . . ." He sighed and threw the dishcloth he had over his shoulder onto the counter. "I was baking."

She shouldn't have been surprised. He was a domestic god, clearly. But she *was* surprised. Couldn't have been more surprised if he'd admitted he'd murdered someone.

"You were baking."

"Yes, Gemma." Annoyance blended into his tone. "I was baking."

She took a second, and told herself to snap out of it. "What do you bake?"

"Stuff."

"Levi," she said in a reproach. "I've spent the last almost month living with you, and not once have you offered me any baked goods. The least you can do is tell me what you bake."

She paused. "I would also like to know who you're baking for, if not me."

"You'd want to eat my baking?" His frown made it seem as if he didn't care about the question, but there was a hopeful tone in his voice that he couldn't hide.

"Depends on what you make. I'm not a huge fan of coconut, so if your expertise lies in that area, I'd probably be disappointed."

"Cupcakes."

"Coconut cupcakes?"

"No." He folded his arms. "Red velvet. For example," he added gruffly.

"Red velvet cupcakes."

"Why are you saying it like that?"

"Cupcakes are hard to get right. You have to make sure your cake isn't dry, and the icing can't be that sickly sweet stuff. That's even truer when it comes to red velvet cupcakes. Plus, if you don't have the right icing-to-cake ratio . . ." She shook her head. "They're tricky."

"I didn't realize you had such strong opinions on cupcakes."

"Well, you've been giving the ones you've been making away. Maybe I'd have brought it up before."

"I'm beginning to think my decision was right."

"Are you afraid that your cupcakes are too sweet?" she asked him.

"No."

"So you're worried about them being dry."

"My cupcakes are never dry."

She tilted her head, shook it. "No. I'm not going to go there."

"Your brain is a minefield," he informed her.

"Yes, it is."

"You sound proud."

"It is what it is."

He snorted. "I'll make you cupcakes tomorrow."

And he did. A variety, too. As if her questions had activated his pride, and he needed to prove that sweetness and dryness did not plague his baking. He was right, and she readily told him so between bites.

He pretended her compliments didn't matter, but she knew a stroked ego when she saw one. She didn't address it, too afraid that doing so would cause him to give his cupcakes away again. She still hadn't solved the mystery of whom he was giving them to—she hadn't really tried, to be fair—but she wasn't taking the chance that someone else would enjoy them. So she kept praising him, he kept pretending he didn't care, and she got some form of cupcake every day.

It was easy to focus on their daily lives together. Easy to slip into a routine where she actually *wanted* to get up early to see him before work, and looked forward to coming home for the same reason. It was so easy, in fact, that Gemma didn't ask when he'd be moving out, and he didn't bring it up. Their sexual tension was a simmer now, anyway, one both of them could ignore, and they seemed to be living in peace.

She liked it, in ways she didn't care to examine, which was enough for now. Probably because she had other things keeping her up at night.

Mainly, she thought about her family. She'd told Levi she hadn't had a big family growing up, but she did have a new family member now. Her sister. And while Gaia spent a lot of time occupying Gemma's mind, Gemma had little to show for it. Yes, she'd met her. Yes, they'd had a decent conversation. But that was it.

Gemma wanted more. So she decided to act.

"Good, you're up," she told Levi one Saturday morning.

"You say that as if I haven't been up before you for weeks."

"Put on something nice," she said, ignoring him. "We're going to a book signing."

CHAPTER 16

"I hope you know what you're doing," Levi said as the elevator went up to the floor the signing was on.

Gemma whirled around. "Why would you say that?" she demanded. "I absolutely don't know what I'm doing! I'm trying to have a relationship with a sister I never knew I had, who doesn't know I exist, either. Or maybe she does? I don't know. I don't think so, though. None of her bios mention family."

"Should they?"

"I think so? Most bios I've read are like, 'So-and-so lives in this city with three dogs and seven children.'"

"Naturally, she should include that she has a biological twin sister she's never met because said sister was adopted and she wasn't."

A burst of pain at his shin made him look down. She'd kicked him.

"That's what you get for being unhelpful," she told him. "Let it be a warning for everything else you intend on saying from this point on."

He frowned, waiting until the doors opened—until he had witnesses in case she tried to hurt him again—before he said, "I can't believe you kicked me."

"Oh, hush. It was a tap."

"Tell that to the bruise I can already feel forming."

"Really?" she asked, whirling around. She was lowering before he could stop her. Then she was lifting the leg of his pants. "It does look a bit pink."

"Gemma," he hissed, placing his hands under her arms and pulling her up. "We're in public!"

"I was checking your bruise."

"It looks like you were doing something else."

"Having flashbacks?" she asked with a grin—and immediately sobered. "No, I'm sorry. We have an agreement."

He grunted in response. Mostly because she was right; he had been having flashbacks. Especially when she'd looked up at him, her eyes questioning. His hand was already itching to cup her head as he had that night . . .

"There she is!" Gemma exclaimed, and he let out a sigh of relief. He would have done anything, literally anything, to escape those memories. Even if it was an ill-advised visit to Gemma's sister's book signing.

It wasn't that he thought contacting her sister was a mistake. It wasn't. But the way Gemma did things . . . like this, for example. She'd looked up her sister, did what she called a "social media background check," and discovered Gaia was having a book signing.

Something she thought was a good idea to reveal to Gaia minutes into their conversation.

"Hey! I heard about this online. Well, when I was looking you up online, there was a social media link that told me about this event, and I thought, hey, that sounds like fun! So here I am." She paused. "This is great."

"Is it?" Gaia asked.

Levi had trailed behind, letting Gemma take the lead before making his presence known. But even from where he stood, he could see Gaia didn't seem disturbed by Gemma's confession.

He didn't know if he should be amazed or exasperated. No one seemed to be disturbed by Gemma for long, even when she essentially confessed to stalking. It was a gift, one only Gemma possessed, and it annoyed him to no end.

Because she had done it to him, too.

"Yeah!" Gemma answered enthusiastically. "I mean, I've never been to one of these before, but it looks great."

Levi listened to their conversation, trying to be supportive without seeming threatening. He inched forward, saw Gaia's eyes on him, and nodded a hello. He sort of lingered behind Gemma after that. Sometimes he moved closer, sometimes farther. It felt odd, and wrong, and when Gaia said something about it, he wasn't surprised.

"Hey—do you know there's a man standing really close behind you?"

Gemma looked at him. Her eyes warmed. It was a minimal change, but it happened. He almost smiled in return, but he remembered himself and merely lifted an eyebrow.

"Yes," Gemma said, turning back to her sister. "This is Levi. He looks big and scary because he is big and scary. He also doesn't believe in smiling or personal space. He's fine, though."

She thought he was big and scary? She certainly didn't act that way. And he believed in smiling! He smiled at her all the time, didn't he? And the personal space remark was awfully rude, considering he was trying to support her. When this was over, he was going to have a word with her about her glowing assessment of him.

Not to mention that Gaia knew who he was from the café, so really, this entire exchange was unnecessary.

Proving his point, Gaia replied, "So you keep saying."

They were definitely sisters.

"Hmm," Gemma said in a noncommittal way. Even he wasn't convinced. "Well, will you sign my book?"

Gemma had taken a large bag with her, but she always did.

The first time he'd asked about it had also been the last time. He hadn't wanted another lecture about how the size of a woman's bag related to liberation and expression of freedom. But perhaps today, he should have taken that risk. Because now, he was watching Gemma take one book out after the other, none of which seemed to be the book she wanted signed.

Eventually, Gaia asked, "How many books of mine do you have in there?"

"Er . . . a few."

He snorted.

"I'm assuming that your partner's snort is because you have more than a few."

"Oh, no, he's being annoying," Gemma replied. He could hardly deny it. "Signing this one would be really great."

She slammed a book on the table—and jumped.

"I'm sorry! I—"

"Gemma," Gaia interrupted. "This still isn't the right book."

"Right. Okay, hang on."

"I'll sign them all," Gaia said with a laugh. "Give them all to me, and I'll sign them."

"Yeah?"

Gemma's aura exploded in happiness. He drank it in eagerly, like a kid who'd been given free access to a slushie machine and was standing under the tap with his mouth open. He couldn't describe what it felt like when she turned to look at him. When she squealed and wriggled her shoulders as she did whenever she was excited. Almost as if her body couldn't contain her happiness, and it had to do something to relieve the pressure.

He clenched his hands to keep from reaching for her. It would be like holding the sun, and even in this state, he knew that would be dangerous. When Gaia suggested they get coffee and Gemma's entire demeanor changed, his chest loosened. Guilt weighed him down for feeling that way, but he could breathe, and that seemed more important.

He missed most of the discussion after that, distracted by the range of emotions he'd experienced in the last few minutes. It was confusing and messy, and yet it seemed so perfectly suited to Gemma. That might have been the reason his feelings weren't coated with the resentment he expected them to be.

Gemma hooked her arm into Levi's and said, "Come on, darling, let's go get some coffee," which probably should have wound him up, but instead sent a warm thrill through him.

He looked to the sky. He *knew* Jude could see him, even if Levi hadn't seen his Guardian Ghost in weeks.

Why me? he asked.

He only got silence in answer.

"Gemma."

She blinked at Levi, who was looking at her like a man who'd said her name several times. He said her name again, and she realized that's exactly who he was.

"What were you saying?"

"Your name."

"Hmm."

"Gemma!"

"What?" she said, eyes wide.

"I've said your name several times in the last few minutes."

"It wouldn't be the first time," she muttered. "You didn't seem this angry then."

He took a deep breath. Let it out slowly. She could all but see the smoke dissipating as he tried to regain control.

"What's wrong?"

"Who said there—" She sighed. What was the point? "It's never going to be the way I want it to be. With Gaia."

He leaned against the wall—she was *barely* attracted to it now—and looked at her. She didn't turn away, even though under different circumstances, she would have. There were a lot of things she would have done under different circumstances. She would have used the time waiting for the coffee to look around the small shop. She would have studied the vintage pictures on the brick wall, enjoyed the plants that rested in every corner.

But she wasn't interested in doing that now. She was interested in what Levi had to say.

"How do you want it to be?" he asked softly.

"I don't know. Easy?" She placed her hands over her eyes. Dropped them. "What's it like having a sibling?"

"Some of it's easy," he agreed. "You have things in common. Parents, experiences. That bonds you." His eyes flickered to over her shoulder, his gaze unfocusing. "More often than not, it's hard. You're different people. Sure, you're family, but at the foundation, you're different. You fight that for a long time. Pretend that your relationship isn't forced because you happen to have the same parents. The same experiences."

He stopped, gaze coming back in focus as he looked at her. She caught the surprise in his frown before he smoothed it over.

"I don't even have the things in common," she said, not addressing his surprise. He deserved a chance to process it. "I was adopted; she wasn't. I had parents; she didn't. So what bonds us?"

He didn't answer her for a long time. The barista called out their names, and they went to collect their drinks. Gemma stared at the red cappuccinos. She'd ordered herself one, like Gaia, even though she wanted coffee. But this made her feel closer to Gaia. It was stupid. So stupid.

She closed her eyes when they began to sting. Bit her bottom lip when it started to tremble.

A hand pressed against her hip, gently pushing her out of the way. Levi put honey in the cappuccinos. She wasn't sure how he knew she'd want that, or if Gaia did, but she had a suspicion he cared less about what Gaia wanted. He picked up the cardboard container with the drinks in one hand, and used his free hand to guide her out of the shop. He stopped at a bench in a quiet corner, set the cappuccinos down, and looked at her.

Just . . . *looked* at her.

The tears came almost immediately. She wasn't surprised at that. The intensity she hadn't expected. Her shoulders started to shake, and the sobs wracked her entire body. When Levi's arms folded around her, it felt like he was holding her together. Like she would completely shatter if it weren't for him. She put her arms around him, too. Clung to him as if he could somehow make the pain stop. As if somehow, holding on to him would change that her parents had lied to her. That her sister had suffered in ways she couldn't even imagine. That she'd spent her life being grateful for being chosen—and now it all felt like a lie.

She hated herself for it.

"Shh," Levi said softly into her ear. "It's okay, baby. I promise."

He kept repeating those sentiments as she tightened her hold on him. As she buried her face into his chest. There was a part of her that wanted to become part of his body. She could hide in there, for sure. And he'd protect her, hold her close, promise her that everything was going to be okay.

Except he was already doing that, wasn't he?

"I'm sorry." She pulled away and folded her arms around her waist, trying not to feel cold now that she wasn't in his arms anymore. "I know you don't like . . . comforting people."

He shifted and shoved his hands into his pockets. "I don't mind it." At her look, he shifted once more. "With you."

She almost started crying again.

Instead, she sniffed, but discovered her nasal situation was more than a delicate sniffle could solve. She dug into her bag for tissues and blew her nose. As she was about to pull the tissue away, she turned. No one needed to see what would come away with that tissue. She was right, so she took another tissue, did the same. And did the same with a third, for good measure. She turned around.

"What?" she asked when she saw him staring at her.

"Nothing." He shook his head. "Do we need to talk about . . . this?"

"No."

He waited a beat. "Do you *want* to talk about what happened?"

"No."

"You want to talk about everything," he pointed out.

"Not this."

"Fine. So you'll listen to what I have to say." He didn't allow her the choppy reply she'd come up with. "You asked me what could bond you and Gaia earlier, but I didn't get the chance to answer." He stopped, only continuing when she looked at him. "It's love, Gemma. You love her."

She shrugged. "She's my sister."

"And you don't think that she'd feel the same way about you?"

"I don't know."

"You'll never know if you don't tell her."

Could she tell Gaia? Finding out had changed so much of what she thought she knew. When she'd hired that private investigator, she thought she would find out about a distant aunt or some long-lost cousin. She hadn't expected to find this. Nor had she expected to find out that her parents had made a conscious decision to take her and leave her sister. That was the only way she could interpret it when they were both at the same orphanage at the same time.

And she hadn't been the one who'd been left behind.

"It'll upend her life."

"Probably." Levi reached out, brushed her hair out of her face, tucking it behind her ear. "I suppose the thing you have to ask yourself is if you were her, would you have wanted to know the truth?"

An unfair question, since they both already knew the answer.

Maybe that was the point.

CHAPTER 17

"Sorry, it took so long, but Levi said you would probably need time to sign the books. I told him it was just a signature. Then we argued about that for a while, and then we came here," Gemma said with a bright smile.

Levi had to admit that was an adequate excuse for where they'd been the last forty-five minutes. It sounded plausible. Plus, there wasn't a single thing that gave away that she'd been crying in his arms not that long ago. She'd excused herself to freshen up before they'd come back, and when she'd emerged from the bathroom, her face looked almost exactly as it had before she'd cried.

Her nose was still slightly pink, her eyes the smallest bit puffy, but he could see that because he'd been looking for it. No one else would, especially not when she was back to her sunshine self.

She turned to the two men hovering at the table. Levi recognized the one from when he'd seen Gemma and Gaia at the bookstore, but the other was unfamiliar. Neither was a threat to him, but he still felt a pang of jealousy when Gemma offered them a smile and greeted them.

A *threat*? *Jealousy*? He'd become unrecognizable.

"Who are you?" one of them asked.

It took Levi a second to realize the man was talking to him. The question had come out vaguely menacing, too, but Levi could hardly blame him. The situation was strange to an outsider with no knowledge of what was happening.

Didn't mean he had to answer.

"Oh, we haven't really introduced ourselves, have we?" Gemma said, giving Levi a look before smiling again. "I'm Gemma; this is Levi. We're . . . a thing."

She said it with a wave of her hand, and exasperation. As if she couldn't believe they were continuing with the lie. He almost smiled, but remembered himself. The amusement would have to remain on the inside.

"And you are . . . ?" Gemma asked them.

"Jacob. And this is my brother, Seth. We're friends of Gaia's."

"Yeah? That's awesome."

"I must have missed how you two know Gaia," Seth, the brother, said.

"Oh." Gemma's eyes widened, and she turned to Gaia. "I'm a fan. Of Gaia's." She pointed to the stacks of books in front of Gaia. "These are mine. Because I'm a fan."

There was a stretch of silence. Levi felt an irrational urge to fill it, but only because Seth was looking at Gemma too closely for his liking. He was feeling another irrational urge, to protect Gemma this time, even though she wasn't in danger. At least not physically.

"I haven't got to the last pile yet," Gaia said, "but I'll do them now and you can get going if you want."

He sensed Gemma's body go still before he saw her face. She was blinking, rapidly, and now Gaia, Jacob, and Seth had focused their attention on her.

Levi stepped closer to her, and she shifted so that her back was almost entirely aligned to his front. Her shoulders loosened, she started breathing again, and her blinking slowed to normal.

"Yes, of course. We'll leave." Gemma smiled again, but it was strained. "Because I'm just a fan, and this is a signing, and there are other people here you need to talk to."

He barely resisted the urge to look to the sky again.

"Yeah, lots of people," Gaia said dryly. "All of them standing in line for me, as you can see."

There was no line.

For the first time, Levi noticed how well Gaia indulged Gemma. She was hesitant about it, and not entirely comfortable, but he suspected that was because of him, not Gemma.

Maybe Gaia did know more than she let on.

No—that didn't make sense. She hadn't recognized Gemma in that coffee shop. Unless she was a superb actor, which Levi doubted. She didn't seem the type. So whatever was happening between Gaia and Gemma was natural. He'd never tell Gemma in case he was wrong, but they looked as if they'd already begun the process of bonding.

"You can stay if you want," Gaia interrupted his thoughts. "All of you. Um . . . all of you can stay."

Gemma beamed again but looked back at him. He didn't know what she saw on his face. It must not have been good, because her shoulders straightened, and she turned. After Gaia's friends had told her they'd leave her to it, Gemma asked, "Do you want us to stay, Gaia?"

Gaia's eyes flitted to the direction her friends had left in, and settled on Gemma. "I have this stack still to sign. Why don't you keep me company while I do?"

When Gemma looked at him again, he winked at her. She bit her lip to hide her smile, and sat in the free chair next to Gaia.

"I'll leave you two to it," he said, looking around, his mind already on what he could do to give the sisters their privacy.

"Oh, you don't have to," Gemma replied. Gaia shifted in her seat. He saw it, and quietly said, "I need something to eat anyway. I'll see you in a while."

He left before she could try to talk him into staying. Hoped that she wouldn't blurt out the entire story to Gaia before thinking it through. His legs slowed when he considered that she might do exactly that.

It would solve a lot of your problems, wouldn't it?

He stood completely still at that thought, unsure of where it had come from. Actually, he was pretty sure he knew where it came from. His time was running out. He had under two months left. She was making progress, but at this rate, she wouldn't be in a good enough position for him to move on.

And then what happened? He ceased to exist here. It wouldn't matter that he was certain he'd never been satisfied with the life he'd left behind. That there was a part of him that wanted to stay in this time, in this reality, to see where a life free from the responsibilities he'd had back home would lead him. But that wasn't an option. The only option he had was to go back. He wanted to see his sister again. He didn't want her to live a life where she thought she was responsible for his death.

She would, too. As stubborn and feisty as Haley was, she was also sensitive. She absorbed emotions and made observations without much thought. It meant that she took on emotional labor that wasn't hers to carry. He'd talked to her about it, and he usually managed to get through to her. But he wouldn't be there to talk her through his death. His father wouldn't even try—he'd left most of the emotional heavy lifting to Levi when Levi had been alive.

He *had* to go back. For her.

And because he had no choice.

But mostly for her.

So yes, Gemma blurting out the truth would propel them forward. He didn't know if moving forward would mean Gemma would finally face her problems, or if it would only cause more of them. He hoped, for her sake and his, that it would move them forward.

He might have been underestimating her, though. Earlier,

when she'd looked back at him, asked Gaia if she wanted her to stay . . . she'd highjacked whatever she was going to say. She'd filtered herself. Maybe she was doing so now. If she was—and he was beginning to think she was—he'd have to talk her through telling Gaia the truth.

How did he do that without feeling as if it were self-serving? He didn't know. Probably because it *was* self-serving.

He forced himself to walk again, but went outside this time instead of to the coffee shop. There was a bench a few steps from the sidewalk, except it was already occupied, so he rested his back against the wall next to the convention center's entrance.

There was no guilt-free way of moving forward. Even though he wanted to help Gemma more than he would ever admit out loud. Holding her as she shook from crying had been . . . an experience he never wanted to repeat. If he could save her from hurt, he would. Talking her through telling her sister the truth was one way he could do that. But it was also to help her through the emotional obstacles in her life. That would help him succeed in his mission.

Objectively, it was a win-win situation. She got a relationship with her sister, sorted through the shit with her parents, and he got to go home. In reality, it was much more complicated. And it was time he admitted that a large reason for that was because she didn't know the truth.

Telling her the truth would only cause trouble. But not telling her the truth . . . felt worse now. He didn't know why—was happy leaving that question unanswered—but he wanted them to be on equal footing.

He looked up. "Now would be a great time for you to make an appearance, Jude."

He waited. Nothing.

"Am I ever going to see you again?" he asked. He got a dirty look from a passerby but ignored it. "For someone who's supposed to guide me through this, you're doing a shitty job." He paused. "I hope swearing isn't allowed, and you're getting a black mark for me being a terrible charge."

With a deep, heavy breath, he went back inside.

"Tell me what you did."

Gemma turned her head to Levi, and quickly looked back to the road. Because she was a conscientious driver who paid attention, and not because he kept looking at her face and she was afraid of what he'd find.

"I didn't do anything," she said.

"You've been quiet since we left the book signing."

"So? I can be quiet."

He snorted. She narrowed her eyes but kept them ahead of her. She was going to get them home safe, even if it killed her. Besides, focusing on driving meant she wasn't talking, and if she wasn't talking, she was proving Levi wrong.

Except a few minutes later, she heard herself say, "I'm a very reflective person, Levi. When I reflect, I'm quiet. I can't believe we've been living together, and you haven't noticed."

"My mistake," he answered a little too quickly for her liking. It also sounded like he was smiling, but she refused to look. "Does this mean everything went well with your sister?"

"Yes."

She said it primly, which might have implied that things hadn't gone well. That wasn't true. Things had gone amazingly. She'd talked to Gaia about her career, about her books, about the fair. Gemma had read two of Gaia's books so far, but now she was determined to read them all. The passion her sister had shown as she talked about her writing . . . it was special. And Gemma wanted to be a part of it.

Sure, the conversation was largely superficial, but Gaia had asked her about what *she* did for a living, too! She got to tell her sister about her job. And then Gaia had said Gemma sounded "passionate," and that was the best compliment she had ever got, because it meant they had something in common.

When she'd left, she'd floated, courtesy of that realization. But the farther away from Gaia she got, the more she lowered, until she found herself buried in the ground as she got into her car. She'd spent some of the time driving trying to figure out why the good feelings had dissipated so quickly. Before Levi had spoken, she'd come to a conclusion: It wasn't enough. Sharing a conversation about their careers simply wasn't enough.

She wanted to know how her sister had found living in the foster system. How bad were her abandonment issues? Did she sleep okay? What was it like to find stability and success when the first years of her life had been so unstable?

Did she hate Gemma for being adopted when she wasn't?

Yeah, that was the *real* question. She wanted to know if her sister blamed her for what happened. Gemma would understand if Gaia did. Feelings weren't logical, after all. It didn't matter that she had nothing to do with the decision.

Anger boiled under that, making her think that was a lie. She could see it pretty quickly these days. What with her spending the last months of her life making excuses for her parents, only for anger to burn every single one of them to ashes. She was angry with her parents, couldn't see why they'd done what they had. Didn't want to see it yet, if she was being honest. And now, after months, she could face that.

So what was it about what she'd thought with Gaia that was the lie? That she wouldn't blame her sister for being angry at her? A faint *ding* went off in her head, and she realized that was exactly it. She *would* be angry, because *she* hadn't done anything wrong.

And that was what she was afraid of.

A car honked behind her, and she startled. Saw the green light and quickly put the car into gear before she took the turn.

"Things didn't go well?"

She glanced over. Hmm. She'd almost forgotten Levi was in the car with her. "No, they did."

"Why are you acting so strange?"

"I'm not acting strange," she said defensively. "I'm thinking."

"Think out loud."

"No."

"Because your thoughts are embarrassing?"

"Because they're none of your business." When it didn't feel right in her mouth, she sighed. "I'm sorry. Today's obviously been a lot. I forgot my manners."

Levi didn't accept her apology, but he did reach out a hand and squeeze her leg. Was that a form of forgiveness? Maybe. But she never knew with him. What she did know was that he was waiting for her to tell him her thoughts. He didn't ask again—twice was his limit—but she could sense the anticipation in the air. It smelled like Levi and expectation.

She sighed again. "My thoughts are shameful."

He took a second. "It's okay to imagine me naked."

"I don't have to imagine that." She slanted a look at him. "I only have to remember."

His lip lifted, but he didn't say anything. Waiting again. She could pretend like she didn't know for what. Go inside her house and order takeout, since they'd pulled into the driveway.

Instead, she sat, looking at the quaint little house she'd bought. She'd only had it for a year, but it meant more to her than anything else. She didn't care that the roof over the garage leaked every time it rained, or that the shower head fell off every time she adjusted it. Or any of its problems, for that matter. She had bought it; it was hers. The first thing she'd bought entirely for herself. The first thing she could say she owned.

It shouldn't have had that much significance. It wouldn't have, if she'd had exactly the same upbringing she'd had, and she hadn't been adopted. The fact that she had been adopted changed things. She didn't know how or why, felt immensely guilty for feeling it, but it changed things. Ownership meant more.

"I want to tell Gaia the truth," she finally said. "I'm going to."

"When?"

She turned to look at him. To check if there was judgment in his eyes, since there was none in his answer. She'd expected a *Why?* or an *Are you sure?*

When? When was a surprise. A typical Levi surprise—with no judgment at all.

"Tomorrow, I think." She turned to look ahead. "The sooner, the better. I might chicken out otherwise."

"What will you say?"

"I'll give her the folder the private investigator gave me. I'll tell her I was adopted and my parents chose to leave her. I'll apologize for it."

"You don't have to apologize."

"I know," she said. "But I want to. Because I am sorry. For both of us."

A minute or so passed by before either of them spoke again. "What's her ideal reaction?"

"I haven't thought about that, believe it or not." She frowned. "I don't know. Maybe a 'my sister? My darling sister?' and a hug and a kiss or something."

She could feel him looking at her.

"Seriously?"

She returned his gaze. "Would be nice."

"Fine. What's her ideal reaction that's also realistic?"

She stuck out her tongue, but said, "Some questions. Why, when, that sort of thing. And then . . . then I guess I'd want her to say we can be sisters."

He studied her for a moment. Took her hand. His touch, comfort, were more forthcoming now. Easier to accept, too. Warm and soothing, the touch made her want to climb into his lap and curl into a ball. The same feeling had come over her when he'd been holding her when she was crying. That intense desire to let him protect her.

She swallowed. "What?" she croaked, before any more errant thoughts came her way. "What are you going to say that makes you think I need comfort?"

"It might be like that," he said softly. "Eventually. She'll need time to process. The same time you had to process."

Gemma blew out her breath and looked at the house again. Usually, it made her feel anchored. It wasn't working now.

"You're right," she said. "I know you're right. But is it wrong for me to want it to be the easy way? That she'll realize that I love her, and I want to be there for her? That she'll want to do the same for me?"

"It's not wrong." He lifted her hand and pressed it to his lips. "Just not realistic."

"There you go with that word again." She sighed. "It's almost as if you don't think I know what it means."

He chuckled, and her skin shot out in goose bumps. She angled her head to look at him, caught her breath at his beauty. His dark, angry hair; his sharp facial features; his intense expressions. They were all *Levi*. A man who was complex and caring. A man who was strong and supportive. A man who accepted her as she was. Didn't expect her to change. To jump through hoops so he could love her.

Her mind looped around that thought. It was a confusing one, on multiple levels. The first, most obvious problem, was that it seemed to be talking about love, and that wasn't possible. He didn't love her; she didn't love him. There—simple. So maybe that part wasn't as confusing as she thought.

The second thing most certainly was. Who was making her jump through hoops for their love? Her parents? Her friends? When both those answers came back as yes, she didn't know how to handle it. So, she set it aside, and turned to Levi.

"Will you go with me? Tomorrow?"

There was something strange in his eyes, but he said, "Of course," and her heart exploded with the gooeyness of having someone support her, so she didn't think too much of it.

But when they got into the house, that strangeness moved from his eyes to his entire demeanor. He stared at her as she put her handbag down, kicked off her shoes. As she went to put the kettle on for tea.

So, when he told her that they needed to talk, she wasn't surprised.

CHAPTER 18

Levi took in Gemma's stricken expression. She tried to hide it almost immediately, but he'd already seen it. Already knew she was worried about what he was going to say.

He wanted to pretend like it wasn't anything serious, but that had been his approach throughout their time together. It wasn't getting him anywhere, and it wasn't fair to her.

"My future depends on whether or not you work through your issues," he said. What was the point of preamble? "When They offered me the assignment, They told me that if I succeeded, I could go back to my time and continue to live my life. I said yes."

She was looking at him, her face carefully blanked, but she was also folding her arms. She had done it after she'd cried earlier, too. Even if it hadn't been an obvious defense mechanism, the fact that this was how she was responding in each situation was clear enough.

She was holding herself together. This time, because he'd broken her.

"What happens if you don't succeed?" she asked, her voice firm, revealing none of the hurt he was imagining.

"I cease to exist."

Her eyes widened. "As in, you disappear? No heaven, no hell, no in between?"

He nodded.

"No *nothing*?" Her tone was incredulous.

"Yes."

She unfolded her arms and put them on her hips. Blew out a breath. "So what you're telling me is that you're invested in my life not because you're simply a ghost trying to help, but because your existence, your *essence,* literally depends on it?"

"Yes."

She nodded—and moved so fast he didn't have time to respond when she threw her lip balm at him.

"*Why?*" she demanded, reaching into her bag again—that huge bag with endless ammunition—and throwing a pouch with who knows what in it at him. It hit him in the chest, like the lip balm had, but it was decidedly heavier. Almost as if it had coins in it.

But that was dangerous. Surely, she'd know not to hit him with something that could actually hurt him?

"*Why* would you make me believe that you actually cared about me?"

"I do!" he said. She took out something bigger this time and threw it. He ducked, and it hit the kitchen cabinet with a thud. "Hey!"

"You're lucky I forgot my pepper spray today!"

"You forgot your pepper spray? No, wait—you'd use pepper spray on me?"

"Yes! I was in a hurry this morning, okay? I didn't take it out of the bag I usually use. And I wouldn't have sprayed you with it! Just thrown it at you. And I would have aimed at your head, too, so you'd have a nice round bruise to remind you of what a *dick move* it was to pretend to like me!"

She stormed away in the direction of her bedroom, dropping her handbag in the passage, as if her hands couldn't handle carrying it while she was upset with him.

"Whoa," he said when she tried to slam the door. He put a hand out to stop her. "Who said anything about pretending to like you?"

"I don't know, Levi. You just told me that your support for the last month has had an ulterior motive. If you pretended to support me, what stopped you from pretending to like me? To care about me?"

She tried to close the door again. She put all her weight behind it and pushed, and he had to put in some real strength to angle through.

"Do not force your way into my bedroom," she huffed.

And when she put it like that, she had a point.

"Fine." He stopped fighting back. The door closed with a bang. "Come out here and talk to me like an adult."

"You don't get to tell me when to act like an adult!"

"Are you sticking out your tongue?"

There was a pause that told him she was sticking out her tongue. But she said, "No."

"Liar."

The door opened. "You're calling *me* a liar? You're the one who spent almost a month living with me, and you couldn't have the decency to tell me the truth?" All her spunk went out of her. Her shoulders sagged, her eyes open and sad, as she asked, "Why didn't you tell me?"

"My Guar—"

He stopped. He was about to tell her that it was Jude's fault. That his guardian had warned him against telling her the truth. But he hadn't done it because of that. Jude *had* warned him, but he had provided Levi with a convenient excuse to do what he'd always done: play his cards close to his chest. He had a much better handle on a situation when he did that.

But sometimes, those cards were hidden, even from him. He didn't know how he felt until . . . well, until he died. Now he could see that his life at home hadn't been happy. Raising his sister had sucked up a lot of his time.

Oh, he'd gone through the motions. He'd had a job. He'd dated. He had some friends. But that job was one of the few jobs he could get without a degree. He hadn't gone to university, because it would demand too much from him. He needed to be home to look after Haley. He needed to contribute to the household finances. He'd even worked to become a store manager, because it meant more money.

The dates he'd gone on hadn't ever been serious. When something had the potential to turn serious, he pushed the person away. Or they left, too intimidated by his responsibilities. And his friends? They were colleagues. He couldn't say he'd still be friends with them if they didn't work together.

The motions had contributed to him not seeing the truth: that he wasn't living his life. He was living *a* life, but not the one he wanted. Or even the one he'd dreamt about before his parents had divorced. He'd forgotten about those dreams. Forgotten about the person who'd had those dreams. Now, he was facing it, facing *him*. The real him. Might as well, since his existence was coming to an end, anyway.

The real him couldn't use someone else as a scapegoat for his decisions.

"There was no good outcome if I told you the truth. You'd either feel responsible for my future, and you'd help me at your own expense. Or you wouldn't, and I wouldn't even get the chance to help you through what you're going through."

Emotion flickered in her eyes. "That first part . . ." Her throat bobbed as she swallowed. "No," she said, but she was talking to herself. "What changed?"

That was directed at him. "You deserved to know the truth."

"I deserved that from the beginning. So why now?"

"I . . . I don't know." But he did. Only he couldn't say it out loud. Now wasn't the right time to proclaim his feelings. With them, there'd never be a good time. "Maybe I was thinking about what we were talking about with your sister. Tell her the truth, and let her decide what she wants to do with it."

"So that's what you're doing with me now? Letting me decide how to handle this bombshell?"

He knew it was inadequate, but the only thing he could manage was a shrug.

She pursed her lips. "I think maybe I should spend tonight somewhere else."

"No, Gemma," he said, watching as she turned and started pulling out clothes. "Don't go. This is your home. I'll go."

"Where?" she asked, not bothering to look at him. Instead, she got a suitcase from the top of her cupboard. "Where will you go, Levi?"

He opened his mouth, but had no answer.

"Besides," she continued, putting toiletries into a bag now, "being here will remind me of you, and I'll get angry, and I need . . . I need to focus on tomorrow."

He spent the next few minutes watching her, searching his mind to figure out what he could say to get her to stay. Nothing came to mind. But he thought that she deserved to go. To have space and think about things. Hadn't he told her that's what Gaia would need? He couldn't employ the same strategy they'd decided on for her sister, but not expect the same outcome.

It did give him something to say, but she was already rolling her suitcase toward the front door when he said it.

"Do you still want me to go with you tomorrow?"

She stopped, her shoulders so tight he could see the slight hunch in them. It was a long while before she answered. She didn't bother turning around it.

"Yes." There was a pause. "Damn it."

And she was gone.

Gemma considered going to Lacey and Chet's, but she didn't have the energy to deal with the questions. Instead, she booked herself into a hotel nearby. The room was pretty. It looked out onto a small pond on the hotel's property and was decorated in whites and blues. She idly thought about how she might have approached the design, but Levi's confession kept popping into her head, interrupting even her mundane thoughts.

She stared longingly at the bed.

Too bad she wouldn't be sleeping in it that night.

She ordered room service and tried to focus on the next day. She was finally going to tell her sister the truth. That was more important than what Levi had told her. That was what should have her focus.

But as her food arrived, as she ate and drank and tasted nothing, she realized that it didn't matter. Each issue took up space in her mind in equal measure. She had to focus on both.

Except it wasn't focusing as much as playing things over and over, a loop going round and round in her head until she blinked and realized the sun was coming up. She made herself a cup of tea and gave herself a pep talk.

"You can do this," she said to her reflection in the mirror. "You can tell your sister what happened. She deserves to know. And you deserve the opportunity to have a relationship with her. But only if she knows the truth."

She turned away from the mirror when her reflection seemed doubtful. She downed her tea, burning herself in the process. Then she checked out and got into her car. She knew her sister's address, could go straight there. And it would be cleaner that way. She would tell Gaia the truth and leave. Or stay. Whatever.

Her heart clearly wanted it to be stay, but she knew it would likely be leave. Because of it, because of the very uncertainty of it, she needed Levi there. She didn't want to think about what it meant, or about how she could even want him there after what he'd told her. Instead, she drove to her house and honked the horn.

She might need him, but she didn't have to be polite about it.

She reminded herself of that when he walked out, dressed casually in jeans and a T-shirt, and her body immediately wanted to jump him.

"Hey," he said when he got into the car. "Are you okay?"

"Of course!" she said brightly. But it wasn't for his benefit. It was for hers. If she could be bright, it meant that everything would be okay. And she would ignore every voice in her head that told her that was a lie. "Why wouldn't I be?"

He only looked at her. She could feel his gaze burning a hole through her. Burning a hole into her brightness.

"Put on your seat belt," she told him flatly. She started the car and drove to Gaia's place.

CHAPTER 19

"Gemma?"

It took Gemma a second to process this turn of events. She'd practiced how this would go in her head, but in none of those scenarios did her sister not open the door. She hadn't thought about anyone but Gaia being around when she told her the truth. Seeing someone else—her sister's friend, or boyfriend, she supposed, since friends weren't generally at their friend's houses this early, certainly not wearing that *I just did something naughty* expression, anyway—put her off.

"Hi, Jacob. I didn't realize you would be here."

Jacob frowned, his eyes searching her face before he stepped outside, closing the door behind him. "You want to see Gaia?"

"Yes." She paused. Smiled. It was the universal *I come in peace* sign, wasn't it? "Is she home?"

"How do you know where she lives?" he asked, not bothering to answer her question.

"I . . . um . . ." She tried to think of an excuse, but couldn't. Today was all about truth. She would try it here, too. "Look, I only need a second, okay? Is she inside?"

"Gemma," he said, taking a step forward. Automatically, she stepped back. It wasn't that she was afraid of him. He was just . . . intimidating. But a bush rustled behind her, and she was reminded that she had her own Lord of Intimidation. She squared her shoulders.

"You told Gaia you're stalking her, right?" Jacob asked. *Oh, definitely boyfriend,* she thought, but told herself to focus. "Forgive me if I'm a little concerned that you're now showing up at her house. It was bad enough that you showed up at the café. And the signing."

Well, when he put it that way . . .

She lowered her head, closed her eyes. She'd gone about this the wrong way. What was she thinking, telling Gaia she was stalking her? Showing up at the café? At the signing? It was ludicrous, and of course, her boyfriend was worried about it.

When she looked at Jacob again, his brow was furrowed. It only deepened at whatever he saw on her face.

"I have to tell her something," Gemma said. "I should have told her at the café, the signing"—that had been the real reason she'd gone, hadn't it?—"but if I don't do it now—"

"Is there a problem?" Levi asked from behind her. She closed her eyes again. Tried to summon the strength to be annoyed that he'd chosen now, of all times, to show his face. It didn't work. The only thing she felt was relief.

And a deep, deep desire to leave.

"No," Gemma said. "No problem. We should . . . we should come back at another time."

She turned. Levi looked at her. And said, "No."

"What?"

The *betrayal.*

"We're not leaving," he said, more gently this time. As if that would make her less angry that he didn't have her back. "Can she see Gaia?" he asked Jacob.

"No," Jacob replied. "I'm not letting someone see Gaia who's admitted to stalking her. Not in her home."

"You really think she's going to hurt Gaia?" Levi asked flatly. "She's a literal piece of sunshine."

Now is not the time to feel triumphant, Gemma, a voice scolded her when she felt exactly that.

"She just wants to speak with her," Levi continued.

Jacob waited a beat. "Tell me. If someone pitched up at several of the places Gemma was at, claiming to stalk her, then showed up at her home, would you give them access to her?"

Levi opened his mouth, but didn't say anything. That led to a fairly cocky expression on Jacob's face—until the door opened behind him.

"What's going on?" Gaia asked, looking all fresh in a white dress and matching headband. "Gemma? What are you doing here?"

"I'm your sister," Gemma answered honestly. Well, it was less of an answer and more a series of words that had marched out of her mouth. Much like the rest of the words coming out her mouth. "Your biological sister, I mean. I don't know if you have any foster sisters you still keep in touch with."

Gaia didn't answer, and oh, look, Gemma's brain was responding with more words.

"I know that sounds like a lie, but we're sisters. We were both put into Angel's Care foster house when we were two. I . . . I was adopted," Gemma said, forcing it out, "and my parents didn't take you. I didn't know, and I'm sorry. I'm so sorry."

She stopped, even though she wanted to say more. What, she didn't know. She had said all there was to say; everything else would simply be platitudes.

So maybe she did know. She wanted to give platitudes. She wanted to apologize. She wanted to make everything okay.

But it wasn't. The long silence that followed proved that.

"How do we know this is true?" Jacob asked eventually. Gemma noticed he was holding Gaia's hand. Irrationally, she wished Levi were closer, holding hers.

"I have papers. Documents." She was reaching for her handbag before she realized she'd left it in her car. Levi stepped forward and handed her a file. "You can have it," Gemma said, offering the file to Gaia. "All of it."

When Gaia didn't take it, Gemma offered it to Jacob. He took it, skimmed through the papers. As he did, a paper fluttered out. Gemma didn't have to see it to know what that paper was. Though she'd only allowed herself to look at it once, when the investigator had given her the file, she had it committed to memory.

It was a picture of them in the same crib, cuddled together as if their lives depended on it. When she'd first seen that picture, she'd wondered if those girls had known that their parents were gone. That someday, they'd be separated. Were they comforting each other, or saying goodbye?

Those thoughts had made her actually use the gym membership she'd signed up for years ago. *Twice.* Was it any wonder she could never bring herself to look at it again?

"And I have this," Gemma said, lifting her hand and twirling the ring around her finger. "You have a pendant from this set, don't you? It was our mother's, and—"

Gemma stopped when Gaia walked back into the house and slammed the door behind her. It took all of a minute before the tears prickled at her eyes. She could feel herself falling apart, but she forced herself to swallow. To remember how she'd felt when she'd found out.

"It's a lot to process," Levi said from behind her, a quiet reminder of what he'd told her before. "You have to give her time."

"Of course," she answered, because Jacob was there, and he didn't have to see her fall apart. Or scream and shout. Either option seemed viable at this point.

She turned, walked to her car, and got inside. She only waited for Levi to get in to turn it on and drive back home.

They didn't speak, which Gemma was grateful for. She needed time with her thoughts. She needed them alone. She didn't want to have to think about Levi outside her bedroom when they got home. Pacing, probably, while trying to figure out how to speak with her. When she'd come out, he would stammer or grunt or do something equally as disarming and she'd tell him exactly how she was feeling, even though she desperately didn't want to.

She was trying to figure out how to tell him she was going back to the hotel when she saw their car.

She immediately pressed the brakes, not even checking behind her to see if there was a car. There was no honking, no crash, and no scream from her or Levi, so she assumed they were safe.

"What?" Levi asked, an urgency she'd never before heard in his voice clear. "What happened?"

"My parents," she breathed, staring at the blue vehicle, "are outside my house."

"That's it? That's why you almost killed us?"

"You're already dead," she reminded him.

He grunted.

But because he still seemed concerned, she maneuvered into a parking space on the side of the road.

"So this is the plan," she told him. "I'm going to reverse—"

"It's a one-way road."

"That's why I'm *reversing*. Anyway, I'm going to reverse," she said again, "down this road, so that I don't have to drive past my house. And . . ."

She trailed off when someone honked at her. When *Lacey* honked at her. And waved. And parked behind her parents' car and got out of her own, looking over at them with a frown. Her parents got out their car, too, and Lacey pointed at Gemma and Levi, and Gemma's plan fell to pieces right in front of her.

"I'm guessing that plan isn't going to work anymore," Levi said softly.

She showed him her teeth.

"Are you snarling at me?"

"I'm showing you my displeasure."

He bit his lip—to keep from smiling, she knew. But he became serious so quickly after that that she thought maybe there'd been another, different intention.

"If you want to reverse down this one-way road, I'd support you." His voice was all low and comforting and it went straight to her heart. And then her heart dropped to her panties. "You've already conquered one thing today. This can wait."

Oh, yeah, she'd told Gaia that they were sisters today. She'd almost forgotten about it in the time she'd been panicking about seeing her parents. It probably added to her reaction. But she had been avoiding her parents for almost two months, and she would have reacted in the same way whether or not she'd spoken with Gaia today.

That conversation had already become part of her, though, consciously or subconsciously. She was under immense pressure. There was so much going on that she was being snarky, and a tad horny, because that was a simple outlet. Rather that than crying. Or being all-out horny, which would have involved taking Levi to the hotel she'd stayed at the night before and begging him to make her forget about everything that happened.

She might have done that anyway if she wasn't meant to be mad at him. He'd betrayed her, and he shouldn't be making her feel safe, comforted, *or* horny.

Her gaze settled on her parents. Now wasn't the time to focus on what Levi had done to her, either. She needed someone on her team, and damn him, he was the only one she had.

She blew out a breath. "Okay, we can't sit here forever. Lacey's about two seconds away from marching to the car and dragging me out by my hair."

Levi grunted, narrowing his eyes.

"I'm going to have to introduce you as my boyfriend."

She sighed and lowered her head onto the steering wheel.

Didn't realize the force until the horn went off. She lifted her head again, looking around to make sure she hadn't alarmed any of her neighbors. Her eyes settled on Levi, who was regarding her with a stern expression.

"What?" she asked.

"Our fake relationship isn't that bad."

She didn't answer. Because no, it wasn't. But admitting that felt like she was forgiving him for lying, and she wasn't there yet. She took a deep breath and said, "Come on. Let's go put my flair for the dramatics to good use."

Together, they went to face her parents.

"Gemma," her mother said, as soon as she was within hearing distance, "Lacey's been telling us some interesting things about your life."

Gemma looked at her friend. Lacey winked at her, which Gemma was sure was meant to be harmless, but she didn't find it funny. Were it any other time—had she not met Levi and had all these realizations—she would have pretended it was. But she didn't want to. At least she wouldn't want to when she and Lacey were alone again. For now, she went along with it for her parents' sake.

One thing at a time.

"That's nice," she said breezily. "Can I introduce you to Levi, Mom?" She stepped aside to let Levi through. When he offered his hand to her mother, Jasmine took it, eyeing him suspiciously. "This is my mother, Jasmine." Gemma turned to her dad. "And this is my father, Simon."

Simon took Levi's hand much more enthusiastically. Levi turned away for a brief moment, and her father mouthed, *Nice.*

It was a far cry from the way he'd been when she was a teenager. He'd chased several of her love interests away, in fact. He'd even made one of them cry. But when she turned twenty-one, he'd eased, as if that key he'd bought for her birthday had magically opened a treasure he'd been guarding. Now, anyone could do the looting. And, if his reaction to Levi was anything to go by, he was encouraging said looting.

"Lacey said you were my daughter's boyfriend," Jasmine told Levi.

Levi opened his mouth, but Gemma jumped in. "Nothing that serious, Mom."

She glanced at Levi, whose eyebrows were raised. She widened her eyes—he should know by now that he should take her lead. Also that looking into her mother's eyes had put a little bit of fear into her heart, and having a "boyfriend" suddenly felt a lot more serious than it was.

"Have you told him that?" Lacey asked, taking in Levi's expression, as well.

"Maybe you should stay out of this for a second, Lace," Gemma suggested, her tone sharper than she intended. When Lacey blinked, she tried to smile to soften the blow. She wasn't sure it worked, so she looked at her parents instead. "We met about a month ago, and we're still figuring it out."

"Lacey tells me he's been over at your house quite a bit."

Gemma bit her lip. Harder than she probably should have, but the pain kept her from swearing at her best friend. "Yeah. Um. We've been getting to know each other."

Her father laughed. "Is that what the kids are calling it these days?"

"I believe we called it that, too," Jasmine said, sending her husband a fond look. But her eyes were sharp when they landed on Gemma. "I'd much prefer you 'get to know' someone who is willing to put a label on the relationship, darling."

"Oh, well—"

"You're right, Mrs. Daniels," Levi interrupted.

Gemma turned. "Are you sure?"

"Very," he said firmly, giving her a look that said *trust me*. She ignored the thrill that went down her back. She hadn't ever cared for men taking control, so she wasn't sure what that was about.

She didn't trust it—or him.

"I've been following Gemma's lead here," he said, clearly not taking her hints, "because I didn't want her to feel pressured. But maybe I've been using that as an excuse not to let her know how I really feel."

He looked at her and smiled.

The sweetest smile she'd ever seen from him. Like he'd eaten cotton candy for an entire day, and it was starting to seep from his body.

"Gemma, will you be my girlfriend? Officially?"

She resisted the strong, very strong, urge to kick him. "Yes," she said, with a smile that also meant *I'm going to kill you.* "Of course I'll be your girlfriend."

His smile widened.

To her parents and Lacey, Gemma was sure this looked as sweet as his initial smile. Hell, it probably even looked like a happy smile. She had, after all, said yes to being his girlfriend. Clearly, he was thrilled.

She knew better.

His smile had gone from sweet to pure evil.

She could tell by the glint in his eyes, the way one side of his mouth lifted higher than the other. She had no idea what had motivated this change—this entire act—but she didn't like it. Not in the least, because it looked a lot like the smile he'd given her when she'd been shuddering in his arms.

"Great! So we'll see you at dinner," Simon said, interrupting Gemma's memories with words that dried up every inkling of wetness from her body. If someone blew hard enough, she'd disappear in a haze of dust. "If you're dating our daughter, we have to get to know you."

"Oh, no," Gemma said, shaking her head, "you don't."

"Why not?" Levi asked, blinking innocently.

Really, leaning into this, huh?

"Because our schedule is so busy, *honey.*"

"This busy schedule," Jasmine repeated, her voice deceptively pleasant, "is the reason we haven't seen you much?"

"No, Mom," Gemma answered automatically, but shook her head. "I mean, yes. You know what it's like when you start a relationship."

"Relationships come and go, Gemma." Jasmine's voice hardened to the same tone she used when Gemma would come home late without letting them know. "Family is forever."

"Oh, look at the time," Gemma said, making a big show of looking at her wrist. She wasn't wearing a watch, but she was committed. "We have to go. Levi is . . . hungry."

"Dinner," Simon said, his voice hard now, too. "Friday. Or we'll come inside and do it right now."

"That won't be necessary."

"Good."

They both kissed her on the forehead, her mother lingering, and they greeted Levi and Lacey and went on their way.

Gemma waited until they were out of sight before she turned to Lacey. "Sorry about that. I didn't expect . . . any of this."

"Yeah, I got that." Lacey studied her face, before her gaze moved to Levi and rested there for a second too long to be polite. She looked back to Gemma. "Obviously, you and I have some things to discuss. But maybe now's not the best time."

With a nod, Lacey left, too. Gemma turned to Levi. "Are you staying?"

"If you want me to."

She looked at the sky and asked for patience. "Do you have somewhere to go?"

"No."

"Guess that's a *yes*."

"Guess it is."

She narrowed her eyes. "You can stop this now."

"I don't know what you're talking about," he said, but that glint was still in his eyes.

Oh, she'd do anything to take it away.

Her body apparently got that message before her brain could say *not anything*, because suddenly she was leaning toward him, pressing a hard kiss to his lips, slipping her tongue in for good measure, and pulling back. She waited for the shock she was looking for.

Yes, there it was.

That was much, *much* better.

CHAPTER 20

Levi went over the events of that fateful day too often to count. Every time he did, he concluded that he deserved the punishment Gemma was doling out. Even if, according to her, she was doing no such thing.

What he could remember of his motives were that they were pure. He'd wanted to distract her, and he'd entertained the situation with her parents for that reason. It worked, too. She was mostly back to herself. Yes, it came with snark, and sure, it was a little more dull than usual, but it was something other than the hurt. He didn't want her to linger on that. Unrealistic, perhaps, considering everything that was going on, but true.

Beyond that intention, things got vague. Maybe he was drunk on the power of creating a narrative. Maybe he liked sparring with Gemma. Maybe he was desperate to share anything with Gemma after he'd told her the truth and he'd spent a night not sleeping, too worried about how she was doing.

Any one of those could be true, but he still didn't deserve what she'd been doing this week.

She did the dishes with music now. And she danced. Shook her shoulders, moved her hips. He couldn't help watching, even when he didn't want to. He'd watch her breasts, her hips, and went back to her breasts again because he was a man with specific tastes. She inevitably caught him looking, and she'd quirk her brow, causing him to look away like a twelve-year-old caught with a skin mag.

She also opened the door when she was done showering. Not when she was done in the bathroom, but when she was done showering. Mist poured out of the room—which was why she opened it, she claimed—while she stood in front of the mirror, doing unnecessary things like putting cream on her face. He'd walked past the bathroom unsuspectingly the first time, and he'd almost tripped over his feet when he saw her standing in her towel.

Another fun punishment was how she put her perfume on as she walked into the kitchen. Her scent lingered long after she was gone, too long to be possible, and he wasn't sure if that was his imagination or not. Not to mention that she left the perfume bottle on the table while she was at work, and he'd have to stare at it all day.

He was almost glad when Friday rolled around. She was quieter, more introspective. When she called him to her bedroom that night, he was confident it wasn't to torture him.

Then he saw her.

She was wearing a black dress. It fell somewhere between formal and casual, ended at the knees and skimmed every curve of her body. She paired that with a bright green statement necklace, matched it with simple earrings and flats, and had a denim jacket thrown over her shoulder. Her hair was tied back in a ponytail, her makeup subtle but striking.

The effort clearly put his white T-shirt and jeans into perspective.

"Give me a second to change."

"What? Why?" she asked, eyes sweeping over him. "You look fine."

"Yes, but you look *great*. I don't want this to be one of those things where people look at us and think, 'see how much society expects from women, and how little they expect from men.'"

Her chin dropped. She recovered quickly, and smiled at him. "My, my, Levi. You *have* been listening to my rambles."

He turned away with a roll of his eyes, hoping she hadn't seen his smile. He exchanged his T-shirt for a shirt, put on darker jeans, because somehow that felt better than light jeans. Gemma was in the kitchen when he was done, drinking a glass of water. Every time she brought it to her lips, there was a faint tremble in her hands.

"We need to leave here at six forty-five to be there at seven, since my mom wants us to eat at seven-thirty," she said, turning. How had she known he was there? "We didn't have to bring anything but ice cream, but I thought we could take some of your cupcakes. Or wine? No, not wine. My mom doesn't like it when I drink in front of her."

She picked up the water again, but lowered it before it made it to her lips.

"She was also asking me about what you like to eat. I told her what I've learned over the weeks, so I hope you like meat! Wait—you like meat, right?"

"I like meat," he confirmed, even though they both knew the answer.

"It's funny, when I was telling her all this?" Gemma said, "My mother didn't even notice that I wasn't talking to her the way I usually do. Like this." She waved a hand in the air. "Without punctuation. And I realized: She rarely does! During the important stuff, sure, she'd listen and give advice. But the day-to-day? Nope! It's almost as if my opinions don't matter!"

She shook her head. "No, no, I shouldn't say that. She's a good person. My parents are good people. So what if my mother sometimes doesn't care about what I want, and does what she wants for me? So what if my father sometimes doesn't include me in the plans he's made for my life? I'd be dealing with much bigger things if they hadn't taken me in."

Levi waited to make sure she was done. She drained her water, set the glass down, and gave him a shaky smile.

"Let's go."

"Gemma."

"I'm fine!"

"Pretending to be fine when you're not isn't necessary with me."

"What do you want me to say?" she asked softly. "That I'm worried about how much things are changing in my relationship with my parents, and they don't *know* it's happening?"

"That works, yes."

"Yes, it worked so well I'm realizing what a bad idea this is. We shouldn't go."

She was already walking to her bedroom when he tried to intercept. She didn't stop, ramming into him so hard, in fact, that his arms went around her in some misguided attempt at absorbing the blow. It worked, to an extent. They didn't tumble to the ground, but her nose was still smooshed against his chest, the rest of her body so tightly pressed against his own that he swore he felt her heart beating. Or perhaps that was his own, thudding, knocking against his chest as it recognized the person who owned it.

He shifted back at that thought, a discovery that made him feel . . . he didn't know. It just made him *feel*.

She stepped away, too. "Sorry."

"Don't mention it."

"Okay," she agreed. "This dinner is a bad idea."

She really wasn't going to mention it?

"Why?" he asked, forcing himself to act like the Levi he actually recognized.

"They're going to know that something's up. They'll ask me about it, and I won't be able to lie! Or maybe they won't care. They won't care about how I feel about this, because they'll see it as a small thing. Or a big thing? A big thing," she confirmed. "Of course it's a big thing. It's a big thing that my parents kept the fact that I have a biological sister from me. But will they care?" she asked. "Will they care when they obviously didn't care in the first place or they would have never—"

"Gemma. Stop."

"—done this. They would have thought about how I felt, and they wouldn't have—"

"Gemma. Gem." He lifted her chin with those words. She stopped. "You're spiraling."

"No shit."

He smiled. "It's going to be okay. I'll be there at your side the entire time."

"That doesn't make me feel better." Her eyes were wide and vulnerable when she looked at him. And she sighed. "No, that's a lie. It does." She paused. "It's annoying when I don't know if I can trust your intentions."

His smile faded. "I . . . understand. I'm sorry for it. I never meant—"

"Don't. Don't apologize now. Don't be nice to me now. My anger fuels me."

She shook her arms, bounced on her feet like a boxer.

"You've got it," he replied easily, amused, but a little stung, too. "I'll be a jerk and concern your parents with your dating choices. The focus will be on me, not you."

"That . . . is a pretty good plan."

"I was joking."

She studied him. "Half joking."

He angled his head in acknowledgement. "I'll be myself. I'm told that gives parents plenty to be concerned about."

"Someone *told* you that? Who?"

He shuffled his feet. "A girlfriend."

She pursed her lips. "How long did that relationship last?"

"Until the day after I met her parents."

"Really?"

He nodded.

"What a bitch."

The word wasn't without heat, but she'd said it so casually, it took him a second to realize the content.

"She wasn't wrong," he said, not so much to defend the woman. More because it was strange to hear someone defend him. "I was quiet. Polite, but quiet. Not particularly engaging."

"None of that sounds like a reason to break up with someone," she said indignantly. "What did she expect, for you to magically turn into someone you're not? Hmph."

"Did you just huff?"

"No." She shook her head to emphasize her point. "The only thing I want from you tonight is to be yourself. Yes, that's quiet, and yes, sometimes that's grumpy, too. Well"—she scrunched up her nose—"not only sometimes. Anyway, you are those things, but you're also someone who has a passion for cooking and baking and talking about the intricacies of reality shows."

He frowned. "We agreed never to talk about that."

"No one is going to think poorly of you because you're passionate about something that connects you with your sister. But you're missing the point." She set her hands on her hips. "The point is that there are parts of you that are clouds, yes, but there are also parts that are rainbows. There's nothing wrong with either of those things, of course, but you're both, and there's nothing wrong with that, too. It's okay to let people see that.

"Now," she said, picking up the jacket from the kitchen chair, "let's get this over with."

CHAPTER 21

Her parents didn't do things half-heartedly, that was for sure.

The wooden patio had been decked out to full effect. Fairy lights had been wrapped around the banisters; the table had been set with the pastel blue plates her mother only kept for special occasions. Soft music played through speakers placed at the kitchen windows, and drinks were chilling in steel buckets.

Gemma was tempted to think they'd controlled the weather, too. The sky was turning purple and pink, the moon steadily rising. There was a light breeze that rustled through the oak tree that was her parents' pride and joy.

They'd placed a swing there for her when she was younger. Would use it to lure her out when she was too focused on her dolls or playing teacher to get fresh air. She loved that swing. It was like being in a storybook or a movie, especially when her mother or father would come out to play with her. When they'd push her and laugh with her and make her feel like the only person in the world.

Those memories felt tainted now. Feeling like the most special child in the world reminded her that her sister hadn't felt that. How could she have? Gaia had never been adopted. Had stayed in foster care. It didn't take inside knowledge to know the foster care system, with its instabilities, didn't make for the easiest of circumstances.

Gemma's stable childhood and her stable parents had been blessings that she had done nothing to deserve. There was a part of her that had always felt that, had always tried to make up for it. That part was stronger now. Fiercer. She saw it in every way she'd tried to make her parents proud. In every way she tried to make herself small, easy, so that they never regretted their decision. That desire had shaped her life, her personality, her relationships. She bent over backward for her friends, her family, for anyone, really, because she wanted them to like her. All because she was afraid that if they didn't like her, they'd send her back.

It didn't make sense in the context of any relationship outside of that with her parents, yet somehow, it felt like the right conclusion.

She had no idea how to manage that.

"Gemma," Jasmine said, her chiding tone the clue Gemma needed to know her distraction had been noticed—and wasn't appreciated. "Have you offered your guest something to drink?"

I thought he was your guest, not mine, she nearly replied, but bit her tongue. Literally bit her tongue. She winced and stopped.

"Er, yeah, sure. What do you want to drink, Levi?"

"What you're having is fine."

"Oh, Levi," Simon said, frowning. "We have many options."

Levi blinked. Gemma bit her lip, some of her tension subsiding as she realized what was happening.

"It's fine," Levi said again, slowly, as if that would make her father understand. "Gemma and I share a lot of the same tastes."

"You do?"

They absolutely didn't.

"I . . . er . . . yes. Yes, sir."

Simon looked at Gemma. Gemma shrugged, keeping her expression neutral. "Is it in the fridge, Dad?"

"Got it ready this morning," Simon said proudly.

Her heart softened. Ached. "Thanks. Levi, would you like to help me get it?"

Levi opened his mouth, but thought better of whatever he was about to say and nodded. He got up, and they walked into the kitchen.

Her parents had done some work on the place since Gemma had moved out. They hadn't asked for her advice, which smarted—why were parents like this? It was literally her job to design homes, but still, they knew better—but she couldn't fault the outcome.

They'd replaced the old dark gray counters with lighter gray marble and painted the cupboards white. It made the kitchen look bigger, more modern. They'd made similar changes to the rest of the house, and the house was looking much less traditional. A good thing, should they ever need to sell it. Might be something that happened sooner rather than later, too, considering they'd used Simon's retirement money to make the changes.

The same retirement money meant to sustain them for the rest of their lives.

Levi suddenly heaved out a sigh. "Am I about to drink blood?"

She gave a startled laugh. "No! Well, not straight up. I usually only use a drop or two." She laughed again at his expression, rolling her eyes. "Of course it's not *blood*, Levi. Don't you think you would have known by now if I was a vampire?"

He chose not to reply to that, which somehow amused her even more.

"It's nothing disgusting," she assured him after a bit. "Just a combination of grapefruit juice and lemon with a touch of honey and sparkling water. My parents think it's gross, hence the *are you sure*s. But they still make it every time I come."

It was those types of things that made her doubt talking to them about Gaia. They had good intentions. The best.

Unless it was all to make up for what they hadn't told her.

Oh, man, she needed to get a grip.

With a deep breath, she got the mixture and the sparkling water out of the fridge, and was about to ask Levi to hand her the glasses when she noticed he was staring at her.

"What?"

"You drink grapefruit and lemon with a touch of honey." He paused. "Probably not enough honey to make me regret agreeing to drink this, right?"

She shook her head apologetically. "I can add more, if you like, but I doubt it'll do much to change the taste. Grapefruit juice and lemon is a *combination*. Which brings me to my next question." She bit the corner of her lip. "Why? Why did you ask for what I was drinking?"

"I don't know," he said, rubbing the back of his neck. He was frazzled. How adorable. "I thought it was supportive? I don't know. I don't know what happened."

"You were trying to be supportive," she said, affirming his decision. "But I'm afraid you may come to regret it."

She added the sparkling water to the mixture, feeling all warm and fuzzy inside. It was a strange feeling to have, considering the other feelings inside her. But she had come to expect this sort of whiplash with Levi. And denied what it could mean at every turn.

She slid the glass toward him. He took it tentatively, drank a sip, gagged. "Poison!" he rasped. "It's poison!"

She did her best not to laugh. "Yes, get it out now." She patted his back. "Because when we go outside, you're going to have to pretend like you drink poison on a regular basis."

To his credit, he didn't wince once when he sipped from his drink. He didn't drink very often, though. And when he did, he took the tiniest sips. His glass was still mostly full when her mother announced it was time for dinner.

"Another?" Simon asked him, glancing at the drink with suspicion.

"Oh, no. No, thank you," Levi amended. "I'm a slow drinker."

"Okay," Simon replied, unconvinced. "Do you want another, honey?"

"Sure, Dad. Thanks."

Her parents went inside, Simon to get the drinks and Jasmine to get the food. Gemma stared after them. Usually, her mother would have asked her for help. She hadn't. Which meant that Jasmine wanted to speak to Simon alone. Gemma couldn't think about what.

"Are you always this snarky with them?" Levi asked.

Oh, yes. Maybe it was that.

"No," Gemma said with a sigh. "But I can't help it. It's out of my mouth before I can control it. I try to make up for it with whatever I say next, but I end up doing it again." Gemma continued before Levi could reply, because she didn't have the energy to be chided. "You're doing well. I think they like you."

"Good." There was a pause. "Why don't you tell them?"

"Tell them what?"

"The truth."

She sat back. "That's what I thought you meant, but I decided to check, because I'd like serious suggestions only. I can't tell them the *truth*," she hissed, leaning forward. "They don't even know I went looking for the truth."

"So tell them."

"No."

"Why not?"

"Why are you *pushing*? No, never mind," she said, "I know why you're pushing."

He exhaled harshly. Inhaled deeply. Like he needed strength to manage her. "I don't have any ulterior motives."

"Your entire existence is an ulterior motive!" She pushed up from the chair. "Why? Why did I bring you here when I know I haven't resolved my feelings about what you told me? I should have known you were going to do this."

"Gem—"

"Don't! Don't call me that."

He fell back, watching her as she paced. She should have sat down. Taken deep breaths like he did, so she could present a cool and calm exterior once her parents returned.

Of course, she did nothing of the sort.

She kept talking.

"Do you know why I don't want to tell them? Because it will disappoint them. It'll be like telling them that I wasn't happy with what they gave me, and I was! I *am*. I just . . . I also wanted to know about my family. I wanted . . . I wanted more."

She was breathing faster by the end of it, her heart racing, and her father emerging from the kitchen didn't help her body's reaction. She searched his face, worried he'd heard her, but he was smiling. Until he saw her face.

"Are you okay? What happened?"

Consciously relaxing her features, she smiled. "Nothing. Nothing."

"It's not nothing." Simon looked at Levi, the politeness he'd been treating Levi with disappearing. "Did you upset her?"

"No, Dad—"

"I did," Levi interrupted.

"Levi," she said.

"Gemma," he replied gently. "I can't keep this secret forever." To Simon, he said, "I'm sorry, sir, but I actually do not care for this drink at all. I've been pretending to like it since she and I started dating, and it's been a huge mistake."

He was making a choice. Actively deescalating. Allowing her an opportunity to go back to pretending everything was okay.

After what she'd said to him, after how she was treating him . . . she didn't deserve it. That made her angrier than anything else. Angry at herself. Because yes, Levi might have been pushing, but he was doing so respectfully. He wasn't forcing her to tell her parents. He was supporting her however he could. And what was she doing in return? Biting his head off.

The silence stretching wasn't uncomfortable, but it took

Gemma a second to understand it was stretching because she was lost in her thoughts, and she should be replying.

"I was telling him that our entire relationship has been built on a lie," she told her father. "How can I trust someone who lied to me about something this important?"

She'd started off lightheartedly, but as she heard the words, as they spilled out of her mouth, she realized that's what she wanted to tell her parents.

"Well, honey, surely it's not that serious," Simon said, relief clear in his voice.

"Not with him, no." She spoke quietly, surrendering to the turmoil. "But with you and Mom . . . yeah, I'd like to know how you could keep something as important as a sister from me."

Simon stared. There was no more relief, only tension. Only a tight expression, his white eyebrows drawn together, his lips forming an *oh*.

Gemma's heart fluttered. Throbbed. Ached. Doubt filled her—until she felt the warmth at her hand. She lowered her head, saw another hand. Levi's hand. In hers. The warmth seeped into her bloodstream, went straight to her heart. The fluttering, the throbbing, the aching . . . They eased. She threaded their fingers together and squeezed. Held on tight. And gave herself the grace not to question it.

"How did you find out?"

Her head lifted at that. At the confusion and the . . . the *betrayal* she heard in her father's voice. It was exactly what she'd feared, except she didn't feel the way she thought she would. At least, not to the extent she thought she would feel it. Yes, there was shame, and she hated that she'd heard disappointment, but anger and indignation topped the list. Hot and passionate, it burned out all her doubts, zeroed in on his words.

"I hired someone to look into it," she replied, proud of how in control she sounded, despite the heat. "I thought I'd find some family. Maybe a distant aunt or a long-lost cousin.

I didn't expect to find out that I had a biological twin sister."
She paused. "You and Mom never hid that I was adopted, and
I appreciated that. I tried to model my life after that kind of
honesty. I thought our relationship was stronger because of it.
But you hid a sister from me. Actively," she added, "if the way
you responded to my questions about siblings and the orphanage was anything to go by."

"Gemma."

Her mother was standing in the doorway of the kitchen with
a bowl of salad in her left hand and plate of bread in her right.
Based on her expression, she'd heard most, if not all, of what
Gemma had told her father. Jasmine had spoken in a warning
tone, but the emotion on her face was very far from that. In fact,
Jasmine looked . . . scared.

It deflated Gemma's anger, her indignation, and only left
space for the hurt. "Why?" she managed. "Why didn't you tell
me?"

Simon went over to Jasmine, took the food from her, and
went into the kitchen. When he came back, he stopped next to
his wife, putting his arm around her.

They were forming a united front, as they had whenever
they wanted Gemma to do something she didn't want to do.
Or when they were disciplining her. She didn't begrudge them
needing each other's support, but it felt like they were preparing to lie to her.

Maybe they thought they would convince her to drop the
topic. Maybe they wanted to discipline her into accepting whatever they were going to say.

It wasn't going to work this time.

"The truth, please," she said softly. "We can fix this if we're
honest with one another."

Her parents exchanged a look.

"We couldn't afford her," Jasmine said, opening her hands.
"'The adoption was expensive. We used all our savings. When

they told us . . . when they told us you had a sister, we just . . . we couldn't afford to take her, as well, without going into debt we might not have recovered from."

Had something so simple really kept her and her sister apart?

No, she knew money wasn't a simple thing. Not for those who lived paycheck to paycheck, as her parents had for a long time. They'd been young then, still at the beginning of their careers. A new wave of guilt hit her—that she'd been the reason they'd struggled for such a long time—but she didn't allow it to knock her over. They'd survived, and they had been happy. Her parents lived comfortably. Maybe that would change if they weren't responsible with their money, but that wouldn't be because of her.

It didn't change her resentment. Even made her ask why they'd taken her if they couldn't afford her sister.

"You were ours," Simon answered. "You were our baby. We knew it the minute we saw you and you smiled."

A smile. That's what had drawn her parents to her. She felt the weight of it on her chest, her shoulders, her limbs. It was significant, that answer. But she couldn't face it now.

"Why keep her from me?" she asked. "Why not tell me?"

"How could we, honey?" Jasmine replied, desperately. "Look at how you're reacting now. Do you think it would have been easier when you were younger?"

"So instead you told me not to worry about my biological family. You said you told me all I needed to know." She waited a beat. "You lied. My twin sister was someone I needed to know about. I deserved to know about her."

They didn't answer, and Gemma couldn't blame them. There was nothing they could say that would make things better. They knew that. Of course they knew that—they were her parents.

And that's what made all this hurt as bad as it did.

"Levi, I think we need to go." She gathered her things. "Thank you, Mom and Dad. I'm sorry we didn't get to talk more, but apparently, we've never really talked about what's important, anyway."

"Gemma," Jasmine said when they tried to pass. "Don't be like this."

"It won't be like this forever," she assured them, because something inside her demanded that she did. "But it has to be like this now."

"We love you."

"I know. I . . . I love you, too."

She walked away before they could see her anger, her resentment that she had to say it back when all she felt was . . . too much.

But love was somewhere at the bottom.

CHAPTER 22

"Do you want me to drive?" Levi asked when they got to the car.

"No." She stopped at the driver's seat and looked at him. "I've never asked you whether you could drive."

"I can drive," he confirmed. "Why would I offer if I couldn't?"

"Some kind of compulsion? Men have done that to me before."

Men? What men?

Ah, jealousy. It was irrational and had the worst timing. Fortunately, Levi was able to control the urge to ask the question. Instead, he got into the car and let her be annoyed with him.

He was realizing more and more that he'd rather be the target of Gemma's frustrations than having her feel hurt, impractical as it was. He had experience with the feeling, since that's how he felt with Haley, too. It was confusing to think of his sister and Gemma in the same way. Confusing to feel anything remotely related. He told himself it was because he cared about them both, which was true. But with Gemma . . . well, *care* didn't feel like the right word for it.

What the hell did he do about that? What did he *want* to do about it? He didn't know. His life had never been as messy as it was now. Maybe that was what happened when someone died. They got embroiled in so much drama that they forgot about the drama of the life they left behind.

That wasn't possible with him, of course. His life drama and death drama were entwined. He knew he didn't have a choice, but this situation gave the illusion of choice. Like he had to choose between Haley and Gemma. But it was just that: an illusion. It was Haley, or nothing.

So his feelings about Gemma didn't matter.

Except they did.

"Well, *that* didn't go as planned, did it?" a voice said from the back seat.

Levi didn't have to turn to know who it came from, but he forgot that Gemma didn't have the benefit of his knowledge. She screamed, whirled around, tried to get out of the car. Fortunately, they were at a red light, her handbrake was up, and the only thing that happened was that the car stalled. When her car door wouldn't open—she'd apparently forgotten she'd locked it—she leaned over to the cubbyhole and took out a gun.

She pointed it at Jude. "You better leave this car right now."

Jude looked unperturbed. "Gemma, you and I both know that gun is a toy."

Gemma's eyes widened, and her panic faded. "I'm sorry. I'm sorry. I don't know why I did that. I guess I'm used to ghosts only appearing when I'm alone? And especially not when I'm with another ghost. Also, my mind isn't exactly in the 'thinking logically' space right now."

"It happens," Jude said agreeably.

There was silence, pierced only when someone honked. Gemma started to roll down her window, but Levi grabbed her hand. "Don't."

"It's impolite to honk at someone!"

"It's illegal to point a gun at someone."

She looked at the gun. "Oh."

"Why do you have a toy gun in your car?" he asked.

Another honk sounded. Levi grabbed the offending item before she could do something stupid with it, and she started the car again. But not before she gave the guy the middle finger as he passed her.

Levi bit back his laugh. Tried desperately not to even show his amusement when Gemma looked at him with her eyes narrowed. *I dare you to say something,* they said.

He cleared his throat, "Gemma, this is my Guardian Ghost, Jude."

Gemma glanced at Jude through the rearview mirror. "What does that mean, exactly?"

"Oh, you know. This and that." Jude stared at his nails.

Gemma took a turn before looking at Jude in the mirror again. "So do *you* know why I have a ghost who's trying to help me after twelve years?"

"Yes," Jude said, but didn't elaborate.

Gemma's brow knitted. "And you must also know why I can see ghosts?"

"Yes."

"Am I the only one with this ability?"

"Hmm."

"Are there other abilities in the world?"

Jude shrugged.

"What about my sister?" Gemma asked. "You all knew about her. Why didn't you tell me earlier?"

"Earlier wasn't the right time."

She opened her mouth, but seemed to think better of it.

They drove in silence after that. It bothered Levi that she wasn't peppering Jude with more questions. Perhaps she'd gotten tired of the non-answers, but normally, that wouldn't have stopped her.

He looked at her, really looked at her. There was fatigue in the lines around her eyes, in the tightening around her mouth.

She wasn't wearing her rings, not even the one with the stone in it, and though they'd never spoken about it, he knew how much that ring meant to her. It was her connection to her family. To her mother, yes, but now, to her sister, as well. The fact that she wasn't wearing it . . .

How had he only noticed that she was off *now*? She must not have been sleeping well. Must have been struggling to process everything that happened with Gaia. Or maybe she didn't want to wear her rings to her parents' house, because she didn't want the reminder of her biological family tonight. Either way, she obviously needed support. Yet all he'd noticed this week was her teasing.

The rest of the drive felt painfully silent. Not only in the car, but in his head. It was like there was a layer of ice separating him from his thoughts. Had it always been there? If so, why was he only noticing it now?

Suddenly, he was remembering how often people accused him of having no emotion. Of being cold. It had always bothered him, because it wasn't true. But it had never bothered him enough to examine why people thought so. Now that he couldn't access his own thoughts—and perhaps even his own emotions—they might have had a point. And, like everything else he seemed to be going through these last weeks, he had no answer for it.

Did things like this have an answer? How did he find out whether he was a normal human being or a robot?

"You're clearly of the enigmatic ghost variety," Gemma said suddenly, directing the statement to Jude.

Jude smiled. "Not entirely."

"He's lying," Levi said, grateful for a reprieve from the confusing thoughts. "He does stuff like this to me all the time."

"Do all ghosts have guardians?" Gemma asked. "It's been twelve years, and this is the first time I've heard of it. And if all ghosts have guardians, what's my purpose here? Why do I have to help them? I'm like a low-level consultant, but they have managers? Shouldn't *you* be supporting them?"

"Not all ghosts, no," Jude answered, and for some reason, this time he elaborated. "Ghosts who have a purpose beyond simply resolving their human lives get them. You have encountered ghosts like this in the past, but your part in their purpose was small in the grand scheme of things. Now, you're part of a ghost's purpose, so you get to see a different side to it."

She took in the information without comment. Levi stared at her, as if mentally trying to persuade her to ask more questions. This was the first time he was hearing about how the universe—or whatever They called it—worked, and he wanted to know more.

But Gemma was in a different mood today. The one time he *wanted* her to keep asking questions. He'd have to take matters into his own hands.

"So all human beings become ghosts when they die?" he asked Jude.

"Only those who have obstacles to moving on."

"Do I have an obstacle?"

"Do you?" Jude asked sweetly.

Gemma snorted. Levi shot her a look. "Why's that funny?"

"You're only asking him this *now*? Didn't you read the terms and conditions before you signed up for this?"

"There were no terms and conditions. There was a yes or a no."

"Why did you say yes?"

He glanced at Jude, but not long enough to see more than a quirked eyebrow. Obviously, Jude knew Levi had told Gemma the truth. And since Gemma knew the truth, it took him a moment to figure out what she was really asking. Had the answer changed since he'd taken on the mission?

When They'd first offered it to him, he'd said yes for Haley. He'd sacrificed his life for her; why not do it in death, too? It had taken doing it in death to realize that living for her hadn't been enough for him. It was a terrible thing to admit, especially when she hadn't asked him to sacrifice anything for her. Nor had his father, for that matter. At least not in so many words.

But his father had *expected* it from him. Levi had been so eager to meet those expectations that he'd done it without question. It was too late now to have regrets.

So again, he asked himself—had his answer changed?

"It was the right thing to do," he finally answered. She had already stopped in front of her house, but he kept talking. "For Haley and for you."

"You didn't think of me."

"Of course I did. You forget They made sure I knew what your situation was when I said yes."

Gemma angled against her door, her eyes never leaving him. "Your instinct to help is amazing."

He expected that to be sarcasm, but as he replayed the words in his head, he found no trace of it. "You make me sound altruistic. I'm not."

"Aren't you?" she asked quietly. Pointedly. "You put your life on pause—or lived it in slow motion, at the very least—because your sister needed you. You agreed to help me, a random person, not only for Haley's sake, but for my own. You stepped in for Chet and Lacey's wedding, and Mr. Redding next door told me you go over there sometimes to help him out. Said you bring him baked goods, too, if he's lucky. Mrs. Helsing down the street told me you saw her cleaning out her gutters the other day and did it for her. Wouldn't take money or, to her utter shock, her famous lasagna in thanks. So, please, tell me again how you don't help *the stupid people* in *the stupid world*."

"Was that supposed to be an imitation of me?" Levi asked, aghast.

"It was almost as if you said the words yourself."

Jude chuckled. Levi ignored him.

"Your neighbors are a bunch of gossips," he said. "Maybe I

was doing all that as a front, anyway. To balance the scales or something."

"Balance what scales?" she asked with a frown. "You lived a good life from what you've told me."

"I did nothing remarkable in my life."

"Raising your sister wasn't remarkable?"

He had no answer to that, which she seemed to take as encouragement.

"I've known you for over a month now, Levi. I know the kind of person you are."

"Why don't you believe me when I say I never wanted to hurt you, then?"

"By not telling me the truth?" she asked, her voice sharp, but her body relaxed. She had sunk into the door almost, and didn't look like a person gearing for a fight. "Because it hurt my feelings, Levi. I trusted you. I thought you were in my corner. That for once, someone didn't need anything from me to be my friend or to care about me."

She sure as hell didn't look like a person ready to stop every single one of his defenses in their tracks.

"I don't need anything from you," he said gruffly. "And I care about you because somehow, you got me to like you."

"Don't sound so disgusted."

"It's not at you."

"All disgust is aimed at me in this situation."

"See?" he said. "This is exactly what I'm talking about. I would hate this on anyone else. On you, I tolerate it."

She laughed. "That's what I strive for: tolerance."

He rolled his eyes, but smiled. Eventually, he said, "I can't say I wouldn't do it again if I was given the chance. I couldn't burden you with my existence. Not only because it put my existence on the line, but because it wouldn't have been fair to you. You're not responsible for my life. Still aren't."

"So why did you tell me? The truth this time," she said when he opened his mouth.

He sighed. "Because I *do* care about you. I think you care about me, too. As my friend"—he almost didn't say that word, but it felt like the best one to use under the circumstances—"I guess I trusted you enough to burden you."

"That's a strange way to put it, isn't it?" she asked slowly. "But I guess that's true. I haven't told my friends the truth about my parents, and I didn't tell my parents the truth about Gaia, for that reason. I didn't trust them enough to burden them with my problems."

"You trusted me," he pointed out, hopeful, and confused by it.

"Yeah, I did. Not that I had a choice, but I did." She took a deep breath. "Feel free to impart your wisdom at any time, Guardian Ghost." Gemma turned to the back seat, but Jude shrugged.

"I don't have anything to add to this particular discussion."

"Nothing?" Levi asked. "You usually have so much to say."

Jude smiled sweetly. "Not today."

Levi sighed. Sighed again when Gemma nodded sagely. They were all silent for a bit. It gave Levi the chance to feel the shift in their relationship. It felt almost tangible to him, that shift. There were knots easing in his body, tension releasing. He hadn't been aware of any of it until now, but it didn't surprise him. He hadn't allowed himself to admit how much the distance between him and Gemma was getting to him. If he allowed himself to admit it, he'd be forced to answer why, and he knew why.

He didn't want to think about why.

"I can't believe you don't think raising your sister is a re-markable thing," she announced, throwing her hands up.

He blinked. "Why does it matter?"

"It speaks directly to how you see yourself, and that matters. *You* matter. How many times do I have to say that to you?"

"Probably at least one more time," Jude offered. "He's got a hard head."

"Don't I know it," Gemma agreed. "You matter, Levi. You know that, right?"

He rolled his eyes at the silliness of it. Of the two of them ganging up on him. What he didn't do was say it. Logically, he knew that he mattered. He had to, or he wouldn't have survived. Feeding himself mattered, taking care of his mind and his body mattered. He'd done that, hadn't he? So, of course he understood that he mattered.

Except even in that, he hadn't done a good job. He fed himself whatever Haley or his dad wanted, because it was easier to eat whatever they were having. When he planned dinners, he never even considered what he'd like to eat. Taking care of his mind? Could he really say he'd done that because sometimes he did some deep breathing and thought about things that bothered him for longer than a second? And his body . . . well, that he'd spent much more time on. But in the gym, not hikes or marathons or anything that required more than the set time he'd allowed himself for the task.

"Tell me you matter, Levi," Gemma urged softly.

"I . . . I matter. I do," he said more firmly. "Now you do it."

"No, no, no. You don't get to turn this on me. Say it again, and this time, believe it."

"I believe it."

"You're a terrible liar."

"And you're deflecting," he shot back. "You know you need to believe it, too."

"Fine," she said after a moment. "I matter. My feelings matter."

There was a beat of silence, and he all but heard her brain working. The fact that she was saying the words, the emotion behind them as she tried to believe the sentiment . . .

"I matter," he whispered. "I might not believe it fully right now, but I . . . I want to."

She studied him. Nodded. "That's better."

"It is," Jude said cheerfully. "And now that that's sorted, I can finally tell you why I'm here."

Levi braced.

"I've found you somewhere to stay."

CHAPTER 23

She and Levi were not talking about Jude's offer.

To be fair, they weren't talking at all.

When she got inside her house, she'd gone right to her bedroom, taken off the dress he had said nothing about—not that she had worn it for him or anything—and cleaned her face. She popped her hair into a messy bun at the top of her head, put on a stretched sweatshirt from her university days and some cotton shorts. She kept her bra on—she didn't need him to think she was seducing him—and for good measure, she had on her only pair of holey panties.

As a rule, Gemma didn't wear holey panties. Her mother had drilled it into her head that Gemma's underwear should always be in a state that wouldn't embarrass her in an emergency. That *her* referred to both Gemma and Jasmine. Her mother liked to think of herself as an all-knowing, all-seeing presence, even in hypothetical situations.

Tonight, though, Gemma needed them. She was tired, she was vulnerable, and this man in her home was her weakness. There was no doubt about it. She had been clinging to his lie, using it as a shield against her feelings for him. She couldn't do it anymore. Not only because she understood his position, even if she didn't like it, but because they were past it. She was already carrying too much baggage, holding on to too much hurt, and this . . . she didn't want to hold on to this.

Besides, there was a bigger shield she could use to protect herself here: the fact that he was a ghost. He would disappear and he'd be gone, literally ghosting her. So she couldn't let him climb any further into her heart, especially with his *I'm so busy taking care of other people, I don't know that I matter, too* vibe.

A fine lecture from her when she'd just started realizing she was doing the same thing. But she'd said the words in the car, hadn't she? Besides, the manifestations of it in her and Levi's lives were different. He took care of the people around him, and she wanted to make them happy.

She didn't want them to leave.

But that wasn't important. What was important was that the necessary protections needed to be taken, considering the circumstances. The circumstances being that her vagina wasn't convinced about the whole *he's a ghost* situation.

As she certainly wouldn't be allowing anyone to see her in holey panties, let alone a man who'd already seen her naked, she would be keeping on her pants. And if that didn't work—it would absolutely work, but if it didn't—she hadn't shaved, either.

You know Levi wouldn't give a single damn about that.

She blew air out her mouth.

"What?" he asked. He'd come to sit beside her on the couch. She'd tried not to shift when he first sat down, but now that she was thinking about how he wouldn't care about what her vagina looked like as long as he had access to it, she had to.

"Nothing."

He gave her a look. "I find that hard to believe."

"Why?"

"You've had a traumatic night."

"Oh." Guess she didn't need holey panties to cool her down,

only the reminder that she had blown her relationship with her parents to smithereens. "What do you want me to say about it?"

He stared. "Anything?"

"I don't have anything to say."

"Gemma."

"I'm serious." And she was. "My parents made a decision about my life a long time ago. They thought they'd be able to keep the truth from me because . . ."

"Because?" he prompted, when she didn't go on.

"Because they knew I wouldn't push them. I never did. I was too busy being grateful for the life they gave me."

He was quiet for a few seconds. "Did they make you feel that way?"

"Like I should be grateful?" she asked. At his nod, she sighed. "Yes. No. I don't know. I think . . . I think my mother would have expected perfection from a biological daughter, too. She didn't consider what such high expectations could do to an adopted child. And I can't blame her—it worked! I'm successful, well-behaved. Mostly, anyway. I spent twenty-nine years being content with the information they gave me. Being grateful that they'd taken a chance on me. Then I find out the truth."

"So you decided to pay them back."

He had the gall to nod, as if that were the most logical solution. As if she would have done something like that.

"I didn't 'pay them back.' What are you talking about?"

"You didn't tell them you knew the truth for months."

"I didn't know how to approach it."

"Maybe they didn't, either."

She opened her mouth. Rolled her eyes. "Fine. Fair enough. But if we're going to talk about revenge, let's not pretend what you're doing right now isn't to pay me back for telling you you matter."

"I'm not that—"

He stopped, as if realizing that whatever adjective he was

about to use would describe her, too, based on his accusations. She smirked and scooted back so that her legs were on the couch. They sat that way for a while. Her mind went over the night. It had been traumatic, yes, but it had also been . . . productive. For once, she didn't feel overwhelmed by the secret she was keeping. It wasn't a secret anymore. Her parents knew. Gaia knew. Gemma had no idea what came next, with any of her family members, but at least there was that.

"Do you remember how you told me you felt bad your mother didn't visit Haley?" she asked him. "That Haley didn't deserve an absentee mother?" He nodded. "That's how I feel about Gaia. She didn't deserve to be the one who stayed in foster care. She deserved . . . she deserved what I got. She deserved *me*." She paused. "We could have gone through it together, like you and Haley did. All because of a *smile*. Because I smiled at my parents and they thought, oh, look, this must be our one." She swallowed. "I'm grateful. I am. But . . ."

Emotion had crept into her voice, into her heart, and she didn't have energy for that. "Your turn."

His lashes fluttered. "What? No, we're not done talking about you."

"I am. Which is a pretty slick move, mister. Getting me to admit my shit when I didn't want to."

"There were no slick moves. No moves whatsoever."

"Hmm."

"I don't have shit," he said, shifting focus.

"You don't think what happened in the car is shit?" She didn't wait for him to answer. "Levi, you can't even admit that you're not the first priority in your life. Or death," she added. "You're doing this for Haley. Now, you've added me to that, too. I'm not saying you should be somewhere in heaven, sipping a martini, but you should be . . . I don't know. At peace."

"What does peace look like?" he asked after a moment. "What did it look like for that ghost you met at the wedding?"

She sighed. "I guess she's happy that her boyfriend will know she made the ultimate sacrifice for him." She thought back to how she'd gone to the boyfriend's house, slipped the letter under the door, and hightailed out of there. She did not want the wife to know she was involved in any way. Seemed safer. Later that night, Bridal Gown Ghost had come to thank her.

"I was there when he read the letter!" she'd enthused. "He seemed happy."

"Happy?" Gemma had asked doubtfully. "How do you know?"

"He had this little smile on his face."

He's a psychopath. Clearly, she'd dodged a bullet with both the husband and wife. "I'm glad. I hope you can move on."

She shook her hips in a way that told Gemma she'd have no trouble moving on, and disappeared.

"I don't want Haley to think that," Levi said softly, bringing her back to the present. "I don't want her to believe I made the 'ultimate sacrifice.' I didn't step in front of a bullet for her; I ate a slice of cheesecake that she made and had an allergic reaction. It was an accident. I want her to see it was an accident and not blame herself."

"Which is why you can't be at peace. If you think she thinks it's her fault, you'll never rest."

He didn't respond, but Gemma knew by now that was because he didn't feel one was necessary. He agreed with her. Her heart broke for him, but there was nothing else she could do. Except, of course, let him help her through her family crisis.

"Don't."

She turned to him. "Don't what?"

"You're thinking about how you can help me. Don't."

"I was not—" She frowned. "How did you know?"

"I've spent every day of six weeks with you. I know." He stood. "Do you want some tea?"

He knew that about her, too.

She nodded absently, too taken aback by his observation to insist that she make it. She snuggled into the couch, hugging a pillow, watching him as she thought about what he'd said. About how he'd seen through her and how he didn't want her to help. Genuinely didn't want her help, even though he might cease to exist if she didn't. She had been right all along: He didn't expect anything from her.

She gave up thinking and only watched.

He moved easily, smoothly in the kitchen. He was clearly comfortable, and after tasting his cooking and baking, she knew why. It was yet another thing that made him stand out. In her memories of the other men she'd watched—it was somewhat of a hobby of hers when she had dates over; she blamed it on the cooking shows she loved—they almost always looked like they were trying too hard. That effort told her that they weren't used to working in the kitchen but were trying to impress her. Which was fine and sweet, but it struck differently when it was from someone who wasn't trying so hard.

Levi poured that hot water into that mug like a champ; stirred in honey and left it black, because that's how she liked it. Something unwelcome was happening in the region of her underwear, and she focused on it, determined to stop it. Now was not the time to get horny. Watching a man make her tea was not sexy. Making tea was not an inherently sexy activity.

But when Levi did it . . .

She gave up with a sigh, and told her body to do whatever it wanted. Closed her eyes, surrendering to the moment. Somehow, her eyes remained closed, even when she told them to open. Even when she heard the faint click of mugs meeting the glass of her coasters on the coffee table. She wanted to thank him, but she was suddenly feeling weighed down.

Was that the light pressure of a blanket? It was! Levi had put a blanket over her. She needed to say thanks. She needed to open her eyes and her mouth and say—

Another pressure, firmer this time and on her forehead, stopped her thoughts.

He'd kissed her. He'd kissed her on the head.

Tenderly! Affectionately! Romantically!

Who knew this was going to happen when she'd first seen Mr. Harris in her bedroom? Not her. Hell, she hadn't even expected her second ghost, Marley. Mr. Harris had been so sweet and gentle that Gemma had thought the purpose Mr. Harris had outlined—that she help ghosts where she could—would be manageable. It had felt so right, too. Like she'd been chosen out of everyone in the world because she could do it, because she was special, and that had made her feel . . . a lot like her parents had made her feel by adopting her.

But she'd had doubts about those feelings, too, when Marley had handed her a note to pass on to a boyfriend that had said,

I can't believe you cheated on me, you lying sack of shit.
You'll never have a day of peace now that I'm a ghost.

Her first lesson from her experience with Marley was to never read the notes. Because she had, she hadn't wanted to pass the message on to Marley's boyfriend. It was cruel. But Marley had insisted it was necessary for her to move on to the next phase of her existence. She hadn't seemed worried about her vengeful spirit. Gemma had asked.

"Aren't you afraid of what might happen if you do this?"

"I'm already dead," Marley had replied. "What's the worst that could happen?"

Gemma grimaced and pointed down.

Marley laughed. "You have no idea what you're talking about."

She didn't. Of course she didn't. She was just a girl who saw ghosts and had to deal with the fact that she saw ghosts. She didn't know anything about the afterlife. Had never wanted to ask. It had seemed best to leave it unknown, so that she could continue her life as normally as possible. The most she'd learned had been from Levi.

She gave up on trying to get Marley to change her mind, but had still refused to pass along her note. And Marley spent every day making Gemma regret that decision.

She followed Gemma around, disappearing only when Gemma went to bed at night. She narrated everything in Gemma's life, including pointing out things that human beings—living ones, anyway—didn't say. While Gemma could live with the general annoyance of it, she couldn't live with being questioned about everything she did. Sabotaged, really. Marley had made Gemma doubt *every* decision. From what she wanted to wear that day to what she wanted to get her parents for their anniversary. Gemma didn't know how Marley knew which buttons to push, but she did.

Gemma did not like it. So she'd put the note in Marley's boyfriend's postbox and hoped it would be enough for Marley to move on.

It had been. She hadn't even minded when Marley had said, "See ya, bitch," as a goodbye.

After that, Gemma had expected any kind of ghost to show up in her life. She'd tried to help all of them, too. She'd had a range of experiences with a range of people.

And still, she hadn't expected Levi.

Not that he'd come into her life, not that he'd want to help her, not that she would be attracted to him.

Not that you'd fall in love with him.

It was her final thought as she drifted off.

CHAPTER 24

Watching someone sleep was stalker behavior. That's what Haley had told him when they'd watched that vampire movie together. He knew this, was neither a stalker nor vampire, yet here he was, watching Gemma sleep.

He hadn't been able to leave her. After the day she had, he needed to make sure she was okay. It was unlikely that something would happen to her in her sleep, but Gemma had a knack for getting herself into situations that would hurt her. If he didn't stay and make sure she was okay, it might happen to her again.

It was why he couldn't move out.

Even he could admit there were flaws in his reasoning. That there was emotion in it, too, deeper and more complex than protecting her. He didn't have the energy to analyze the layers of it. Didn't want to, either. What he wanted to do was keep staring at Gemma. Memorize her like this: messy hair, her body covered in baggy clothes. Vulnerable. Open. Was it any wonder he was drawn to her in a way he hadn't ever been to anyone else?

What could have happened if they'd met in his time, when he was alive? Would she have made him see the things he hadn't seen until now? Probably not. Because if they had met in his time, when he was alive, he would have ignored her. Turned away from her or made up some kind of excuse as to why they couldn't be together. She would have distracted him, made him question what and whom he was living for. She would have made him feel selfish, and he couldn't allow that.

Because he hadn't mattered then. He hadn't considered his own feelings. Now, when he was dead and in a position where he had nothing else to do but think, he could finally see it. And he could do nothing about it.

Enough of that, he told himself as he stood. He'd do some exercise in Gemma's garage or go for a run or do whatever he needed to to stop thinking. He glanced at Gemma.

She's sleeping. She'll be fine.

Just as he convinced himself that was true, Gemma's eyes fluttered open.

"Levi?" she asked, her voice soft, tentative. A little husky and a lot sexy.

Yeah, he definitely needed to go.

"I'm going to bed."

"I fell asleep! I'm sorry." She rubbed her eyes. "You don't have to go to bed. Let's drink our tea."

"You're tired. You were sleeping. You'll close your eyes as soon as I'm gone and fall back asleep."

She rested her weight on her elbows, dropping her chin to her chest. Her hair fell forward, the band popping off, causing her hair to tumble over her shoulders. It looked like a hair commercial, that thick, brown hair falling in slow motion.

Wait—slow motion?

"No, no." Now she sat up fully, ignoring her hair. Why was she ignoring her hair? Why wasn't she tying it back up? "Let's have our tea."

She reached for it on the table, but stopped. "What?" she said. "Why are you looking at me like that? I only slept for like"—she looked at the time—"fifteen minutes."

He shoved his hands into his pockets. Tried to figure how to respond. It had been a long night, full of revelations they both needed to process. That was all this was. This . . . urge to do something stupid like kiss her. He was looking for a way to resolve the turmoil.

No, what he was looking for was a way to *add* to the turmoil. That's what kissing her would do. She had made him want a life different to what he'd had with Haley and his father, a life where kissing her—making love with her—wouldn't be taboo.

"I'm going for a run," he said, his voice hard.

"What?" she asked. "It's after midnight."

"I don't have to explain myself to you."

"I know that." She fell silent for a second. "What happened? You weren't upset when I fell asleep. Oh no!" Her eyes widened. "Did I say something while I was sleeping? Did I say something to upset you?"

"You didn't say something to upset me. *You* upset me. The fact that you're sitting there asking me if you said something to upset me upsets me."

She gave him a bewildered look. He didn't blame her, but he couldn't stop talking, either. Was this the type of person he'd be when he thought he mattered? A *talker*? An unreasonable talker?

Because he was being unreasonable. *He* had made the choices that brought him to her. Their shared emotional turmoil this evening had been because of him. He had pushed her into seeing her parents, and that had led to the conversation in the car, which had led to him figuring out that the life he'd had before wasn't the life he wanted.

Despite that—despite knowing all of that—he *was* blaming her. Because she was beautiful and full of sunshine and happiness and *life*. And he . . . he was dead. He'd been dead long before he had actually died.

What was the point of living if he wasn't going to live for himself?

The guilt hit him so hard, he was surprised he didn't stagger backwards. He didn't even notice that his fingers were in a fist. Not until a soft hand curled around that fist.

He looked down. Her eyes were big and brown, full of concern he didn't deserve. Her lips were pink, a little glossed from what he could only assume was lip balm, and need heated his chest. Wrapped around his heart.

He had already known he'd fallen for her. Had known it long before this evening. But now? Now he thought it might be something more serious than simply falling. Something more dangerous. Why else would he have this desire to taste her again? So he could keep trying to recreate it in some sweet dish? Would he ever tell her that was why he baked so much? To remember, even if it was for a brief moment, what it felt like when they'd done things that made him feel more alive dead than he ever had living.

He stepped away from her. It took all of his strength to do it, to not give in to the impulse to lower his head and open his mouth and taste.

And she undid all of that by stepping forward and putting her hand on his chest. Over his heart.

"This isn't fair," he told her shakily.

"I don't know what you're talking about, but I don't care." She waited a beat. "Kiss me."

Heaven help him—he did.

She tasted exactly as sweet as he remembered. Light. As if there were clouds of cotton candy he was sinking into headfirst. It should have alarmed him. If he was going to suffocate, on principle, it shouldn't be in *cotton candy*. Except now that he was experiencing it, suffocating in the overwhelming sweetness and lightness that was Gemma didn't seem like such a bad idea.

He had never experienced anything like this before. Had

never kissed someone he really wanted to kiss. Sure, there had been plenty of kisses before Gemma. From his first kiss on the rugby field of his high school, to the back of cars, the front of houses. Couches. Beds. And he had thought he wanted to kiss them.

Clearly, he had been naïve. Clearly, he hadn't known what it was like when his heart was involved. Suddenly, he didn't think it was such a bad thing to have his heart involved. Suddenly, he was thinking that maybe having his heart involved was the key to the best kisses of his life.

He tried to memorize the way her lips moved against his. The way she softened and surrendered, opening up to him, dipping her tongue into his mouth. He tried to remember the lick of fire that started when their tongues met. That traveled down, down until it settled between his legs. Until he had to pick her up, settle himself there, against her heat.

He lowered them both to the couch and stopped trying to memorize things. Memories were for later; now was for feeling.

For tasting.

For enjoying.

He ran his hands over the thick, plush thighs he'd admired whenever she wore . . . well, whenever she wore clothes. He thought of that day when she had been in that dress, when he'd seen her thighs jiggle, when he'd imagined them around his hips. He thought about the way they looked in jeans. If he hadn't already been out of his mind with desire, this would have given him an express ticket right to the door.

What a gift that he could squeeze her thighs, sink his fingers into their cushioning, use them to bring her closer to him. When he was done—for now, because heaven knew he'd never be done forever—he rested his hands at her butt. Then got antsy and ran his hands up her back, moaning in protest when the thick hoodie she wore prevented him from touching her skin.

"Off," he mumbled into her mouth. When she didn't respond, he pulled back.

Her eyes opened, the expression in them a tangle of desire, confusion, indignation. "Why are you stopping?" she demanded.

"I said *off.*"

"What?"

"Your clothes. Take them off."

"Oh," she said with a saucy smile. "Okay."

She shimmied off his lap, pulled her hoodie over her head. She was wearing a gray strap top underneath. It gave him a view of her shoulders, golden brown and smooth. Made him think about how he wanted to lick the line of it. Shocking, he thought, since he'd never wanted to do that to, or with, anyone else before. And yet, honestly, he wasn't all that shocked.

She hooked her thumbs into her shorts, gave him another saucy smile, rocked her hips in a way he hoped she would imitate on his lap. He held his breath, waited not-so-patiently for her to take them off, but she stopped. Her eyes widened, and her face went blank.

"I'm sorry. I . . . I . . . I thought I could do this, but I can't."

"Oh," he said. "Okay. Yeah, of course. Fine."

"Not because I don't want to," she added quickly. "I think you know I want to. I'm saying no because . . . of something else that I thought would be a good idea, and now I'm thinking it wasn't? Or maybe it was." She gave him a pleading look. "I know that sounds . . . confusing."

She walked toward him, tentatively gesturing to his lap. He nodded—why, he couldn't say—and she sat down primly, her legs to one side, as if she hadn't been straddling him minutes earlier.

"This isn't a good idea," she said softly. "We both knew it after the first time." She took a breath. "The reality is . . ."

"It won't work," he finished when she didn't. "Doesn't matter how much we hope it will." He placed his hand on the small of her back, rubbed it to comfort her. Or himself. "We shouldn't complicate things anymore."

She sighed. "Okay."

"We'll focus on what we need to do."

"Yes," she agreed again.

There was a long silence. When emotion, longing, began to fill it, he said, "Let's go to bed."

"We said—"

"I didn't mean together."

"I know." She sighed again. "Wouldn't it be nice, though?"

He half-snorted. Patted her butt to get her to stand and stood, too. He was about to leave when he remembered. "Are you going to tell me what that thing is? That made you stop," he clarified.

"Oh," she replied. "No."

"Why not?"

To his surprise and delight, her cheeks began to redden. "It's not relevant to the discussion."

He lifted his brow at that. Her blush deepened.

"Okay, now you *have* to tell me."

"I'm entitled to my secrets."

"Gemma." He made it sound like a plea. And for good measure, he added, "Please."

She looked to the sky. "I'm wearing my chastity panties."

"Your what?"

"My chastity panties. They're meant to keep me from—" She gestured between the two of them.

"What . . . um . . ." He swallowed his amusement, or she'd never tell him a thing again. "What makes them chaste?"

"They're not chaste," she said stiffly. "They're meant to keep me from sleeping with you."

"Ah." He waited a moment. "So, you wanted to sleep with me. And you knew that from the moment you put on your panties."

"Duh." She rolled her eyes. "Not only from then, either.

Now," she said, turning around, "I'm going to bed. Alone. And annoyed, now, too."

"Welcome to my world," he called out after her. She turned around, stuck out her tongue, and walked away.

And he realized that since he'd been living with Gemma, he hadn't been going to bed annoyed at all.

CHAPTER 25

They still weren't talking about Jude's offer.

Instead, they continued to live together. Levi became the sexiest housekeeper in the world, and when Gemma came home from work, he'd have a meal prepped for her, often paired with the most delicious dessert.

It was an unspoken agreement at first: They'd dealt with a lot of shit in a relatively short time, and they needed each other's support. There was no rush on Levi moving out, so they could delay dealing with it. She didn't know when it had turned into something else. When they'd decided not to talk about it, because living together suited them fine.

Even with the occasional make-out session that always stopped before it could become more.

She didn't need anyone telling her it was a bad idea. She said it to herself often enough. Hell, they both said it to each other every time it happened. But that didn't stop her from straddling Levi every time he was on the couch. Nor did it keep him from pushing her against things. Walls, cabinets, counters. She had no idea when she'd started liking that—maybe since she'd started reading her sister's books—or when that like turned into love. She was finally discovering the true purpose of her fat wasn't to make her look good, but to cushion her when she was being Levi-handled.

Maybe she was avoiding her problems. Wouldn't be the first time. And certainly, she had many problems to avoid. Her sister hadn't made contact. The ball was in Gaia's court there, and Gemma wouldn't push. Gaia needed time, and Gemma would respect that.

Gemma wasn't speaking to her parents. *She* needed time there, and though her mother had reached out once, with a tentative message that Gemma hadn't responded to, Jasmine seemed to have gotten the picture. Gemma hadn't heard from either parent since, and she was grateful for the chance to breathe.

Lacey, on the other hand, had been calling Gemma non-stop. Gemma had been ignoring those calls, too, though she should have known better. She shouldn't have been surprised when Lacey showed up at her door two weeks after the incident with her parents.

She and Levi had been eating dinner. Or, more accurately, she'd been eating, and he'd been watching her intently. It was his new thing. He was expanding his cooking and baking repertoire, trying recipes that pushed him out of his comfort zone. She always thought they were delicious, but he'd get this really cross face every time she'd say that if something didn't turn out the way he wanted it to.

It was cute, but also super annoying.

When the doorbell rang, he stood. "I'll get it."

She waved her fork in thanks and kept eating the short-rib dish Levi had made. He'd paired it with rice and a sauce that was rich and creamy and perfect, and she didn't care who was at the door.

"It's Lacey," Levi called.

Her chewing slowed. She set her fork down and shook her shoulders. She couldn't avoid her friend forever. She couldn't even avoid her friend for the duration of this meal, which she desperately wanted to finish. No, she couldn't make Lacey wait like that.

Could she?

"Gemma."

No.

She stood and went to the door, where Levi was standing like a guard dog. He hadn't let Lacey in. Usually, that wouldn't have stopped Lacey. Something had changed. The thought brought Gemma anxiety, but she checked herself. Something should have changed. *She* had changed.

But what if Lacey didn't like who Gemma had changed into?

She would deal with it, she promised herself. But she wouldn't anticipate it. Not when Lacey was her best friend, had been for years. That meant something. That deserved some faith.

"It's okay," she told Levi. "I can take it from here."

His eyes swept over her face, and he squeezed her hand as he walked back to the kitchen. Some of her anxiety eased, and she faced her friend.

"Hi."

"Hi," Lacey said, her expression merely inquisitive. It was her lawyer expression.

Gemma bit her lip. "What are you doing here?"

"Really?" Emotion rippled across Lacey's face. "Is this how it's going to go?"

She thought about it. "No," she replied. "Let's sit outside."

Lacey's expression tightened, and now, Gemma could see the hurt, the confusion. She ignored her desire to fix it. Lacey could have emotions without Gemma feeling the need to fix them. A faint shimmer of pride rolled over her body, and she clung to it as she led Lacey to her outdoor patio set in the garden.

By some miracle, the square table and its four chairs had yet to be stolen, something she'd expected when she set it up. Sure, it was heavy, but criminals were motivated. She fully attributed the fact that it was still there to her neighbors. Mr. Redding watered his garden an illegal number of times, so he had a reason to be outside.

Lacey didn't say anything until they sat down. Gemma was tempted to start speaking, to fill the uncomfortable silence, but that would have undone all the progress she'd congratulated herself on. She folded her hands into her lap and waited.

Lacey cleared her throat. "There seem to be things we need to talk about."

"Yes."

Her friend frowned, as if she hadn't expected the agreement. "Let's start with your parents."

"No," Gemma said. "Let's start with the wedding."

"The wedding?"

"Yeah." She paused. "You know I went out of my way to make that day special for you?"

"I . . ." Lacey's frown deepened. "Yeah, I know. Of course I know."

"Do you?" Gemma pressed. "I mean, do you *really* know? I intervened with your mother countless times, trying to make sure she didn't impose. Same with Chet's mother. And Izzy, for that matter. I fetched the cake, I made sure the thank-you cards were printed and written, I went to get your dress, I spoke to the chef to make sure every single thing would be to your specification." Now that she was listing it, it sounded endless. How had she managed to do it all? "So, Lace, *do* you know?"

"I feel like you're blaming me for that," Lacey said, leaning forward. Her confrontational pose. Being a lawyer, Lacey didn't back away from even the hint of a fight. Something in Gemma wanted to stand down, but she knew if she did, she would never forgive herself. "I didn't ask you to do those things."

Gemma gave her a look.

"Okay, fine. I asked you to do *some* of those things. But you wanted to!"

"I didn't want to do those things. I wanted to make you happy. There's a difference."

"And now you're blaming me for it?"

"I'm blaming myself, actually," Gemma admitted. "For making you feel like asking me to do some of those things was okay."

Lacey's lips parted, surprise shimmering in her eyes. Gemma swallowed. Took a breath, and told Lacey what she'd figured out about herself over the last two months.

"I don't remember a time before my parents told me I was adopted. There wasn't a big reveal, or anything. They spoke of it casually, didn't make me feel different in any way because it was a simple fact. I was adopted. It wasn't a *thing.*"

She traced a pattern on the table.

"It worked. At some point, I don't know when, I started thinking that maybe they kept talking about it for a reason. Like I was meant to earn it or something. They would be horrified to hear me say that . . . I am, too, if I'm honest."

Her fingers stilled. She curled them into a fist and dropped her hand to her lap.

"My point is that I've practiced pleasing people for a long time. The longest. I didn't mind it, because I didn't know any different. Besides, I wanted to make the people I care about happy. I wanted my parents to not regret deciding to be my parents. Or my friends," she added softly. "But I found out—" She hesitated, not ready to delve into the Gaia situation yet. "I realized that it was less want than need. A desperate need to be loved and cared about. To not . . . regret me," she said again, because that was the whole point, wasn't it?

Lacey was entirely focused on Gemma. Another one of her lawyer skills. She had the ability to make a person feel as if they were the only person who had anything of importance to say. Usually, Lacey would use that skill to lull them into a false sense of security before she got them to confess to a multitude of sins. Gemma had seen Lacey in action once, and it had scarred her forever.

"You didn't tell me any of this," Lacey accused.

"I just found out myself."

"Because of Levi?"

"Some of it, yeah. Well, a lot of it," Gemma corrected. "I would have got there eventually, but he helped. He's annoying like that."

Lacey bit the inside of her lip and sat back. "You're saying you did this with me? With the wedding?"

"Not only with the wedding," Gemma said. "With our entire relationship."

"So it's a lie?"

Gemma rolled her eyes. "No, you dork."

"I'm the dork? You're the one telling me our entire relationship was built on a lie."

Gemma stared, and started to laugh. "That was not what I said."

"Well, it felt like it!" Lacey said, but she was laughing, too. "You're so dramatic!"

"*Me?*"

They kept laughing, probably because they knew they were both being ridiculous. Probably because things were going to change, and it was scary, but necessary, and laughing . . . laughing felt like this issue wouldn't keep them from being friends.

"I took advantage, didn't I?" Lacey said when they'd calmed down. "With the wedding. Maybe other times."

"Definitely other times," Gemma corrected. "With my parents, for one. That was not cool."

Lacey opened her mouth, her expression fierce. It crumbled quickly after, and she closed her eyes. "I knew that was wrong. I knew I was crossing a line, but . . ." She opened her eyes. "Don't be mad, okay? I know how this sounds, but . . . well, I was jealous."

"Of me? Why would you be—"

"Not of you." Lacey shifted. "Of Levi."

"Of Levi?"

"Yes." Lacey sniffed. "This is not the easiest thing for me to admit. Please do pay attention."

Gemma rolled her eyes at the faux formality. "Fine. Tell me why you were jealous of Levi."

"Because he had you."

"Lacey, I have no idea what that means."

Lacey sighed. "It sounds terrible now, after everything you've told me, but . . . but I used to have you. Whenever I needed you. I'd call and you'd tell me you were coming."

"Because I wanted to make sure you didn't stop being my friend."

"Yeah, I get that." She bit the inside of her lip. "I absolutely took advantage of that. I won't apologize for it."

"Rude."

"You didn't let me finish. I won't apologize, because of course I took advantage of it. It was *you*. I got access to the warmest, kindest, sweetest, sauciest person with one phone call." Lacey rolled her eyes. "It's annoying, actually, how wonderful you are. How being your friend makes me feel like I'm likable and funny and important." She took a breath. "I didn't know it made you feel the way it did."

Gemma didn't respond immediately. This conversation was making her aware of yet another layer of what she was feeling. She didn't regret doing any of the things she did for Lacey. Or for any of her friends, really. She just . . . didn't want to feel like she *had* to do them. Plus, it was kind of nice to hear that she was a good friend. That Lacey seemed to need her as much as she needed Lacey.

When she told her friend that, Lacey rolled her eyes again. "You're an idiot. I need you. I need you so much, I'm jealous of your boyfriend, because he gets all of that, and I come second."

"Third," Gemma corrected. "I'm trying to put myself first these days. So technically, the ranking would be me, Levi, then you."

"Thanks for the clarity," Lacey said dryly.

"You're welcome."

There was a pause. Lacey laughed. "You're such an idiot."

"So you've said. You still love me, though."

She didn't know why her heart was beating so hard at that. Or why it went back to normal when Lacey replied.

"Yeah, I love you." She leaned forward. "I'd love you even if you didn't ask me how high when I wanted you to jump."

"That's a weird way of phrasing it," Gemma said, but tears were pricking at her eyes, and she was blinking rapidly.

"My brain works weird. You know that."

"I do."

"I'm sorry," Lacey said after a while. "I'm sorry that we had to have this conversation for me to see that I shouldn't be taking advantage of your kindness."

"Thank you." Gemma took a breath. Exhaled, and felt the tension leave her body. "It wasn't only you. I taught you how to treat me."

"I should have known better."

"Yeah, you should have."

They smiled at each other.

"We're going to have to talk about boundaries and shit now, aren't we?" Lacey asked.

"Yep."

"And about Levi. Is he living here now?"

"Yep."

"Talk about moving fast."

"I believe you started planning your wedding to Chet after the second date."

"That's different."

Gemma snorted.

"It is!" Lacey insisted, but pivoted. "We also need to work on your self-esteem. It's at like, a one, and it needs to be at least a ten."

"Our level system is only out of ten."

"A minimum of ten."

"You can't change the rules because it suits you," Gemma accused.

"Yes, I can," Lacey disagreed. "Especially in this case." She crossed her arms. "You're trying to distract me. But—if you can't see that people are going to love you because of who you are, it's a self-esteem issue."

"No—" Gemma broke off. "Maybe it is."

"You're awesome."

"Is this you working on it?"

"Indeed."

"Well, then," Gemma said. "I *am* awesome. Thank you for the reminder."

"Don't mention it."

There was a longer silence this time. Lacey reached out and squeezed Gemma's hand. "I'm grateful that you're my friend. Even with the boundaries and shit."

"Me, too." She squeezed back. Released. And felt something shift. She looked her friend in the eye. "Do you want to know what started this entire thing?"

Lacey's brows lifted. "Sure."

"I have a sister."

CHAPTER 26

Things were going well until he said *I love you.*

It was a mistake, obviously. Levi hadn't changed so much that he would proclaim his feelings like that intentionally. They were in the kitchen, she was nagging him about something, and it just kind of came out.

"What did you say?" Gemma asked, after an awkward silence.

"Nothing. Here." He took a spoonful of the chocolate baking mixture he was about to turn into a cake. "Eat this." That usually distracted her.

But not this time.

"Did you say you love me?"

"No."

"Levi."

"Gemma."

"You said it. I heard you say it."

"I believe," he continued—clinging to the lie, because what else could he do?—"what I said was that you're annoying."

"You said 'if I didn't love you, I'd find you more annoying.'"

"Doesn't sound like me."

"It sounds exactly like you," she insisted. "Apart from the *I love you.*"

"What's that supposed to mean?"

"You love three things: your sister, your father, and cooking-slash-baking. Wait, four." She cleared her throat. "Your mother."

He'd never told her any of that that, but he supposed it was true. The fact that she knew it proved the nature of their relationship.

"And now," he said quietly, "apparently, you."

Gemma stared at him—and moved. Gently, she took the spoon out of his hand, pushed the bowl aside, and kissed him.

He didn't think about what she was thinking, only took her in. Eagerly, desperately, as if they hadn't been doing some iteration of this for the last month. He'd never get tired of the sweetness and spice he tasted when she opened up to him. When her tongue swept into his mouth, and he hardened, and his body became entirely hers.

She did the little shimmy that usually meant she was gearing up to jump him. It would always remind him of a cat, a comparison she had not appreciated when he'd mentioned it to her. He found it sexy, he assured her, and though she clearly didn't believe him, she also didn't stop doing it.

And when she jumped, he caught her. She wrapped her legs around him. He pushed her against the wall. Their kiss deepened. Her hands were everywhere: over his shirt, under. She dragged her nails over his shoulders. Again, over his chest. He'd told her once he liked it, that it made him feel like he belonged to her, and she'd responded by doing it every time.

He pulled off his T-shirt, pulled off hers as he steadied her against the wall. She was wearing a simple cotton bra. Red, with a trim of lace at the top, pressing into the generous curves of her breasts. The sight never failed to arouse him. Never failed to make him submit to the temptation to take that flesh in his mouth. Soft, oh, so soft. He grazed his teeth over it, before sucking her nipple through the fabric. She arched her back, pressing her lower body closer to him as she offered him her chest.

Knowing what she wanted by now, what she needed, he took

his time licking. Sucking. She nudged against him, and he gave her the space to lower her legs to the ground, but then he was back at his task. She fiddled with his pants, pulling his belt out of the loops and throwing it on the floor somewhere behind him. Opened his buttons in one aggressive movement, and soon her hand was closing over his erection and moving.

He moaned, his mouth still open, pressed against her breast, and she stilled.

"I thought we've been over this," she panted.

"Over what?"

"You stop, I stop."

He chuckled, moved his tongue. She shuddered, the vibration going through him, in him, and taking hold of his entire body when her hand resumed stroking. His hips thrusted, hands moving over her butt, one hand staying there while the other slipped into her panties. His fingers moved through the tangle of curls—she'd told him she hadn't shaved once, along with the chastity panties, to which he'd told her he didn't care, and she hadn't shaved since—and began to play.

His mouth found hers again, and they kissed, desperately, passionately. Suddenly, they weren't kissing anymore, only breathing, panting, their hands touching and squeezing and teasing.

"Let's do it," she whispered.

He stopped, pulled back so he could look into her eyes. "Are you sure?"

"I love you, too," she said simply, and undid him. He pressed a hard kiss to her lips, wrapping his arms around her before kissing her again when he could hold her tight.

"What about . . ." he trailed off, not sure how to ask.

"What about everything?" she finished. "I don't know. I don't care."

"That's . . ." He shook his head, something deep and heavy shifting inside him. "Okay." He took a breath. "So let's talk about condoms."

She blinked. "Condoms?"

"Protection."

"Yeah, I know what condoms are." She frowned. "Do we need them?"

"I was tested before I—"

"No," she interrupted with a huff of laughter. "I mean, yes, that's good to know, assuming you were going to say you were tested before you died and everything's good to go. Here, too, by the way. But . . . you're a ghost. Do we need condoms?"

"I . . . yes? Yes," he said again. "I don't know if we need them, but it's better to be safe, right?"

"Right." She nodded. "Don't want to end up with a ghost-specific STD. Or a ghost baby. Sheesh. Can you imagine?"

"I cannot," he said, even though he could. Even though the image of a baby Gemma made him feel warm and full.

"But maybe your sperm are ghosts, too. With their little ghost capes."

He made a strangled sound.

"What?" she asked. "You don't think it would be cute?"

"Gemma, this is not what I'd like to be talking about right now."

"Why n—" She broke off when he pushed his hips forward again. "Oh, right. Of course. Let's use condoms to be safe, and we can—"

"Not to interrupt this," came a voice from behind them, "but we all should probably talk."

Jude truly had the worst timing.

Levi shifted his body to give Gemma some privacy, and waited as she put her top back on, putting on his own when she was done. She walked behind the kitchen counter, disappearing from view before rising and offering him his belt. He took it, looped it into the bands of his pants, searching her face the entire time for any signs of distress. She seemed remarkably calm, even winking at him as she stopped beside him to face

Jude. When he was done, though, she took his hand. Threaded their fingers together and held on tight.

"Jude," Levi said, finally facing his Guardian Ghost, "your timing is well and truly shit."

Jude's bright red lips made his black-as-night hair and goth-styled clothing seem even more striking. Even more . . . ominous. Something rumbled in Levi's chest, and it took him a moment to realize it was concern. Jude wasn't there for a quick chat; he was there to tell Levi something awful. Not only Levi, but Gemma, too.

That worried Levi the most.

"My timing is perfect, actually," Jude said cheerily. "Would you like to have a seat? What I'm about to tell you might not be the easiest to hear while standing."

Levi almost growled in warning. *Don't make me make you regret this* were the words that accompanied that warning. Jude lifted his eyebrows, but said nothing. Levi clenched his jaw— the asshole *could* read his mind—and followed Gemma to the couch.

She took his hand again when they got there, and eased some of his anxiety. But it didn't make that big of a dent, which said more about the extent of the anxiety than her.

"Now that you've both proclaimed your love for each other—congratulations, by the way"—was Jude beaming? He *was* beaming. *Why?*—"you've come to the end of the test."

"Test?" Gemma and Levi said together. Levi followed it up with, "What test?"

"Your assignment, Levi, was less about Gemma and more about you." Jude sat down and folded his legs. "Your real mission was to get to a point of self-awareness. You've reached that point now, haven't you?"

Levi opened his mouth to provide an eloquent answer, but the only thing that came out was, *"What?"*

Jude smiled. "Did you enjoy your life, Levi? When you were living in your time with your family?"

He struggled with it. It was one thing to admit it to himself, and an entirely different thing to admit it out loud. Eventually, he said, "No."

Gemma squeezed his hand.

He squeezed back.

"You've found joy now?" Jude asked.

Again, it took Levi a moment. "Yes."

"In cooking?"

"Yes."

"Baking?"

He nodded.

"In Gemma?"

Levi looked at her. She was looking at him, her eyes deep and searching, as if she wanted the answer, too. Which was ridiculous. He smiled at her at least three times a day. She knew that was much more than his usual quota of no smiles. The fact that he had that quota, unknowingly in his time, and here, in fact, until Gemma had asked him about it, should tell him all he needed to know about that life.

But since he had come here, since Gemma had come into his life, three was a minimum. Hell, he was pretty sure there was no quota. He was more relaxed, found cooking and baking a surprising joy now that he had time for it, and he had Gemma to look forward to every day of the week.

Her smile, her laughter, her sense of humor.

Her generosity, her time, the way she ran her fingers across his hand when he was sitting close enough.

She played with her rings whenever she was impatient or nervous. When they weren't there, she rubbed the base of her fingers.

He loved that she immediately headed to the kitchen when she came home, offering him a kiss only after she'd checked what he was making for her. Depending on the answer, the kiss could be any length, any intensity, and the surprise of it always made him happy.

All these things—these stupid, silly, trivial things—mattered, and yes, brought him joy. So of course he told Jude, "Yes."

"Not only would those answers have been different had I asked you before, you wouldn't have admitted them, even if they hadn't been. Growth," Jude said, spreading his hands.

"Is there a point to this?" Levi asked tersely.

"Levi." Gemma poked him in the ribs. "You're being rude."

"You were aware of that part of my personality before you fell in love with me."

"Yeah, but now I can't enjoy the fact that you said I make you happy because I'm worried about your manners."

He took a breath, asking for patience. "Jude, would you *please* get to the point?"

Gemma looked at Jude. "I suppose that's better?"

"Marginally," Jude agreed. "But he's right, I do have a point, and I'll get to it. When we believe that a person might need a second chance at life, we offer them a trial period of three months. When they meet the requirements we set for that trial period, we offer them their lives back."

"Their lives . . . *my* life?" He let go of Gemma's hand, ignoring the heat he lost in the process. If this were going the way he thought it was, he'd have to get used to losing her heat—and her light, her happiness—anyway. "You're saying I can go back now?"

"Yes."

"It has nothing to do with Gemma and her life?"

"You've helped her tremendously already," Jude pointed out, "and we believe that she'll be able to move forward well."

"Really?" Gemma asked. "You all"—she twirled a finger in the air over her head—"think I've got this?"

"You've got this," Jude assured her kindly.

"Thanks," Gemma beamed.

"You're welcome."

"Jude," Levi interrupted, trying to get back on track. It

wasn't that he wasn't happy for Gemma—he was, and it was a huge relief that she'd be able to sort things out on her own, even though he wanted to be there for her—but he was waiting for his future to be clarified. "Do I *have* to go back?"

"No."

"Clarify." He glanced over at Gemma. She lifted her brow. He looked back at Jude. "Please."

"My colleagues will be so happy you've learned manners this time around," Jude deadpanned, but continued. "You have a choice. You can go back to your previous life. You will have no memory of what happened during this time, but you will be the person you are here now. You'll be self-aware; what you do with that self-awareness will, again, be your choice. Alternatively, you can remain here. As you are now."

"What?"

"You can choose to stay, Levi. Live the life you've created for yourself with Gemma."

He didn't dare look at Gemma. "How? I don't have any identification. I don't have a job or money. I—"

"We can, and will, assist with that. You'll be taken care of."

"As I was while I was here?"

"Yes."

"You couldn't even bother to get me a place to stay."

"The plan was always that you would stay here, with Gemma."

His eyes widened. "You told me I should be careful."

"I stand by that," Jude said. "This choice is a difficult one, Levi. You will feel guilt no matter which one you make. I wanted you to be sure, so that when you make this choice, you truly know the stakes."

"You also helped me find a different place to live. Twice."

"Ah, so we did help you then, didn't we?" Jude asked lightly. "Although I suppose it doesn't matter when we ruined the pipes of the first place, and the second . . . well, I said that to push you and Gemma closer to realizing your feelings for each other."

"Diabolical," Gemma commented.

"Hmm." Jude stood. "Now that you know your choices, I'll be off. Feel free to continue what you were doing before I interrupted you."

"Jude!" Levi called before he could disappear. "What happens to Haley if I stay?"

Jude gave him a sad smile. "Everything continues on as it would without you, Levi. That's all I can tell you."

Which, of course, told him nothing at all.

Or perhaps it told him everything he needed to know.

CHAPTER 27

If Gemma had known this was how her impromptu trip to a coffee shop would go, she would have tried to prepare better. Instead, she was taken by surprise when her sister asked to sit opposite her. When Gaia told Gemma that Levi had told her where to find Gemma.

Her surprise had led to small talk about her sister's boyfriend and his knowledge of a vagina—she wasn't proud of that—and now she was asking her sister about magic.

About ghosts.

"Why would you ask me that?" Gaia asked, sitting back slowly, as if she were relaxed. But Gemma could see her shoulders were lifted an inch too high, her fingers curled into a fist she left on the table.

"You know what? Never mind."

She wasn't going to make her sister uncomfortable during their very first conversation where they both knew they were sisters. Especially not when Gaia was wearing her pendant.

She rubbed the backs of her fingers, but she still wasn't wearing her rings. It had felt wrong to after telling Gaia the truth. Now, it felt wrong that she wasn't wearing them.

"Forget I asked."

"You asked," Gaia said deliberately, "about magic, and about ghosts. Why?"

"Hmm . . ." How was Gemma going to get out of this now? She'd told her sister this, and clearly, Gaia wasn't going to let it go. Gemma sighed. "Well, since we're in it now anyway, and maybe it'll break the ice between us, but I asked because . . ." She glanced around, making sure no one was listening to their conversation. "I can see ghosts. I don't think it's magic as much as a supernatural ability, but that's splitting hairs, I guess."

Gaia frowned. "That's something, isn't it?"

"Are you freaked out?"

"No, no." Gaia's hand uncurled, her palm flattening against the table, and Gemma found something inside her unfurling, as well. "Have you always been able to see ghosts?"

"Yeah. I mean, no. It started when I was eighteen years old. On the day, actually."

Gaia made a strangled noise, but she didn't seem upset. "And it's just ghosts?"

"Yes." Gemma narrowed her eyes. "Why are you taking this so well?"

"Am I?"

"Yes. And you were acting weird from the beginning, which is why I even brought it up." She paused. "Can you do it, too? See ghosts?"

"No." The knot re-tangled inside Gemma, until Gaia said, "But, for twelve years, I did live the books I wrote in my dreams."

"Holy crap! Really?"

Gaia smiled. "Yeah."

"That's so cool!" Gemma leaned forward. "Did you get to live the scene where Keaton takes Ilona down to the basement and—"

"Yes," Gaia interrupted, clearing her throat. "We probably shouldn't talk about the details of it, though."

"You wrote those details!"

Gaia pursed her lips. "I did. But I didn't expect anyone would know about my abilities, so didn't think I'd ever be called out on the more sexually adventurous things I've written." She paused. "You really read that book?"

"Of course."

"Only that one?"

"Four of them," Gemma said. "I'm on my fifth now."

"Why?"

Gemma considered lying, but there had been enough of that. She was tired of it. "It made me feel connected to you."

Gaia folded her hands into her lap. "How long have you known?"

"The truth?" Gaia nodded. "A couple of months."

"Why only tell me now?"

"There were many reasons," she answered honestly. "I was ashamed when I found out. My parents had taken me and not both of us, and I was ashamed of them for making such a horrid decision."

Gaia nodded, hands creeping over the handbag now. She did things with her hands when she was nervous. It was almost like how Gemma played with her rings. A tenuous, silly comparison, but a precious link Gemma would hold close to her heart forever.

"You've spoken with them about it?" Gaia asked.

"A bit."

"What did they say?"

"Money. They couldn't afford both of us."

"That's . . ." She blew out a breath and offered Gemma a shaky smile. "Maybe we should stop there? I think it might be easier to process the whole thing if we talked about it over time. For me, at least. Is that . . . is that okay with you?"

"Yeah, of course." A spark of light in Gemma's chest grew. "Does that mean we'll have the chance? To talk about it, I mean."

Gaia didn't answer for a long time. Her eyes were soft and

open when they looked at Gemma, though, and she could see none of the admonishment, none of the judgment she'd been expecting. Something else softened, loosened inside Gemma. And did so completely when Gaia said, "I'd like that."

"Me, too," Gemma said immediately.

Gaia lifted her brows. "You didn't even think about that."

"Why would I need to think about it? You're my sister."

Gaia bit her bottom lip as she went a little teary. Gemma felt tears prickling her own eyes, but she'd be damned if she was going to let this turn into something sad.

"Levi's a ghost," she told Gaia. "We've been faking a relationship to explain why he's been in my life all of a sudden."

It worked. Gaia's tears disappeared, replaced by surprise and a slow smile. "Well, that explains some things."

"How awkward we were around each other?"

"I wouldn't say awkward. Although . . . it was believable that you two were together. You had a bond. And chemistry."

"That's nice to hear, considering we're in love."

Gaia blinked. Her smile widened. "Well, you're going to have to tell me more now, aren't you?"

Warmth took hold of her, spreading in her veins, melting something in her heart. She didn't spend too much time thinking about it. Only enjoyed it. Enjoyed the peace it brought, especially since she hadn't had that kind of peace in a long time.

Perhaps ever.

So she settled in and began to tell her sister the story.

"It all started with a kiss . . ."

The first thing she wanted to do after her meeting with Gaia was tell Levi how it went. But when she got home, he wasn't there. Not in the kitchen, where she usually found him, nor in his bedroom. She searched the rest of the house, her heart beating faster with each empty room.

Eventually, she had to admit that he wasn't in her home at all, no matter how many times she looked.

She took a couple of deep breaths to calm her panic. When that didn't work, she poured herself a glass of emergency alcohol. Only she wasn't much of a drinker, and the emergency alcohol was liqueur she kept to make desserts with, which didn't really have the effect she was looking for.

But what the hell, she'd make the dessert anyway. It would give her hands something to do—other than shake—and she'd be keeping her mind busy and not thinking about the fact that Levi had left her without saying goodbye.

A little voice in her head mocked her after a while. Sure, her hands stayed busy, but her mind? Her mind was taking a run around the *I can't believe Levi left* track. Because she couldn't believe it. He'd just *left*? Without saying goodbye? Why?

Maybe he thought it would be easier. She'd seen his face when Jude had told them his options. He had to choose between the sister he adored and the woman he loved, and . . . well, it would be a difficult choice. Although, maybe not, if he'd left. Maybe he didn't love her as much as she hoped he did. Or was that an unfair thought? His sister, his family, needed him. Even if they didn't, he wouldn't want his sister to carry his death with her, which he was certain would happen.

So, yes, it was unfair to interpret that as a lack of love for her. It wasn't about her at all. But she'd spent her entire life thinking that she had to earn people's love. To keep it. That being herself, only herself, wasn't enough. It was difficult to let go of that, especially when she hadn't tried with Levi. She hadn't tried to earn his love; she'd been herself. He loved her anyway, and she accepted it. For a while, at least.

It was a start though, wasn't it? Usually, she'd struggle to believe it at all. There was always something inside her that didn't, and even though she'd become an expert at ignoring that feeling, she knew it was there. With Levi? That feeling hadn't been there. She didn't know if that was because she'd grown or because it was him. Everything was easier with him.

She should take that as a win, shouldn't she? That he had

helped her see that she didn't need to earn love, that she deserved it as she was. Her relationship with him had been a lesson in self-love, too. Because if he loved her like that, why couldn't she believe anyone else would? Lacey thought she was great. Gaia seemed to want a relationship with her, despite everything. And her parents . . . more complicated, that one, but she knew they loved her. So, really, this came down to her, what she believed she deserved. And that was to know unreservedly that she was worthy of love.

She was.

She was worthy of love.

From everyone, but especially from herself.

She stopped when the realization brought tears to her eyes. Looked up with a small smile as they rolled over her cheeks.

"Thank you," she whispered. "I hope you're happy, wherever you are."

"Who are you talking to?"

She whirled around, taking her cup with her, the momentum spilling its contents onto Levi's shirt. She didn't care. Instead, she ran into his arms, her heart pounding in joy, in relief. She buried her face into his neck, the ice cream and alcohol soaking her shirt and his in a cold, wet circle. Again, she didn't care.

"Gemma," Levi said, his arms around her, but not holding her too tightly. "Gem." He leaned back this time, searching her face. "What happened?"

"Nothing. Nothing. I . . ." She pursed her lips. "I thought you were gone."

He frowned. "You didn't think I'd say goodbye?"

"I thought you might think it easier not to."

He didn't reply, but picked up the groceries he'd apparently gone to the store for and started packing them away. He made no mention of the mess over his shirt, on hers, and the floor, or the faint smell of alcohol coming from all of it. She tidied it up, stealing glances at him every few seconds.

"Are you checking that I'm still here?" he asked eventually.

"No." She snorted—and almost immediately said, "Yes."

"I haven't *poofed* for a while."

"You haven't had to," she pointed out. "Now you have every-thing you always wanted at your fingertips."

He folded the plastic bags into tiny triangles and placed them in the drawer he'd designated for such things. When he faced her after, he leaned back against the counter and crossed his arms.

"We have to talk about this."

"Yes," she agreed, digging into the dessert that was left in the glass. "Wanna go first?"

He took a long time to reply, but since he hadn't agreed or disagreed, Gemma knew to wait for it. She gave herself brain freeze in the process, gobbling up the dessert because it kept her from talking, and now was not the time to talk.

"Do you need me to wait?" he asked softly, watching her.

"No," she replied, mouth full. She swallowed. "I was do-ing this because I didn't want to interrupt your very important words."

His lips curved into an almost smile. "Thank you."

"You're welcome." She shoveled another spoonful into her mouth and gestured for him to continue.

"You said I have everything I've always wanted," he started, "and you're right. Except it's coming to me in this . . . this ter-rible way. I have to choose between you and my family. The woman I love, and the people I've cared for my entire life."

"It's a tough decision," she said, finally putting down the des-sert.

"What do you want me to do?"

"It's not my decision."

"I know that." His answer was curt, but she understood. "I'm asking you what you want me to do."

She took a moment to figure out her thoughts. To work

through what she wanted to say and what she knew was right for him to hear.

"I think you should choose the life you want." When his frown deepened, she elaborated. "Don't choose people, Levi. If you do . . . if you do, you're going to spend the rest of whatever life you choose wondering. So, choose you. Choose the person you want to be and the life you want to have. Let the people, let us, fit into that for once, instead of the other way around."

"You say that like it's simple."

"I know it's not simple, Levi." She moved closer to him. "But it's what has to happen."

His eyes searched her face. "You don't want me to choose you."

She poked him in the ribs. "Don't be an idiot. Of course I want you to choose me. But . . . well, I also know what it's like to try to make up for someone else's decision." She paused. "I spent my life trying to satisfy my parents. Trying to make them happy because they decided to choose me. It's my own fault, I know. Partly, at least. The other part . . . I think they believed that I should be grateful. Grateful enough not to question anything, to agree with everything they said. They knew I was doing it, and they accepted it, because deep down, they believed it was necessary. How else would they keep my sister from me?"

It was the first time she'd said her suspicions out loud. She hadn't wanted to before, afraid of what might happen if she did. But the fear wasn't warranted. In fact, her response was the opposite to what she thought might happen. She didn't feel trapped; she felt free.

"I don't blame them for it. Not that much, anyway. I can see my part in it now, so I'm . . . I don't know. I guess I don't feel like I have to do it. If I continue to do it—and let's face it, I probably will—it will be because I want to." She shook her head. "All this to say . . ." She closed the distance between them and cupped his cheek. "I don't want to feel like I owe you because you chose me. If you choose me, that's what you might expect, too, and it'll make you resentful. And unhappy."

"You don't know that."

"I do. We both do." She dropped her hand. "But if you make that choice for yourself, for your happiness? *That's* the best choice."

"Is it?" he rasped. "How can I choose me?"

"Because it's about time you did. Don't worry about me," she added softly. "I'll be okay. Gaia and I talked today. Thank you for sending her to me, by the way," she added. "I'll tell you about it later." She waited a beat. "And this thing with my parents? We'll work through it and move forward with boundaries. Sure, I'll never love again, but who needs love?"

When he didn't smile, she rolled her eyes. "I'll be fine."

"What about me?"

She lifted to her toes and kissed his nose. "If you go, you won't remember me, and you'll live a new life with your family. You'll be fine, too." This time, she kissed his lips. "Choose you, Levi. Finally, choose you."

She left him with that, immensely proud that she didn't drop to her knees and beg. Promise that she would do everything and anything to keep him with her. That she didn't mind being whoever he wanted her to be.

But the truth was, she had to choose herself, too. And this? This was how she did.

CHAPTER 28

At first, Levi was angry. It was why he didn't speak to Gemma about Jude's information when Jude first offered it. She hadn't pushed, not once. Hadn't mentioned a single word of it. He knew she was trying not to pressure him, but he wanted her to. He wanted her to tell him to stay, so that he could listen to her, and the decision would be made for him.

But she didn't say a word, and he was forced to stew in what could only have a terrible outcome. No matter what he chose, he would be hurting someone he loved.

He tried to look at it logically. If he went back, it would cause the least damage. He wouldn't remember Gemma or his life here. Haley wouldn't be burdened by his death. Everyone would get to live happily. Except Gemma. She would remember him. She would mourn him. And if he was being honest with himself, he knew he wouldn't ever truly be happy, too.

What he shared with Gemma wasn't something he'd simply forget. Her laughter was buried in his heart, the shape of her body inked into his hands, the heat of it embedded in his skin. He would live the rest of his life missing something. He knew that without a doubt.

He also knew that if he went back to his life, things wouldn't change. Yes, Jude had told him he would be the person he was now, but what did that matter when his circumstances were the same? He would still look after Haley. Would still be in a job he did out of duty, not enjoyment. Still play a supporting role to his father in their family. None of which had bothered him much before, but it would now.

Because he was different.

But that didn't mean he would change. Put people who had grown back in the situation that had stunted their growth in the first place, and they'd become stunted again. He would go on doing what he always did, but he'd be unhappier, and he would never know why.

Could he go back to that for his sister?

"Tough decision," Jude said from beside him. Today, the Guardian was young, probably fourteen or fifteen. Her hair was tied into a bun at the top of her head, her clothing simple. She looked innocent and full of potential.

"The point of this entire thing, isn't it?" Levi asked, looking out at the neighborhood that had become his home over the last few months.

He'd come to sit outside after Gemma had left for work, their conversation from the night before still ringing in his head. His anger had dissipated some, but it was still there. Because the conversation last night had highlighted one important thing: He wanted to stay. He wanted to be with someone who supported his growth. Someone who encouraged him, not only with her words, but with the way she lived her life.

Gemma would reconcile with her parents, as she promised, he had no doubts. She'd already navigated her relationships with Lacey and Gaia masterfully. She hadn't let her fear hold her back; she had chosen herself in spite of it. His heart had filled and poured over when she'd rushed to hold him after thinking he was gone. He'd been so sure she would ask him to stay, but she hadn't. Now her words had made the decision even worse.

"I've already explained why we've put you here," Jude replied. "And you've done tremendously. Well done."

He snorted.

Jude waited a while before she said anything else. "Levi, there is no right answer."

"There's always a right answer," he said in a low voice.

"No," she disagreed. "There's the best answer, but not the right one."

"Tell that to mathematics." Why did he sound like Gemma? Why didn't the prospect upset him?

"Mathematics is not life. And thank the heavens for it, or I might have died much earlier."

He turned. "You were human once?"

"Of course. We're all human. Well, not all of us, but most of us."

Levi stared and shook his head. "I'm glad you didn't give me more details about the great beyond. Sounds like a messed-up place."

"A confusing place, perhaps, but not messed-up. We wouldn't be giving humans like you these kinds of opportunities if it was."

"This is not an opportunity. This is a device of torture."

"Levi, you already know what you want to do."

"No," he lied.

"Levi," Jude said again, this time in a voice that was almost pity.

He exhaled. "Fine, I know what I want to do. But how can I do it? How can I abandon my family?"

"You aren't abandoning them."

"How can you say that when I did all this for them, and now I'm saying, no thanks, I'll take another life, not this one?"

Jude took his hand. It felt cold for a split second, then warmed up, as if Jude had realized she was holding a human's hand. Or maybe that was all in his head. Either way, it was disconcerting, and he wanted to pull away, but found he didn't have the strength.

"You have to choose," Jude said. "I can't help you make the choice. Neither can Gemma—nor will she."

"Heard that, did you?"

"Indeed." Paused. "I like her."

"Yeah, I do, too."

Jude didn't speak again, but didn't let go of his hand. Levi didn't let go, either. It was a reminder that he did have to make a decision. And he wanted to choose himself.

If he did, he could stay here, in this life he and Gemma had created. He could pursue a career in cooking, something he'd surprisingly discovered he wanted to do. Gemma would push him to be a better person every single day, just as she had every single day they'd been together. Just as she *did* every day.

He wanted to be the person he was here. He was happy here. Something he could say without reservation for the first time in his life. And if he had to choose between an unfulfilled life and this one? This happy, content life? Why would he choose the former?

"Haley," he choked out. "I know you said you can't give me more, but . . . give me a little, please. Is she . . . Does she . . ."

He trailed off, and Jude loosened her grip on his hand, patting it. "Let me ask you this: If someone gave her the opportunity to live the life you have now, with love and happiness, would you want her to take it?"

"Yes. Of course, yes."

"I imagine she'd want that for you, too."

His lips parted, his breath whistling out. "Unfair."

"Fair," Jude said with a wry smile. She sobered. "You can't expect your family to want things for themselves if you can't even accept them for yourself."

He leaned forward, rubbed his eyes. "How can I do this?"

"By doing it."

It took him a long time to say it. And he only did because he heard a car coming up the driveway. Gemma got out, walked to the door, but stopped when she saw them on the lawn. Her eyes widened, but she quickly hid her emotion behind a smile.

"Hi, you two!"

"You forget something?" Levi asked.

"Sort of." She shifted her handbag from one arm to the next. "Well, no, that's not true." She sighed. "I had a feeling you might need me. So I came back. But I . . . I don't want to interrupt."

He looked at her for a long time, looked at Jude, and stood. "I choose this," he said, before reaching out for Gemma's hand.

She walked closer, but didn't take it. "Don't do this for me."

"I'm not," he said. "I'm doing this for me. I love you, and this life, and . . ." He exhaled. "I want to stay."

She bit her lip, her eyes filling, and she took his hand. "I love you, too."

He lowered his head to hers, closing his eyes. Relief poured into him, and guilt. The guilt would always be there, he knew, but that relief . . . it was rolled in happiness and contentment. He couldn't deny that was stronger.

"I'm proud of you," Jude said from behind him. Levi turned to her smiling face. "You've made a journey not many people do."

"Sacrificed my sister in the process."

Jude's smile widened. "Oh, I have a feeling she'll be fine."

Levi dropped his head. "You're telling me this now?"

With a laugh, she disappeared. When he turned back to Gemma, she shrugged. "The undead. Can't live with them, can't kill them. Because they're already dead."

He rolled his eyes. "I get to have this for the rest of my life?"

"You lucky bastard."

With a chuckle, he kissed her forehead.

He one hundred percent agreed.

Epilogue

Two Years Later

"So, you're married, huh?"

The voice came from beside him. He didn't jump, didn't look at the person the voice belonged to. Even though it had been years since he'd last seen Jude, Levi could still sense the Guardian.

"Yes."

He'd been married for all of twelve hours. It was almost 3:00 a.m. Gemma was passed out in their bed, for reasons he would share with no one but was incredibly proud of. He hadn't been able to fall asleep as easily, though the tiredness seeped into his body, his soul.

The planning of the wedding had been relatively easy, but he'd wanted to make some of the courses served. He could have left it to his catering company, except this was his wedding, and it felt right to be involved. So he'd gotten his hands dirty, made almost one hundred starters, not to mention the cake, a beautiful three-tiered masterpiece that Gemma, when she'd first seen it, had cried about. It was worth it for that alone.

He should have been resting. Sleeping. But something was keeping him up.

"It was a beautiful wedding."

Levi finally looked over. Jude appeared as he had the first time Levi had seen him on earth. A tall, lanky man, though this time, he was dressed in jeans and a shirt rather than leather. When the man looked over, Levi recognized his eyes. Even in the nighttime, he could see the shadow and light.

"Thank you," Levi said. "Gemma did a hell of a job."

"As did you," Jude replied. "I don't think I've seen any cake more beautiful."

"How many cakes are you seeing?"

He laughed. "Touché." He pivoted. "Does Gemma miss seeing ghosts?"

Levi frowned. There was a part of him that wanted to ask how Jude knew Gemma no longer saw ghosts, but it was a stupid part. Of course Jude knew. He'd probably been one of the Beings who had decided to take her ability away.

"The familiarity of it, yes," Levi answered slowly. "But I think not having so many people needing her, dead or alive, has helped her focus on her boundaries." He angled a look at Jude. "Which is probably *why* you took it away."

"We didn't take it away," Jude denied. "It ran its course. Served its purpose." He gave Levi a pointed look.

Levi's brows lifted. "She saw ghosts for twelve years of her life, all to meet me?"

"No one questions the will of True Love." Jude shrugged. "Now, tell me why you aren't sleeping with your beautiful wife?"

"No."

"I see."

Because he likely did see, Levi sighed. "It's my wedding, and my family isn't here."

"Tough," Jude commented. "Does it bother you often?"

"All the time."

It was true. Levi spent almost every moment of his day thinking about Haley and his dad. It didn't matter that he was the happiest he'd ever been, with his company. With his wife. He couldn't stop wondering whether they were happy. Whether they'd been okay after he died.

Mostly, he thought about Haley. About his sister. Witnessing Gemma and Gaia build their relationship had been a privilege, but a heart-wrenching one. Because he'd had a sister, too, and he'd had to say goodbye to her. Without knowing if she was okay.

She'd be eighteen now. Old enough to go to university. Would she be going? Or had her life turned into something else? Something different than what they'd envisioned—what he'd envisioned—for her?

"You have another family," Jude pointed out. "You get along well with Gemma's parents."

"Within reason."

"Yes," Jude said with a smile. "I wouldn't expect an unreasonably close relationship. Especially when their relationship with Gemma has changed so much."

Levi felt compelled to defend Gemma's choices, but he realized they didn't need defending. It was fine to have boundaries. She was no longer willing to twist herself to please her parents, which they viewed as revenge for their decisions. She had tried, several times, to explain it wasn't about them. Levi thought her father might have understood, but her mother insisted Gemma was punishing them. After a while, Gemma stopped trying to explain, and had simply lived the way she thought necessary. Jasmine and Simon were eager to maintain a relationship, despite the differences, so they accepted it and moved forward. But they were all aware that a new distance existed, one no one knew how to bridge.

Perhaps that's just how family was.

"It's been two years," Levi said softly. "Are the rules still as stringent? Or can you tell me whether they're okay?"

"They're okay," Jude replied.

He exhaled. It eased whatever was spinning inside him, but only slightly. Then Jude said, "I *can* do one better than that. Only it would have to be our secret. See it as a wedding gift."

"What?" he asked, tone short, desperate. Hopeful.

"You can see her."

"*What?*"

"Her life is . . . changing, much like yours did." At Levi's raised brows, Jude shook his head. "The details don't matter. What matters is you'd be able to see her for a few minutes. Over the equivalent of a call, I suppose."

Not in person. But Levi didn't care. He'd take a call. A pigeon, damn it. He just wanted to know, from her, that she was okay.

"Please," he rasped.

Jude smiled. "I thought you might say that. Give me your hand."

He stuck out his hand. Levi stared at it. Sighed. "We're going to *poof*?"

"We're going to *poof*."

He looked back into the room. "We'll be back before she wakes?"

"Yes."

"Where are we going?"

"To where we keep the mirror."

"Mirror?"

Jude's eyes twinkled. "A story for another time."

Levi hesitated for exactly a second before reaching for Jude's hand. "Thank you, Jude. For everything."

He only saw Jude's wink before the hurricane took him.

ACKNOWLEDGMENTS

Every book has a behind-the-scenes story of how it got written. The story of this book is that I deeply regretted coming back from maternity leave so quickly (LOL). I had to find time to write this while my twins were sleeping, which could be literal minutes some days. I woke up early and went to bed late. Each word was a challenge, and a victory, and when I finally finished the draft, the words together had somehow turned into this funny, sweet, beautiful romance that I am so, so proud of.

I have to thank my editors, Esi Sogah and Norma Perez-Hernandez, for their expertise, which has strengthened Gemma and Levi's story so much. But mostly, I'd like to thank them for their kindness and support. I desperately needed it as both an author and new mom, and I can't express the positive impact it's had. The same goes for my agent, Courtney Miller-Callihan. Thank you for every single email and call that you've answered with understanding and strategy, an impressive combination that makes you such a rock for all your authors. A massive thank you to the team at Kensington, who have worked incredibly hard to give me the perfect cover and back-cover copy, who've pushed to get my books in front of a diverse group of readers, and who have poured so much, seen and unseen, into making my projects a success.

To Lunelle, Megan, Bianca, Tessa, Jolette, Olivia, Talia, Jenni, and Nick: I'm so lucky to have you. And to Grant, who, on a daily basis, offers me assurance and love, guidance, and hope. There are no words to describe how much you and our family mean to me. Ash and Gabe: I love you beyond anything I can say. I hope you'll see it in everything I do.

And to my readers, who have followed my career, cheered me on, read and reviewed and shared my books . . . I write so that you may know how much love and romance you deserve, and feel hopeful, always.